'Tests carried out o~~n~~ picked out their vict~~ims~~ mugger will steer cle~~ar~~ stride but instantly ~~consider~~ a person of timid appearance or manner as fair game. The same theory applies to murderers; it's just that they home in on a different type of body language. The problem of course is that we have yet to discover what makes the victims so attractive to their killers.'

Malone wrote one single word on the blackboard in block capitals:

VICTIMS

Also by Shaun Hutson
and available in Sphere Books:

SHAUN HUTSON

Victims

SPHERE BOOKS LIMITED

A SPHERE Book

First published in Great Britain in 1988 by
Star Books, a Division of W H Allen & Co Plc
This edition published in 1990 by Sphere Books Ltd
1st Reprint 1990

Copyright © Shaun Hutson, 1987

Printed and bound in Great Britain by
Cox & Wyman Ltd, Reading

ISBN 0 7474 0787 8

Sphere Books Ltd
A Division of
Macdonald & Co (Publishers) Ltd
Orbit House
1 New Fetter Lane
London EC4A 1AR
A member of Maxwell Macmillan Pergamon Publishing Corporation

THIS BOOK IS DEDICATED TO
STEVE HARRIS, BRUCE DICKINSON, DAVE MURRAY,
ADRIAN SMITH AND NICKO McBRAIN –
QUITE SIMPLY THE BEST.
WITH THANKS AND ADMIRATION,
SOMEWHERE ON STAGE . . .

Acknowledgements

Writing this book was not easy but the following people, for various reasons, made the task less painful. For those who offered either advice, expertise, friendship, support, love or inspiration, I extend my warmest thanks.

To Mr Bill Waddell, Curator of New Scotland Yard's Black Museum, who put me right on a number of research points. To my agent, Sheelagh Thomas, and my editor, Bill Massey (thanks for the tea bags). To Bob Tanner, Ray Mudie and 'The Wild Bunch'. To everyone else at W.H. Allen.

Thanks also, for different reasons to Bill Young at Chiltern Radio ('The Attila of the Airwaves', frequenter of more beer tents than Watneys). To Mick Wall (I don't care what you say, I still owe you and by the way, it's your round). To Malcolm 'Miracle Man' Dome (who's going to win the league? And it's your turn to buy the lunch). To Krusher 'Jimmy Page' Joule. To Steve McTaggart, Geoff Barton, Karoline and all at 'Kerrang', thank you from your tea-boy . . .

Thanks to Cheap (from Fulham pubs mighty bands do grow). To Scrapheap (today 'The Comedy Store' tomorrow the world).

Extra special thanks to Rod Smallwood and all those at Smallwood-Taylor who made three days 'on the road' so special for me. To all the road crew as well, thank you.

Thank you to Liverpool F.C. for one of the greatest days of my life. To Queensrÿche, to Joan Ingram (I promise not to pay for any more tickets, honest) and to Ray Pocock (a great 'Harpist').

And finally, as ever, to my Mum and Dad, for everything. And to Belinda, who suffered this one with me. Just being there was enough . . .

Shaun Hutson

'It takes two to make a murder. There are born victims, born to have their throats cut, as the cut-throats are born to be hanged. You can see it in their faces.'

Aldous Huxley

Prologue

A thin mist of cigarette smoke hung like a dirty curtain between the watchers and the lone figure at the blackboard.

The man eventually turned, rubbing his hands together in an effort to remove the chalk dust. Then he pointed to what he had just written.

'I don't know if those names mean anything to you?' he said.

From the subsequent silence he guessed that they were unfamiliar to the assembled throng. Edward Malone jabbed at the first name with his stubby index finger.

'Franz Werfel. A German, as you may have gathered. In 1920 he wrote a novel called *Not the Murderer but the Victim is Guilty*. But it is this man,' he pointed to the second name, 'this psychologist, who concerns us. Dr Hans Von Hentig. In 1949 he was responsible for what has become a classic study, *The Criminal and the Victim*. He maintained that in many murder cases the victim is as responsible as the murderer for the act of violence, albeit by provocation. This is particularly true in domestic killings and in many cases concerning women and sex crimes. Provocative behaviour is often the cause of murder.' He gazed around at his audience. 'As policemen I don't need to tell you that. Individuals often behave in ways which invite violence. For instance, a woman who dresses alluringly and frequents, shall we say, "dubious" premises, one who habitually picks up a series of different men, must be classed as a potential victim. The same goes for a man, but to a lesser degree. It's a kind of Russian roulette. If a woman sleeps with ten different men in rapid succession then the odds are that one of those ten is likely to be either disturbed or perhaps violent. The same premise can be applied in some cases of child murder. If we use Von Hentig's theory then it's easy to see that it is sometimes the child who invites violence by its own behaviour. Many children like to play games with adults and perhaps, if those games get out of hand, the child may struggle . . .' He allowed the sentence to trail off. 'I realize that this is a generalization, the case of the Moors Murders being an exception, but the theory applies in many instances.

'Provocative behaviour was the subject of Von Hentig's studies but there was something which he didn't explore fully. The idea of the *born* victim. Someone actually destined from birth to become a murder victim. It could be anyone. Even one of us in this room now. There is some kind of psychological beacon given off by all murder victims which the killer homes in on, like a dog to a scent.

'No one knows what it is. No one can identify it. Von Hentig and, later, Jung, called it "Victimology". It might just be a case of being in the wrong place at the wrong time, especially in the case of people murdered by total strangers, such as the victim of Leopold and Loeb, but the fact remains that all of us give off certain unconscious signals, *vibes* if you like.

'The killer is triggered, we think, by some kind of subliminal means. As far as we are aware there are no external stimuli, something registers subliminally in the mind *and* eye of the killer. Something he himself may even be unaware of. But the psychological lure is there for a killer to see.

'Tests carried out on muggers showed that they picked out their victims by the way they walk. A mugger will steer clear of someone with a forceful stride but instantly consider a person of timid appearance or manner as fair game. The same theory applies to murderers; it's just that they home in on a different type of body language. The problem of course is that we have yet to discover what makes the victims so attractive to their killers.'

Malone wrote one single word on the blackboard in block capitals:

VICTIMS

Initiation

The coffin was covered by flowers. Bouquets, wreaths and as many other floral tributes as could be balanced on the lid of the box. The child watched as the four black-coated men lifted the casket gently from the back of the hearse and made their way towards the grave which yawned open like a waiting mouth, ready to swallow the offered article.

In the trees nearby birds sang, oblivious to the sound of sobbing, unaware of the moans of anguish which periodically rose from the assembled group close to the grave.

Bees buzzed around the coffin flowers, one of them settling on a wreath of red carnations.

The child looked up and around at the faces of those who stood by, some tear-stained and drained of colour.

As the coffin bearers approached the graveside one of the bouquets slipped and fell into the open grave. The child watched it disappear into the black maw, wanting to go over and look in, to see how deep the hole was, but the restraining hand on its shoulder prevented any such opportunity.

The priest spoke his words softly as the coffin was lowered slowly into the ground. The child watched the clergyman, studying his face – the heavy jowls, the thick lips dotted with spittle which he wiped away after every few sentences.

The sound of sobbing rose to a crescendo as the straps which held the coffin were pulled free and the box at last lay in the waiting earth. Again the child wanted to rush across and peer down into the hole, to look at the coffin. To look through the wooden lid at the body which lay within.

The priest finished speaking and beckoned the first group of mourners forward and the child felt itself being pushed ahead. Towards the grave.

The hand never left the child's shoulder but now, as it looked down at the casket, nothing else seemed to register. There was the grave and the coffin. Nothing else.

The child stood mesmerized, eyes flicking back and forth over the object, from the brass name-plate to the six screws which held the lid down. The polished wood reflected the child's own image for a moment and it was as if positions had briefly been reversed. The child tried to imagine looking up at the faces which gazed down into the grave. Tried to imagine lying in the cold silk which lined the coffin, encased in a kind of cocoon, but one which was never likely to burst forth with life. This encasement was for the slow disintegration of a body, not the renewal.

The child wondered what it felt like to be dead. Never to hear those birds which still sang in the trees nearby or see the insects which hovered around the flowers at the graveside.

Then a handful of earth hit the coffin lid and the child looked at the priest who had thrown it. He was brushing the dirt from his palms as he backed away.

More dirt followed, thrown by others at the graveside, and now the child took a handful and stood over the box, noticing how the name-plate was all but covered by the scattered earth. The child finally released what it held in its hand, listening to the fragments bouncing off the polished wood.

Then hands tried to coax it away from the hole, but the child did not want to move. It wanted to stay and stare, wanted to climb down into the hole and look more closely. It wanted to lie on top of the coffin and look up at the twisted, anguished faces.

The hands tugged more urgently and the child moved away, the sound of muffled sobs now loud in its ears.

The wailing and the chorus of pain grew in volume but the child was unmoved. This was the music of death.

It was a tune which the child found pleasing.

It stared back at the open grave.

Wondering.

PART ONE

'Rather murder an infant in its cradle than
nurse unsatisfied desire.'

William Blake

'He's not a victim,
You can see it in his face.'

Kiss

One

He knew the child was somewhere inside the house.

Since her disappearance two days earlier he had known.

He had known that she had been taken to this decaying shell of a building. A testament to the insanity of some architect now long dead.

He had known but, until now, he had not been able to summon up the courage to enter the house to search for her.

He had been disgusted with himself. Disgusted with his own reluctance to retrieve his child.

But that disgust had been tempered by fear.

Fear of entering the building and searching its dusty rooms and cavernous corridors.

But now he had no choice and, as he moved slowly into the towering hallway, he felt the muscles of his stomach tighten into a hard knot until he found it difficult to get his breath. He trod the floorboards softly, his footfalls deadened by the odorous carpet of mildew which covered the wood. He paused at the foot of the staircase, one hand resting on the banister. Beneath his hand the slime felt like cold mucus and he withdrew it rapidly, wiping the noxious fluid on his trousers. He peered up into the gloom which made the upper landing almost invisible. Then, slowly, he began to ascend.

The steps creaked protestingly beneath his weight and he paused for a moment, ears and eyes alert for the slightest hint of sound or movement. There was none. He continued to climb.

The torch which was jammed in his belt was useless. He had smashed the bulb whilst breaking in. Now its only use was as a weapon should he need to defend himself. The idea brought beads of perspiration to his forehead.

He stood still at the top of the stairs, pulling the lighter from the pocket of his jeans, lifting its meagre flame above his head. The puddle of light which fanned out around him was woefully inadequate in the darkness, but he moved on, one hand gripping the rotten balustrade.

Ahead of him were three doors.

He crossed to the first of them, his hand shaking as he reached for the handle. He turned it and the mouldy brass knob twisted loosely in his grip.

He tried again, putting his weight against the thick wood this time. With gritted teeth he drove his shoulder into it.

The door swung back on hinges which had not tasted oil for years and the pitiful whine which they emitted reminded him of an injured dog.

He stood in the doorway for long seconds, flicking the lighter on once more, trying to discern some shapes in the cloying blackness inside the room.

But for some rotting pieces of furniture, the room appeared to be empty. He backed out onto the landing.

Somewhere ahead of him he heard a low, almost mucoid exhalation. Soft and sibilant.

He squinted through the darkness, trying to pick out the exact location of the sound. Easing the heavy torch from his belt he raised it before him like a truncheon and moved further along the corridor.

Outside the second door he saw something apallingly familiar.

The breath caught in his throat as he recognized his daughter's shoe.

Gasping, he dropped to one knee and picked it up. The tiny article was splashed with blood and he felt his own life-fluid freeze slightly as he held the shoe before him, listening for the sound once more.

Silence.

Only the pounding of his heart and the rushing of the blood in his ears greeted his vigilance.

He got to his feet and tried the handle of the second door,

pausing a moment before shoving it open. Immediately he flicked on the lighter.

The sickly yellow light spilled into the room, illuminating a torn cardigan. He crossed to it, sickness now replacing the knot of fear in his stomach. The cardigan was almost shredded and, like the shoe, it was spattered with blood. He whispered his daughter's name under his breath and turned back to the landing, approaching the third and final door. The lighter was growing hot in his hand and he was forced to flick it off, standing blindly in the darkness for what seemed like an eternity, his eyes darting to and fro in a vain attempt to pierce the stygian gloom. Finally, satisfied that the lighter had cooled down, he lit it again and prepared to enter the third room.

His hand was actually on the brass knob when it was turned from the inside.

The door swung open as if bidding him to enter and he stepped across the threshold, the lighter held above his head.

Had he been able to, he would have screamed.

As it was, all he could do was sag helplessly against the door frame, sickness sweeping over him, his stomach contracting and threatening to expel its contents. His eyes bulged madly in their sockets as he stared at the sight before him.

His daughter was hanging upside down from a hook and chain attached to the ceiling, dangling there like a joint in a butcher's shop. Both her arms had been severed at the shoulders, her throat slashed clumsily. The floor beneath her was awash with blood, some of which had begun to congeal, forming a sticky red porridge.

Of her severed arms there was no sign.

He staggered back, slamming the door behind him, anxious to block out the appalling sight, wishing that he could block it from his mind too. The lighter fell from his hand and the darkness closed around him once more. He felt as if his legs were going to buckle beneath him but, summoning some hidden reserves of strength, he managed to run for the stairs.

He was roughly level with the first door when it flew open.

The creature which came hurtling at him was straight out of a nightmare.

17

It was as tall as a man, its body slightly hunched due to the weight of its large head. A head which was covered by torn and shredded skin, revealing bulging veins and pustules beneath. Long wisps of white hair cascaded behind it as it ran at him, its eyes blazing. Twin orbs which seemed to have no pupils. Two burning red pools like boiling blood. As it opened its mouth a huge tongue flickered out, reaching past its chin, dripping yellow saliva.

In one clawed hand it held a machete.

He raised a hand to shield himself but the suddenness and ferocity of the attack were overwhelming.

The blade of the machete caught him just below the sternum, powering effortlessly through his belly until it reached his pelvis. His body split open like an overripe peach, entrails spilling out like a plague of bleeding ringworm. He screamed and fell, feeling the creature throw itself upon him, its claws burrowing into the cavity of his torso. Digging deeper until they closed around the object they sought.

The creature tore his heart free, squeezing the throbbing organ in its powerful hand, holding the blood-drenched trophy aloft while, all the time, its tumefied reptilian tongue writhed like a spittle-covered worm.

It squeezed the heart more tightly, watching the blood spew from the torn arteries. The creature raised it towards its mouth.

It was then that the lights came on.

Two

'Cut it.'

The voice was accompanied by a sudden explosion of brilliance from the banks of lights overhead and the darkened landing was bathed in a cold white glow.

Phillip Dickinson clambered off the camera crane which was poised beside the two actors and jumped down, careful to avoid the continuity girl who was busily snapping photos of the little tableau. She was taking no chances when shooting resumed. Only last week a character with a scar on his right cheek in one scene had appeared with the disfigurement miraculously transferred to the left cheek in the following scene. Only careful study of the rushes had revealed the mistake but now the actor had returned to America and it would cost too much to recall him. This time she didn't intend anything to go wrong. She measured positions while the two actors remained still, the one on the ground smiling up at her as she busied herself.

With the coming of light the film set once more became a scene of organized pandemonium as technicians consulted the shooting script to see what was next on the agenda. Actors were called onto the set, others stood around smoking and chatting.

Three grips were busily assembling the tracks onto which they intended lowering the heavy panavision camera and its trolley. The next scene called for a travelling shot of the deformed creature carrying the heart of its newest victim down to the cellar to its growing companions.

Dickinson looked down as he heard the voice of assistant director Colin Robson bellowing to some crew members to be careful as they moved a large spotlight into position. Robson was tall and lean, yet to reach his thirty-fifth birthday. He was four years younger than Dickinson who now stood looking at the scenes of activity around him, brushing a hand through his shoulder-length brown hair. He reached into the pocket of his jeans and pulled out a stick of chewing gum which he pushed into his mouth. He looked first at his watch, then at the continuity girl.

'Come on, Sarah,' he said, 'We haven't got all day.'

Despite having been born in Sussex, Dickinson had commuted back and forth between Britain and the States enough times for his accent to carry a slight American twang. He'd been directing for the past eight years, having graduated from scripting a couple of long-running American cop series which he then went on to direct. However, the constraints of television, he felt, had stifled his real creative leanings, so he'd decided to try films. He'd worked as a second-unit director on several films in the States but his big break had finally come when he'd travelled to Italy two weeks after his thirty-first birthday and met the head of DAC Films.

Dickinson had been hired to direct *The Mutilator*, which on release in the States made over ten million dollars and, more importantly, gave him a foothold in the American business. But in his eagerness to succeed he found himself directing a succession of horror movies and now, eight years later, the novelty hadn't so much worn off as been permanently eroded.

Now the director stood, hands planted firmly on his hips, looking down at the actor who was sprawled on the floor, his clothes saturated by stage blood. He shook his head and sighed wearily.

'Something wrong, Phil?'

The voice made him turn and he saw Frank Miller approaching from the top of the landing. Miller was dressed in a dark sweatshirt and jeans and he was carrying a small silver hip-flask in one hand. His brown hair was uncombed and, like his moustache, it carried traces of grey. His face was heavily stubbled, and as he scratched his cheek the bristles made a rasping sound. Miller, despite appearances to the contrary, was six years younger than Dickinson but the deeply cut lines in his forehead and around his eyes belied his youth. He took a swig from his hip flask then jammed it back into the back pocket of his jeans.

'You don't look very happy,' Miller said, patting the director on the shoulder as he passed.

As Dickinson watched, the younger man began pulling a network of thin tubes from around the back of the actor sprawled on the ground. They had carried the blood which had so realistically spurted from his torn stomach in the scene they'd just completed. Worked by three small and well-concealed pumps also attached to the actor's body, the device had been operated by remote control by Miller himself, who now looked on with some pride at his bloody handiwork.

'Can I go and wash this off now?' asked the bloodstained actor.

Dickinson nodded.

'Why not? I think we'll all take a break.' He looked at his watch then turned and, cupping both hands to his mouth bellowed across the set, 'We'll break it here. Everybody back on set in an hour.'

Murmurs of approval greeted his latest instruction and technicians and actors alike trooped off the set, heading for the canteen which had been set up in two large caravans outside the sound stage.

'What about this, Frank?' asked the rotting creature, still clutching the heart.

'Leave it here,' Miller said, watching as the heavily made-up actor deposited the organ on the ground beside him. Then, both monster and victim ambled off for lunch, leaving Dickinson and Miller alone. The silence suddenly seemed oppressive after the frenzied activity of between-scenes preparation.

'Got any of that to spare?' asked Dickinson, pointing at Miller's hip flask.

The younger man pulled the receptacle from his pocket and handed it to the director.

'I could be forgiven for thinking that you're not happy in your work,' Miller observed, winding the bloodied tubes into a ball.

'You'd be right,' Dickinson said, handing back the flask. He wiped his mouth with the back of his hand and watched as Miller stuffed the plastic tubing into a bag. He then picked up the heart and dropped that in as well. 'Christ, they give me a budget of four million bucks, a crew I've never seen before and a piece of shit for a script, send me over here and tell me to come back with a movie that's going to make them fifteen million. What the hell am I supposed to do?' He sighed wearily.

'They call it trying to make a silk purse out of a sow's ear,' Miller said sardonically.

'I'm lucky they let me pick my own special effects man. At least one part of this mess is going to look good.'

Miller smiled proudly. He knew that what Dickinson said was true; he hadn't earned a reputation as one of the film world's top special effects men for nothing. Twice nominated for his work in prosthetics, he'd finally won an award at the Trieste Fantasy Film Festival a year ago for his make-up and effects work on *Brainsucker Part 2*. Although his work throughout the film had been excellent, Miller had been particularly proud of the scene in which he'd been forced to contrive the illusion that the creature of the title was actually inserting its long proboscis into the ear of its victim and feeding on the brain. He'd achieved the effect through a mixture of false heads, stop-frame animation and live action.

Dickinson had directed on that occasion too.

'So why did you take this job?' Miller asked as the two men wandered down the staircase. 'You knew the script was crap.'

'It's a contract job,' the director answered. 'I signed for three movies. At least this one's an original,' he grunted. 'The last two were both sequels to somebody else's work. I sometimes wonder what would happen to the film business if no one had ever thought of sequels. So, what happens? I tell the chief executive that I don't want to direct any more sequels. He hands me this fucking script his son's written.'

Miller smiled thinly as the director continued.

'He rings me at home two days later and asks what I think of it. Fortunately, he told me how much they were going to pay me before I had to give an opinion.'

'It's all about money, Phil, you don't need me to tell you that,' the effects man reminded him. 'If you've got the money, who cares. Like they say, life's a shit sandwich. The more bread you've got, the less shit you have to eat.'

'Very philosophical,' Dickinson remarked. 'I'll just be glad when this damned picture's finished. I'm going to pick up my pay-cheque and run.'

'That's one of the things I love about you, your dedication,' Miller chuckled.

'You're the one who should know about dedication. I've been in this business for nearly fifteen years altogether and I've never seen effects as realistic as yours. Like that heart.' He motioned towards the bag which Miller was carrying. 'It looks so real and you only had twelve hours to model it. I don't know how the hell you do it.'

'Trade secret,' Miller told him, reaching for the hip flask again.

'You coming for lunch?' Dickinson asked.

'I want to take this stuff back first,' Miller said, holding up the bag and its contents. 'I'll leave it in my make-up room. I'll see you in the canteen in about ten minutes.'

Dickinson nodded and walked off.

Miller paused for a moment then wandered off in the opposite direction. Pushing open the exit door from the sound-stage he stepped out into the drizzle beyond. Above, the sky was grey and swollen with cloud. Puddles had begun to form on the tarmac round about. Miller's make-up room cum mobile workshop was a converted caravan as were the dressing rooms of the cast. He looked across towards his own temporary quarters then turned and headed for the toilets.

The special effects man paused as he entered, checking that he was alone. Satisfied that all the cubicles were empty, he entered the first one and slid the bolt behind him.

Locked inside, he opened the bag, recoiling slightly from the smell that rose from within. He picked up the heart then dropped it down the pan.

For long moments he stood looking down at it, bloated and bloodied, staining the water, lying there like the swollen remains of some hideous miscarriage. Then he flushed the toilet, watching as the entire pan turned red.

The heart stuck for a moment then, as he flushed again, it finally disappeared in a cascade of clear water.

Miller hurried from the toilet to his caravan, dumped the tangle of rubber tubing, then headed for the canteen.

On the way he checked in the toilet once more.

The heart had disappeared.

Three

Pieces of chicken stuck to the thick, cracked lips of the creature as it shovelled food into its mouth.

'Fuck this,' rasped Kevin Brady, his words somewhat slurred because he was unable to open his mouth more than half an inch. He pulled the greasy blobs of chicken from the lips of the mask and, instead, attempted to take a sip of his tea. The hot liquid dribbled down his chin but he felt nothing because the prosthetic skin protected his own flesh. Finally he retrieved a straw and sucked the tea through that.

'If this is what they call suffering in the cause of art then they can stuff it,' Brady grunted, his face feeling as though someone had coated it with concrete. He had been in make-up since six o'clock that morning and now, as the hands of his watch reached one-fifteen he was beginning to feel more like the man in the iron mask. Miller had told the actor when he applied the make-up that too much movement would cause it to crack and, as it took over two hours to transform him into one of the 'astro-cannibals' of the film's title, neither actor or make-up artist relished the prospect of a repeat performance that same day.

Frank Miller sat over his plate of egg and chips watching Brady, a slight smile on his face. The canteen was a hive of activity, a blur of sounds and conversation. A number of the cast were in make-up and Miller turned to see two hideously scarred burn victims queuing up for their lunch, chatting happily as the woman behind the counter did her best to look away from them. The effects man grinned more broadly.

'Are you eating that?' asked another man and, as Miller shook his head, a clawed hand with one finger torn off reached across

25

and claimed the jam doughnut which lay close by.

Two men, both with gaping bullet wounds in their foreheads, sat at the next table smoking.

'It took me an hour to get this stuff off last night,' Brady said, prodding his face. 'I know you removed most of it before I left the set but I had to use soap and water to get the rest off.'

'I told you,' Miller explained. 'Use surgical spirit, it's more effective.' He pushed his plate away and reached for his hip flask, glancing around him at his other creations.

A woman with one ear torn off and her throat cut was busily combing her hair. The front of her ripped top was stained with blood and Brady caught sight of a tantalizing flash of nipple through one of the strategically placed gashes in the material. As the actress got to her feet he tried to raise his eyebrows but the make-up prevented that simple gesture. He ran appraising red eyes up and down her long, slender legs as she strode from the canteen.

'There's times when having a tongue like this might come in handy,' he said, chuckling, prodding the long worm-like accessory which he wore over his own tongue once shooting began.

'Especially if you could breathe through your ears,' said Miller, swigging from his flask.

A chorus of guffaws greeted his remark.

'You get to put make-up on lots of actresses don't you?' Brady said. 'You know, body make-up.' He tried to smile but the effort was almost painful as he felt the rubberized skin tighten on his flesh.

'So?' Miller asked. 'It's only like an artist putting paint on a canvas. It's just that I use living canvas.'

'Yes, but artists don't paint on tits do they?' Brady replied lecherously.

Miller took another sip from his flask.

'Oh, I don't know,' he said. 'I mean, I put make-up on *you*. That must class as painting a tit if anything does.'

An outburst of laughter rang around the table. Brady, however, didn't see the joke. He regarded the effects man malevolently for a moment then returned to his lunch.

Miller massaged the bridge of his nose between his thumb and forefinger and tried to shut out the cacophony of sounds inside the canteen. He closed his eyes, as if that act would lessen the noise, shut it out of his mind. Needless to say it didn't work and he sighed almost painfully.

Miller didn't really feel comfortable in crowds, he never had. Probably a legacy of having been an only child, he told himself. He had grown used to his own company and, over the years, had seen the presence of others as, at best, a nuisance and, in the most extreme cases, an intrusion.

His jobs after leaving school had perpetuated his liking for solitude. He'd spent five years at a photographic college then decided, with the help of his father, to go freelance. At the age of twenty-three he had sold his first photographs to a national newspaper. There'd been an outbreak of foot-and-mouth disease on a farm close to where he lived and the pictures of the stricken animals had been used by the *Mail*. When a car crash had claimed the life of a local dignitary Miller had been on hand when the fire brigade were cutting the remains of him and his wife from the wreckage. He had managed to get some shots of the bodies before anyone could drape them with blankets.

The tabloids went crazy for those.

The pay was good but sporadic, so when he was finally offered a full-time position with the *Express* he moved to London and into digs. He made friends easily or, more to the point, he attracted people to him. Miller was hesitant to use the word *friend* about anyone. To him, people were never more than acquaintances; he wanted nothing more from them and he made sure that no one ever got too close to him. He had his work, that was all that mattered.

The assignments began to take on a depressingly familiar pattern. He was always first at any accident, camera at the ready. During the height of the IRA bomb blitz of London in the late seventies he found that his best friends were death and pain. Those friends paid his rent. Wherever there was suffering, Miller was never far away, ready to record the event for posterity and for a big cheque. When a woman had jumped from the seventh floor of the Ritz hotel he had been the one who had captured her image in mid-air as she plummeted to the ground. That photo had won him a prize. The one that he'd taken *after* she hit the ground hadn't been so popular but Miller was nothing if not thorough.

The police work seemed to be a natural progression. From taking photos of accidental deaths it seemed only logical that he should progress to snapping the aftermath of premeditated destruction.

The ten-year-old boy who'd been raped by a homosexual, so badly assaulted that his anus had been torn open. Then his killer had strangled him with barbed wire.

The young woman who had been found with her face pressed onto the ring of an electric cooker, a weighted suitcase holding her head there.

In time he even managed to look on the dead babies with an impassioned eye. Like the six-month-old girl who had been beaten so severely that part of her brain had burst through one of the holes in her skull. She had been killed by her mentally retarded mother who had been so fascinated by the fact that her daughter's fontanelle was still visible beneath the thin skin she had pushed three fingers into the child's head.

And then there had been the bigger jobs. Those that reminded him of his days on the newspaper. He had been one of the first on the scene at the Moorgate tube disaster, he'd watched as the remains of complete human beings were shovelled into plastic bags. Bodies had been mangled almost beyond belief. Certainly beyond any artistic acceptance. For in that blood-drenched tunnel Miller had finally learned that death and mutilation also had an aesthetic face. No one had seen him re-arrange one of the pulped corpses so that all of it was showing when he took the picture. After all, he was a photographer first and foremost and he'd never forgotten that the composition of a photo is important.

Even if, sometimes, it does mean having to wipe slicks of brain matter off your shoes afterwards.

He'd been twenty-six when that happened and it was around that time he had begun to drink heavily.

Miller's thoughts were interrupted by a hand on his shoulder.

He turned to see Dickinson standing there.

'Have you got a minute, Frank?' the director asked. 'I wanted to talk about the scene we're shooting next.'

'I'm all ears, Phil,' he said, swigging from his flask. The effects man got to his feet and followed the director out of the canteen. As he left a young woman smiled at him.

Miller smiled back.

She was a good looking girl.

Even if one of her eyes *was* missing and part of her nose *had* been hacked away.

Four

There was a loud metallic rattle as Dickinson worked the pump action of the shotgun. He raised the weapon to his shoulder, drew a bead on Kevin Brady and gently squeezed the trigger.

As the hammer slammed down on an empty magazine, the director squinted along the sight towards the actor who was standing with both arms upraised while Miller carefully attached a metal plate about the size of a man's fist to his chest. Holding a strip of surgical tape between his teeth, Miller secured the plate to the actor's bare flesh, grinning when he saw that the sticky band covered some of the hair on Brady's torso.

'That's going to be a bit painful when you pull it off,' said the effects man as he inspected his handiwork.

Brady nodded resignedly and prodded the small metal plate. It was backed by foam rubber to absorb what small recoil would come from the detonation.

'I hope these bloody things are safe,' said the actor, watching as Miller attached the tiny explosive charge to the metal.

'That's what we're going to find out,' Miller said, flatly, the solemnness in his voice making Brady feel suddenly nervous. 'OK, hold still,' the effects man said and retrieved a small hand-set from a nearby table. With one eye on the squib he selected the appropriate button on the remote and pressed.

There was a dull bang and a smokeless explosion as the squib went off.

Brady moved involuntarily as he felt the small impact on his chest.

'Do you want to try it with the blood bag, Phil?' Miller asked, taking a swift swig from his hip flask.

Dickinson nodded, handing the shotgun to another actor who was watching in fascination as Miller took hold of the small metal plate and, with one tug, pulled it free of Brady's chest. Several dark hairs came with it and the actor cursed, rubbing his sore skin.

He seated himself on the edge of the table, watching as Miller pulled a piece of rubber from his pocket and laid it out before him. Brady looked at the smooth latex, convinced that it looked familiar.

It took him only a second to realize that it was a contraceptive.

'I left some of my gear at home this morning,' Miller announced, carefully filling the contraceptive with a thick red fluid. 'It's a good job there's a chemist near the set.'

'How many did you buy?' Brady wanted to know.

'Six packets,' Miller told him, smiling. 'The woman behind the counter must have thought I was in for a heavy night.'

Brady and the others who were watching chuckled as Miller completed his task. The teat and the first quarter of the sheath were now full of the imitation blood. The effects man wiped some of it on his jeans and Brady noticed how realistic the stain appeared. As if he'd cut himself and wiped the wound on the material. Next he tied the contraceptive into a tight knot, pushing the blood into the end of its receptacle to form a bag. It looked as if someone had filled it with crimson ejaculate.

Colin Robson, the assistant director, wandered over to tell Dickinson that the cameras were in position, then, that task completed, he paused for a moment to watch as Miller attached another metal plate to Brady's chest. This one he also fastened on with surgical tape then, carefully, he positioned the blood bag on the plate, ensuring that it was directly over the fresh squib. That done, Miller retired a foot or so and picked up the remote control.

'Ready?' he said to Brady.

The actor nodded.

Miller took another swig from his hip flask, then nonchalantly pressed the small red button on the remote.

The squib went off, rupturing the rubber bag which burst

like a throbbing boil, spilling its sticky contents down Brady's chest.

'Terrific,' said Dickinson. 'We'll go for the shot now.'

As Miller set about securing another of the blood bags and squibs to Brady's body the director turned to Pat Sullivan, who was holding the shotgun. Sullivan was in his early twenties, a thin, gangling youth with long brown hair.

'Now, just run towards Kevin,' Dickinson said. 'Lift the shotgun up to your shoulder then stand there as if you're horrified. As if you can't bring yourself to believe what you're seeing. Kevin will run at you and it's then that you fire at him. Don't worry about the gun, it'll be loaded with blanks. There'll be lots of noise but it's safe enough. We'll dub on the sound later. Blanks always sound too hollow.'

'I was supposed to speak a line before I fired, according to the script,' Sullivan offered.

'Fuck the script,' snapped Dickinson. 'The line was crap anyway.'

'I just thought that it was necessary in the context of the character,' the young actor suggested.

'For Christ's sake, this is a horror film not a bloody social documentary. I'm not here to make great movies, I'm here to make money. Now forget the line, right. Just fire the shotgun at him. I'll be holding on a two-shot until you fire, then I'll move in for a close-up on you, then on Kevin when he's hit.'

Miller had all but completed his work. He had fixed four of the squibs and their accompanying blood bags to Brady's chest. With practised care he fastened one last one at the point of the actor's shoulder.

'With five of them on you, it's odds-on you're going to feel some impact,' Miller said.

'I'm more worried about pulling the bloody things off when we've finished,' Brady told him, his voice still slurred because of the thick make-up he wore.

High above them two powerful arc lights were lowered into position while the lighting cameraman checked the scene with a light meter, conferring with the cinematographer who was perched on top of a camera crane.

Miller glanced round as he saw the flash of a bulb and he recognized the photographer as one of the regulars from *Photoplay*. He nodded at the effects man then scuttled off to get some photos of the other technicians who were swarming over the set like flies over a dead dog.

'Are we ready to go?' Dickinson said wearily.

'Come on everybody,' the assistant director shouted. 'We *are* supposed to be professionals.'

A chorus of jeers and laughter greeted his remark.

Lights dimmed as Brady and Sullivan took up their positions.

'Right, no run-through. We go with it first time,' called Dickinson. 'Ready?'

'One ready,' a cameraman replied and his two companions signalled in affirmation.

'Turn over,' Dickinson shouted.

There was the harsh clack of a clapperboard and Miller heard the words 'Fifty-eight, take one.'

Dickinson took one last look around him then stepped back.

'Action,' he called and Sullivan stepped forward onto the set.

Miller moved closer to the director, the remote control panel held in his hand, the hip flask held in the other. He took a long swig from it as he waited for his cue.

The camera crane swung in low over Sullivan as he raised the shotgun.

'Right, Frank,' whispered Dickinson and Miller allowed his finger to hover over the red button on the remote. A few more seconds and he would, through his effects expertise, make it appear that most of Brady's chest had been destroyed by a shotgun blast. He watched the two actors confront each other, Brady now sporting the lolling plastic tongue which he'd worn in previous scenes.

Dickinson watched impassively as the actors played out the scene, his impatience growing as Sullivan paused a fraction too long before squeezing the trigger of the shotgun.

There was a dull boom as he did so, the blank cartridges going off with a deafening roar.

Miller jabbed the button on the remote.

Nothing happened.

'Oh, shit,' hissed the effects man, shaking the small box angrily.

'Cut it,' Dickinson shouted, wearily. 'Right, nobody move. This'll be fixed in a couple of minutes.' He looked at Miller who was already examining the squibs.

'What happened?' Brady wanted to know as the effects man fiddled with the small explosive charges.

'Something could have jammed the signal,' Miller said. 'If it doesn't work this time I'll have to wire them up to a control board.' He bent closer, squinting at the minute detonators, adjusting them slightly.

Brady could smell the whisky on the effects man's breath.

Miller muttered to himself as he re-adjusted the squibs, looking round to see where he'd put the remote.

It was lying on the table behind him.

He decided that he'd be better off trying the squibs first, before the cameras started rolling. He didn't want any more cock-ups.

He bent closer to the squibs, his face only an inch or two from them.

Pat Sullivan rubbed his shoulder, surprised that the recoil on the shotgun had been so violent, considering the weapon had fired only blanks.

Miller prodded the detonator of the fourth squib, bending closer to adjust it.

Sullivan put the shotgun down on top of the remote.

Miller heard the warning shout but there was nothing he could do.

All five squibs went off simultaneously.

He saw a brief blinding light then all he felt was searing pain as the charges exploded in his face, the bursts of fire scorching his eyes. He screamed in pain as he felt sticky liquid spurting onto him as the blood bags burst and splattered him with fake life-fluid. But the most powerful sensation was that of pain. Excruciating agony which seemed to fill his head as he clawed at his burning eyes. Fragments of rubber mingled with the shower of sparks which roasted the sensitive orbs. Miller fell to his knees roaring in pain, striking out blindly.

34

He heard screams and shouts around him but they came from an interminable darkness which would not lift while all the time he clawed at his eyes which felt as if someone had poured acid into them. Stage blood mingled with his own and ran down his face to stain his cheeks which were already blackened by the five miniature explosions.

He fell forward, the pain finally growing too great and, almost gratefully, he felt himself beginning to lose consciousness.

Before he blacked out completely he heard Dickinson's voice loud above the cacophony of shrieks and calls.

'Get an ambulance, quick.'

That was the last thing he heard.

Five

He heard the crash as the ambulance doors were flung open, then suddenly he felt cold air on his face as he was lifted onto a waiting gurney.

At least that was what he imagined to be happening. He could see nothing.

Miller had regained consciousness only minutes after being placed in the emergency vehicle and he had been forced to lie in agony as the ambulance sped through the streets towards the hospital. He'd been vaguely aware of the sensation of speed, he'd heard the strident wailing of the siren and, closer to him, the voice of a medic offering reassurance and, more to the point, morphine. In the darkness he had been grateful for the pain-killing drug.

The journey had taken less than ten minutes but it had seemed like an eternity. Now, in his blindness, he felt himself being trundled towards the main entrance of Casualty.

Voices swirled and eddied around him, disembodied sounds in the perpetual night which had descended upon him. He heard nurses speaking quickly, caught fleeting words here and there.

'. . . his eyes . . .'

'. . . straight to surgery . . .'

'. . . badly damaged . . . in pain . . .'

Miller felt like adding his own contribution to the patchwork of words and sounds, but when he tried to speak his lips merely moved soundlessly. It felt as if someone had filled his mouth with chalk. When he tried to swallow his throat merely constricted, preventing even that simple action.

The gurney bumped against something and, in his blindness,

he called out. A sound he'd felt incapable of making came out as a low croak. The smell of disinfectant was strong in his nostrils now, an odour which meant he was being pushed along one of the hospital corridors. He felt hands brushing his skin. Warm hands. There was reassurance in the touch.

Jesus, if only he could see something.

He blinked but the action only increased his pain and he groaned again, realizing that the effects of the morphine were wearing off.

'Get out the way . . .'

'. . . emergency . . .'

'. . . OR three, now . . .'

Miller could feel the bandages around his head and he prayed that was the reason he could not see. He gritted his teeth as he felt the gurney come to a halt.

'He's lost a lot of blood,' a voice above him said. Miller wanted to say something, wanted to tell them that most of the crimson fluid which covered his face was of the fake variety. Like some kind of joke. Funny fucking joke. You're blind, you stupid bastard, he told himself. Now let's hear you laugh.

'What happened?' the voice asked again and Miller heard brief details of the accident being relayed from somewhere to his right. He also felt hands gently removing the bandages, peeling back the layers of gauze until his eyes were exposed. He braced himself for the onslaught of the light, for the pain which would come when he opened his eyes. And he prayed for that pain.

He prayed for the light.

The cotton wool pads were removed.

Miller opened his eyes.

Darkness.

'Oh Christ,' he moaned, the noise sounding alien. As if someone else had spoken the words. 'I can't see.' His breath was coming in short gasps now. *'I can't fucking see!'* he roared, his voice a mixture of fear and frustration. He turned his head from side to side as if expecting his vision to return, as if everything was going to suddenly become clear, as if the disembodied voices were about to be given substance.

But there was only the blackness.

Miller tried to sit up but the pain tore though him and he slumped back as if he'd been struck by a heavy object, as if the outburst had sapped any strength he possessed. He lay helplessly on the gurney, restrained now by more firm but caring hands.

He heard other words, some he didn't understand, then he felt hands on his right arm, rolling the material of his sweatshirt up, exposing the crook of his arm and the vein which pulsed there. He turned instinctively towards the movements, angered now by his inability to see, wanting to know what these people were doing to him. Wanting to see them.

He hissed as he felt the needle being run into his arm and he tensed momentarily as the steel was pushed home, held there, then withdrawn.

'Lie still . . .'

'. . . get him ready . . .'

'. . . must hurry . . .'

More invisible words. He felt the gurney being moved again and he sank back onto the pillow which supported his head. It still felt as if his eyes were on fire but that pain was gradually beginning to subside. Everything was becoming distant. The voices were beginning to resonate inside his head like words spoken inside an echo chamber. He was floating but he fought against the feeling, blinking his blind eyes hard, squeezing his torn lids together. But even the renewed stab of pain could not prevent his steady slide into unconsciousness. It was a battle he knew he couldn't win, but he fought it nevertheless until, finally, he lay back and the darkness which filled his eyes filled his brain.

'The damage to the left eye looks more severe,' said Doctor George Cook as he gazed down at Miller's face.

Apart from the low breathing of the unconscious effects man and the odd murmurings of the surgical team the only sound to be heard in the operating room was the steady blip of the oscilloscope. Every now and then Greg Vincent would glance across at the machine but the anaesthetist did it out of habit rather than any concern for the patient. Miller was in good hands.

Cook picked up a scalpel from the nearby trolley and with minute skill slid it beneath the upper lid of Miller's left eye, exposing the ruined orb more fully. The surgeon carefully wiped away a dribble of vitreous jelly which spilled from the eye as he inspected it. Tiny clips held the lids open, allowing the doctor and his team a full view of their patient's injuries.

'There döesn't appear to be any damage to either retina or optic nerve,' muttered Cook. 'But the lens of this left eye is completely destroyed.' He sighed. 'I don't think we have any choice. We either remove the remains of the cornea and the lens or he'll lose the whole eye.'

'What about the right eye?' asked Doctor Simon Thompson.

Cook looked at it, using the point of the scalpel to remove a small piece of black matter from the lower lid. The skin round the eye was scorched in places but the orb itself seemed to have escaped damage. He shook his head and returned his attention to its neighbour.

'I'm going to remove the cornea and lens,' Cook repeated.

He steadied himself and, working with incredible delicacy for such a big man, pushed the point of the scalpel carefully into the pulped eye. Using a slight cutting action he sheared a small section of the cornea away, lifting it free with the razor sharp blade. A nurse moved forward and offered a metal dish, watching as the surgeon dropped the piece of almost transparent tissue into it before continuing with his task. He cut deeper this time, ignoring the watery trickle of blood and fluid which ran from the incision. His cut was circular, freeing what remained of the lens. It seemed to float on the vitreous liquid until Cook removed it and placed it in the dish.

The contents looked like slivers of bloodied cling-film.

'The suspensory ligaments and the ciliary muscles are badly burned,' he mused aloud, cutting away a small piece of flesh from beneath the inner lid of the eye.

It joined the cornea and the lens in the metal dish.

The steady blip of the oscilloscope accompanied his expert ministrations.

As if he were peeling away the layers of an onion, Cook separated pieces of translucent flesh and pulled them from the ravaged eye with the aid of a scalpel and tweezers. Then, when the last of the tissue had been lifted away he discarded the scalpel and set to work stitching together the small hole left by the removal of the lens.

'Will he be blind in that eye, sir?' asked a nurse who stood nearby.

Cook exhaled, the breath rasping against his mask.

'Possibly,' he said, thoughtfully. 'However, he does have a choice.'

Dr Thompson threw the surgeon a puzzled glance, his brow furrowing slightly.

Cook saw the other doctor's reaction but didn't acknowledge it. He merely regarded his colleague over the top of his mask.

The oscilloscope continued its tuneless refrain.

Six

At first he couldn't work out whether he was still asleep.

Miller tried to sit up but found the effort beyond him. He sighed and lay back against the pillows, breathing heavily. It was still dark. Everything around him was silent, none of the shouting and yelling in his ears which had greeted him on arrival at the hospital. Maybe it was just night time. Perhaps that explained the darkness. Perhaps.

He opened his eyes.

He saw nothing.

Miller reached up, aware that once more his eyes were covered by cotton wool pads. He touched the tape which held them in place, feeling the pads with the tips of his fingers as a blind person might trace their hands across a page of braille.

A blind person.

You are blind, he told himself. Get used to touching things, because you're never going to see them again. The thought made him sigh once more and he raised both hands to his temples, his breath coming in short gasps.

'Mr Miller.'

The voice startled him.

'Who's that?' he murmured, sitting up awkwardly, instinctively looking round even though he couldn't see who had spoken the words. Immediately he groaned as he felt the stiffness in his back and legs. He lay back once more.

'How are you feeling?' the voice asked. A soft, feminine voice with a slight Irish lilt to it.

He shrugged his shoulders.

'You've been unconscious for six hours,' the voice told him.

41

'Where am I?' Miller wanted to know.

'In your room in the hospital,' he was told.

'And who are you? You'll have to excuse me but being blind puts me at a slight disadvantage,' Miller said acidly.

'I'm Nurse Brennan,' she told him.

'I'd like to say it's nice to see you but, as you've probably gathered, that'd be rather inappropriate at the moment,' Miller said. He raised both hands to his bandaged eyes and exhaled deeply. 'Christ,' he murmured. 'I'm sorry . . .'

'No need to apologize,' she said and Miller heard her move closer to the bed. Next thing he felt her hand behind his back, pushing him forwards. She re-arranged the pillows behind him so that he was sitting upright then he heard the clink of cutlery on crockery and the smell of food reached his nostrils.

'I'd rather have a drink,' he said, listening as she cut up his food.

She took his hand and closed it around the fork, guiding it towards his mouth. He chewed, wrinkling his nose slightly.

'Perhaps it's just as well I *can't* see what I'm eating,' he said, allowing her to cut up more of his food.

He swallowed two or three more mouthfuls then waved a hand in front of him.

'You've got to eat, Mr Miller,' she told him.

'I haven't got much of an appetite at the moment, nurse,' he said, indifferently. 'You could say I've got more important things on my mind. Like whether I'm going to be blind for the rest of my life.'

'I'm not the one to tell you that, Mr Miller.'

'Well, is there any chance of me speaking to someone who can?' he snapped.

The momentary silence inside the room was broken by a knock on the door. Again, Miller turned instinctively towards the sound, aware that a newcomer had entered the room.

'That's all for now, nurse,' Miller heard, noting the authority in the voice. Nurse Brennan left the room, closing the door behind her.

There was a moment's silence finally broken by the new arrival.

'I'm not going to ask you how you feel, Mr Miller,' said George Cook, lifting the chart from the bottom of Miller's bed and scanning it. 'I can imagine.'

'Yeah, it's easy. Just close your eyes,' Miller said sarcastically.

Cook introduced himself, then crossed to the window, gazing out at the rain-sodden sky. High above, hidden from view by the low-lying cloud, a plane passed over, its low rumble sounding like thunder.

'It's not very often we get a celebrity in here,' the surgeon said. 'Someone from the film world. Special effects isn't it?'

Miller nodded.

'Only this time they weren't so special,' he said wearily.

Cook looked across at his patient who was lying with his arms by his sides.

'Am I going to be blind for the rest of my life?' Miller asked, a note of fear in his voice.

'That's difficult to say. The injuries, to the left eye in particular, were bad. It's difficult, as I said.'

'Well, try an educated guess.'

'It's likely, yes,' Cook said, quietly. 'However, it's not certain. In fact, there is a chance that your sight could be restored fully.'

Miller sat up, his head turning in the direction of the surgeon.

'How?' he demanded, the depression in his voice suddenly replaced by a hint of hope.

'I only said that there was a *chance*, Mr Miller. Your right eye may well return to normal in time without the aid of surgery but the left was beyond help by the time you were brought to us.'

'Just tell me what you meant by a possibility of restoring my sight fully,' Miller demanded.

'A transplant,' said the surgeon. 'We've done them before at this hospital, successfully too.' He turned as he heard the first drops of rain spattering the glass of the window pane.

'Is there a donor available now?' Miller asked, involuntarily touching his left eye.

Cook hesitated for a moment.

'Yes there is,' he said quietly.

'How soon could you do the operation?' Miller wanted to know.

'The earliest would be a week – '

Miller interrupted him. 'A week? Why so long? If there's a donor why can't you do it immediately?'

'It isn't like changing a light bulb, Mr Miller,' the surgeon said. 'There have to be all sorts of tests done, tissue-typing, blood-group compatability. It's a complicated process.'

There was a long silence, broken by the surgeon.

'And there is always the possibility that the operation may not be completely successful,' he said. 'There's no guarantee it will work. I'm merely offering you an option.'

Miller nodded.

'I understand. It's a risk I want to take.'

Cook announced that he was leaving and headed for the door.

'Dr Cook,' Miller called after him. 'Thanks.'

'Thank me when the operation's over,' the surgeon said, then he was gone.

Miller sank back further onto his pillows, aware that his hands were shaking as he rubbed them across his forehead. Cook had at least given him something to cling to. Some hope. If Miller had believed in God he might well have offered up a prayer. As it was he rubbed his stomach and wondered if there was some way he could get a drink.

'George, can I have a word?'

Cook turned to see Dr Simon Thompson striding towards him down the corridor.

'Is it important?' the surgeon asked.

Thompson nodded and the two of them continued down the corridor to Cook's room. Once inside the surgeon closed the door.

'You've been speaking to Miller,' Thompson said. 'Did you mention the possibility of a transplant?'

'He's all for it. He wants us to go ahead as soon as possible. I told him that the tests would have to be carried out first, but he's willing to go along with that.'

Thompson exhaled deeply.

'I can't see your objection, Simon,' said Cook. 'We have a suitable donor, we have the opportunity to give Miller his sight back.'

'You know my objections,' Thompson said. 'What did he say when you told him who the donor was?'

'I didn't tell him.'

'Why not?' Thompson demanded.

'What difference does it make? The specimens are in perfect order, why should it matter who they've come from? All Miller's interested in is getting back his sight and, as doctors, our only concern should be in completing the operation successfully.'

'He has a right to know,' Thompson persisted.

'Do you think it's going to make him change his mind? Do you think he's going to choose to remain blind when he could have his sight restored?' Cook said, irritably.

Thompson regarded his colleague angrily.

'He's not to be told about the donor,' Cook insisted. 'You know that's general policy in all transplant cases anyway.'

'I think this case is exceptional,' the other doctor argued. 'I think that Miller has the right to know he's being given the eye of a murderer.'

Seven

He didn't know how long he'd been asleep.

Miller raised his hands to his face with the intention of rubbing his eyes, but when he felt the gauze against his fingertips he realized that instinctive action was impossible.

Miller cursed under his breath. He felt so bloody helpless, not even able to see what the time was. He could hear the steady ticking of a clock on his bedside table and he reached out towards it as if the mere touch of the timepiece would give him the information he sought.

His hand brushed against a water jug and the receptacle topped from its perch.

It hit the floor and shattered.

'Shit,' hissed Miller, slumping back onto his pillows.

A moment later the door of the room opened and he heard footsteps scuttling across to him.

'Are you all right, Mr Miller?' the nurse asked, looking first at the effects man then down at the glass and water beside the bed.

'I didn't know that bloody jug was there,' he said. 'I'm sorry. I didn't know what the time was. I was reaching for the clock . . .' He allowed the sentence to trail off.

'As long as you didn't hurt yourself,' the nurse said, busying herself beside the bed retrieving the pieces of glass. She informed him that she'd send an orderly in to mop up the mess then she retreated from the room to fetch him some more water.

'Put a drop of Scotch in it, will you?' Miller murmured as she left the room. He heard new footsteps and then a male voice close by him followed by the slopping of a mop.

The orderly looked down at the man on the bed, studying his

bandaged features.

'I heard that you were in films,' the orderly finally said sheepishly.

'Sort of,' Miller said.

'Are you an actor?'

'No, I do effects.'

The orderly squeezed some water into his bucket and continued with his task.

'What kind of effects?' the orderly persisted.

'Decapitations, disembowellings, shootings,' Miller said wearily. 'The usual sort of family entertainment.'

The other man didn't pick up the note of sarcasm in the effects man's voice.

'I was reading this book the other day and there was one bit where this bloke had his head pushed onto a bacon slicer. That'd look good in a film wouldn't it?' he chuckled.

'Great,' said Miller with a distinct lack of enthusiasm.

The orderly finished his task, said a cheerful goodbye and left.

Miller lay in the silence, listening again to the ticking of the clock. He smiled to himself. Head on a bacon slicer, he thought. Well, at least it was original. Nearly as original as blinding yourself with your own squibs. His smile faded as he sucked in an angry breath. Under any other circumstances, the irony of the accident might have struck him as amusing. But now all he felt was frustration and anger. And fear. The thought of blindness terrified him. If he'd been deafened by the accident, he told himself, he could have learned to live with that. But to face the prospect of living in never-ending night was one which made him shudder. If the operation worked, though, he would be fine. And if it failed . . .? He tried to push the negative thoughts out of his mind but they showed a marked reluctance to go. He almost smiled again. 'The best special effects man in the business' he'd been called on numerous occasions, and now he was in hospital, victim of one of his own devices. Miller thought back to the first time he'd worked on a film set. His introduction to the film world had been by way of still photography. He'd finally left New Scotland Yard, his mind numbed to suffering, his soul anaesthetized against pain after photographing the dead for so long. He'd found himself in a bar one evening drinking with a man who he later discovered was the second-unit director on a large American production shooting interiors at Elstree. The man – Miller couldn't even remember his name – had offered him a job and he'd taken it without hesitation.

The move into make-up and special effects had also been a piece of good fortune. Filming a scene in which a man had supposedly been shot in the head, Miller had remarked on how little blood the make-up man was using. After all, he'd seen enough gunshot victims to know that the head contains some of the largest blood vessels in the body. Head wounds bled profusely. He had the pictures to prove it. Miller had re-arranged the scene himself, adding the nauseating details of death which he knew so well.

After that episode he was often consulted on such matters and it was just a question of time before he moved into effects permanently. His time as a press and police photographer had been perfect training for the grisly effects he was called upon to create and Miller had read that top American make-up man Tom Savini drew on his own memories as a war photographer in Vietnam to create the gory effects which had made *him* famous.

Miller rubbed his cheeks, feeling the stubble against his finger-tips. There was a further irony to the situation, he thought. He created illusions with imitation flesh and blood, he'd been blinded by fake gunfire and now his only hope of regaining his sight was with someone else's eye. Once more he almost smiled. Almost.

The nurse returned with a fresh jug of water which she placed on the bedside table, away from the clock. Miller heard the sound of something being unscrewed and turned his head towards the noise.

'I've removed the front of the clock,' the nurse told him. 'That way you can feel the hands and you'll be able to tell the time yourself if you need to.'

'Well, it'll be good practice,' said Miller sarcastically. 'I'll start with the clock and work my way up to braille.'

'Why don't you try and sleep?' the nurse said, quietly.

'I've done nothing *but* sleep ever since I was brought in.'

'Try to rest, please.'

'Yeah, good idea. If I don't get eight hours I'll hardly be able to keep my eyes open will I?'

The nurse sighed softly, almost stung by the bitterness in his voice.

She squeezed his arm gently, then turned and left the room.

Outside it was still raining.

Eight

The green light on the switchboard flickered insistently, like some myopic eye in the gloom.

Nurse Brennan put down her book, folding the corner of the page, and reached for the phone. As she picked up the receiver she glanced across at the clock.

It was almost 12.08 a.m.

'Ward Nine B,' she said, stifling a yawn.

Silence.

'Nine B,' she repeated. 'Can I help you?'

The phone went dead and the nurse replaced it, reaching for her book once more, flipping the paperback open again. The words swam momentarily before her and she rubbed her eyes. Only another twenty minutes and she would finish her shift, able to return to the warmth of her bed. She'd been on the ward since eight that morning.

The switchboard light glowed green again and she picked up the phone.

'Hello, Ward Nine B.'

Again silence.

She sighed. Perhaps the receptionist hadn't connected the caller properly.

'Hello,' Nurse Brennan persisted.

'I want to speak to Frank Miller.'

The voice was low and rasping and the suddenness of the words startled her.

'Who is this, please?' she asked.

Silence.

'Who's calling, please?'

'I want to speak to Miller, now.'

'Are you a relative?' the nurse asked.

'Let me speak to him.'

'Mr Miller is asleep. I can give him a message when he wakes up if you'll tell me your name.'

Only silence greeted her enquiry, but on the other end of the line she could hear breathing.

'Who is this, please?' she persisted.

'Tell Miller we've got things to discuss,' the voice snapped, then Nurse Brennan jumped as the phone was slammed down. The sound rattled in her ear then all she heard was the dull drone of a dead line. She held the receiver before her for a moment then slowly replaced it.

As she did, she wondered why her hand was shaking.

Nine

'You must keep your eyes closed until I tell you otherwise.'

Miller heard Dr Cook's voice as he felt the bandages around his eyes being slowly and carefully removed.

Miller was trying to control his breathing but, like his heartbeat, it seemed to accelerate with every passing second. He swallowed hard as the last of the dressings were removed and only two patches of gauze covered his eyes.

The seconds ticked by.

Everything during the last two weeks had happened with what had seemed like agonizing slowness.

The tests.

The waiting.

The operation.

And now, finally, a week after the transplant had been completed, the moment of truth loomed. Miller knew that he was moments away from learning whether he would see again or if he was to be condemned to a life in darkness. The muscles in his stomach contracted like a fist.

Beside him he heard the clock ticking. Someone had told him it was just after two in the afternoon. He heard other voices in the room, low and almost conspiratorial, but above them all was the voice of the surgeon. It was he who now took a pair of tweezers and gripped the pad which covered Miller's right eye. He inspected the lid quickly, dropped the gauze into a dish and then repeated the action with the left eye.

'Close those blinds,' he snapped to a nurse who stood behind him and Miller felt the tension and fear building inside him as he heard them rattle. In a few seconds he would know.

'All right, Mr Miller, I want you to open your eyes. Slowly,' Cook told him.

Miller twitched his eyelids and felt a slight pain but he persevered, gradually forcing them open.

Light flooded into his eyes, despite the relative gloom inside the room, but he ignored the discomfort until his lids were fully open.

Hazy shapes swam before him and he blinked hard, trying to focus. The shapes remained mere blurs.

'Can you see anything?' asked Cook, looking down at him.

Miller glanced up at the surgeon, squinting in order to sharpen his vision, but it did no good. It was like looking at the man through frosted glass.

'Everything's blurred,' he said. 'I can see shapes but not their definition. It's not clear.'

'Close your right eye,' Cook instructed.

Miller did as he was told, gazing through the new eye.

Through someone else's eye. The thought made him shudder involuntarily.

'Now the left,' the surgeon said.

'There isn't much difference,' Miller said. 'I can't make out details. I can see your face but I'm not even sure what kind of expression is on it.' He raised his own hands and looked at them.

'What can you see?' Simon Thompson asked.

'I can see my hands but the fingers are blurred into one,' Miller said. He spread them but still the vision remained the same. He blinked again but found that it achieved nothing.

There was a heavy silence in the room as the nursing staff looked on.

'It'll take time for the eyes to settle down, especially the transplanted one. You've got to give it time,' Cook told him.

'But how much time?' Miller wanted to know.

'Rest your eyes now,' Thompson urged.

'It might be an idea if we kept them covered for another day or two,' said Cook, motioning the nurse forward.

'And after that?' Miller demanded.

'We've done as much as we can do,' the surgeon told him. 'You have to be patient now.'

53

Miller sighed and nodded resignedly, watching the hazy shape of the nurse as she drew closer to him. He closed his eyes as he felt the first of the fresh cotton pads being eased into place.

'Have you any pain?' Cook asked.

'None,' Miller told him as the nurse worked busily at her task.

There was another uncomfortable silence.

'I know it's difficult for you, Mr Miller,' the surgeon said. 'But all you can do now is wait.'

'The fact that you've even got some semblance of vision back is a good sign,' Thompson reassured him.

The nurse finished bandaging Miller's face and stepped back.

'We'll leave you now,' Cook said. 'I'll check on you later.'

Miller merely lay still, his fists clenched beside him. He heard footsteps as the medical entourage trooped out, leaving him alone. Alone in his room. Alone inside the darkness once again. He reached up and touched the bandages, trying to feel the outline of his eyes beneath the pads. He finally gave up and allowed his hands to drop to his sides once more.

'All you can do is wait.'

Cook's words echoed inside his head.

Beneath the cotton pads he blinked but he felt nothing. He rolled onto his side trying to blot out the ticking of the clock.

Each minute that passed seemed like a lifetime.

He waited.

Miller didn't know which floor of the hospital he was on but he guessed that he must be fairly high up as he could hear no sounds of traffic from the car park. Outside in the corridor he heard footsteps passing back and forth, sometimes at a leisurely pace, sometimes more frenetically. Apart from that, all he heard was the ever-present ticking of the clock, and it was a sound which was beginning to grate on his nerves. It was as if the rhythmic tick-tock was growing louder inside his head. Each movement of the second hand seemed to be more pronounced than the last.

Tick-tock. Tick-tock.

Like a splinter in his brain, driven deeper each time.

Tick-tock.

He rolled onto his back.

Tick-tock.

Something warm and wet rolled slowly down his cheek causing him to jump at the sudden, unexpected, sensation.

He wiped the tear away with the back of his hand.

A feeling of vague hope suddenly swept through him. Perhaps his eyes were beginning to function once more. Maybe the production of tears was a sign.

He felt another of the moist droplets dribble from beneath the bandages.

And another.

He blinked beneath the pads of gauze and the flow seemed to increase slightly. Miller winced as he felt a slight pain from his left eye.

He wiped the driblets away with his fingers, the digits brushing against his nose in the process.

Miller froze.

He felt the fluid flowing freely down both cheeks now and, as he struggled to brush it from his face he recognized the coppery stench which covered his hands.

It was blood.

His eyes were bleeding.

The thought struck him like a thunderbolt and he sat up, his hands shaking, trying to wipe away the fluid spilling from the ruined orbs. He put a hand to the bandages and felt that the gauze was soaked.

'Oh God,' he breathed in horror, trying to pull himself out of bed. In his blind terror he gasped aloud, almost falling as he felt his feet touch the cold floor.

He had to get help. Had to stop the bleeding.

Miller could feel the blood running down his face and neck, the smell strong in his nostrils. He tore at the bandages, trying to pull them off, not knowing quite what to do, wondering where the emergency button was, wondering how he could reach the door. He tried to call out but his throat seemed to have closed up. When he tried to scream blood ran into his mouth.

He coughed, gagging on the bitter-tasting fluid which ran

from his eyes.

Miller stumbled, crashed into a wall. He shot out one quivering hand and slapped at the wall leaving a bloodied hand-print on the white paint.

'Jesus, Jesus,' he gasped as he banged into a chair. Fresh pain shot up his leg and he overbalanced, landing heavily on his shoulder, lying helplessly on the cold floor while the blood continued to run from his eyes.

Miller dragged himself upright, arms flailing uselessly. Then he slumped against a wall, his face a mask of blood. With shaking hands he tore the bandages free, tugging at the pieces of gauze which covered his weeping, throbbing orbs. The lumps of gauze were like sodden sponges, soaked in crimson. But Miller could see none of it. He could only smell the odour of life-fluid as it drained from him through the gaping wounds which had once been his eyes. And yet somehow, through that red torrent, he found that he could see.

He could see.

God in Heaven, he could see.

Despite the pain and the blood he almost smiled, the smile of a man who is losing his mind, for, close to him, with almost frightening clarity, he saw a mirror and using all his strength he dragged himself towards it.

Blood had soaked into his pyjamas and run down his legs. In his blind fear he had wet himself and the acidly pungent odour of urine mingled with that of the blood. But Miller didn't seem to care, all he wanted to do was reach the mirror. To look upon his ravaged face, possibly for the last time.

He stared into the reflecting glass.

His eyes were little more than swollen clots of dark fluid, oozing sores which bulged and throbbed like blood blisters which seemed on the point of bursting. Two grotesque pustules of crimson that opened and closed like slobbering, riven lips expelling their thick contents over his face.

As the blood-soaked image stared back at him he finally found the breath to scream.

Ten

His scream brought him hurtling from the nightmare.

Miller sat bolt upright, heart hammering madly against his ribs, the perspiration sheathing his body like a film of condensation.

He put a hand to his face and felt moisture there. He wiped it away, then sniffed it, satisfied that the wetness was nothing more than sweat.

He let out one huge, shuddering sigh and slumped back.

Immediately the door was flung open and he heard someone approaching him.

'Mr Miller,' Nurse Brennan said, her voice full of concern.

'A nightmare,' he said, softly, trying to catch his breath. 'I was dreaming. I'm sorry.' He tried to swallow but it felt as if his throat was encircled by an iron clamp.

Nurse Brennan poured him a glass of water and held it while he sipped.

'I'm all right,' he told her. 'Honest. It was just a dream.' His breathing was beginning to slow down now. He even managed a thin smile.

'Are you sure there's nothing you want?' she asked.

'Maybe something stronger than water?' he asked hopefully.

She smiled down at him, even though he couldn't see the gesture, then she took one of the tissues from beside the bed and wiped some perspiration from his face.

'I'll be back with your dinner at six o'clock,' she told him. 'Try and get some rest until then.'

Miller nodded, listening as she walked across the room and closed the door behind her.

Six o'clock.

He reached out carefully, feeling his way over the bedside cabinet with one hand until he found the clock. He touched the hands gently and worked out that it was almost 3.00 p.m. Miller replaced the timepiece and lay back, listening to the insistent ticking. He rolled onto his side, then his back, but found that he could not get comfortable. Finally, cursing, he sat up, touching the pads of gauze which covered his eyes. Sucking in a deep breath, he swung himself out of bed, steadying himself against the bedside cabinet. He gripped a handful of sheet and seemed to drag himself to the end of the bed, his feet slapping against the cold floor. His breathing was low but rapid as he gripped the metal bedstead. Another yard and he would be walking without support.

Miller knew that the sink was to his left, so he turned slowly in that direction and padded towards it, arms outstretched like some grotesque parody of the Frankenstein monster taking its first faltering steps. He reached out, hissing in pain when his fingers touched the radiator. He stood still, trying to re-orientate himself for a moment, then he continued onwards towards the sink. Every step seemed a monumental effort, as if someone had weighted his legs with lumps of lead, but he finally reached his goal, his hands closing over the cold porcelain.

Miller smiled thinly and exhaled deeply. Then, after a moment, he reached up and began undoing the bandages around his eyes.

He wobbled uncertainly for a moment but propped himself against the sink as he persisted with his task, his heart thudding faster.

The first layer of bandages came away and he dropped them into the sink.

He set to work on the next layer until finally, only the gauze pads remained.

His hands were shaking as he removed the one over his right eye, keeping his lids firmly closed.

He repeated the procedure with the left. Then, with agonizing slowness, he opened his eyes.

It felt as if someone had glued his lids together, but he persevered, gripping the edge of the sink more tightly as he struggled to open them.

The right eye opened first and Miller was aware that he was now sweating profusely.

Miller opened his left eye, allowing the lids to roll back gradually until both glistening orbs were exposed. He gazed ahead of him towards the mirror above the sink.

Staring back at him was a clear image of his own face.

He tried to swallow but couldn't.

'Oh God,' he breathed, scarcely able to believe. Not daring to believe.

He could see.

Miller regarded his reflection as if he were looking at a stranger, but gradually the realization began to sweep over him. He turned to one side, wincing at the light which streamed through the window, but the brightness was glorious. He didn't care if he had to shield his eyes. He could see and that was all that mattered. He could see the bed, the door of the room, the four white-painted walls. Miller crossed to the window and looked out.

Below him, he guessed seven or eight floors, he could see the car park, vehicles and people coming and going. And he could see it with amazing clarity.

He closed both his eyes for as long as he dared, fearing that simple act might cost him his sight, but when he opened them again everything was as clear as before.

Miller turned towards the bed, towards the emergency button above it.

Shooting out a hand he hit the button, smiling as he did so.

He stood by the bed and watched the door.

By the time it was opened, he was laughing like an idiot.

Eleven

'Does that hurt?'

Dr George Cook aimed the pen-light at Miller's left eye.

'Nothing I can't get used to,' Miller said, sitting up in bed.

Cook inspected the right eye, watching the pupillary dilations and enlargements as he shone the light at the sensitive orb. Finally he flicked it off and dropped it into his top pocket.

'It would be wise to keep your eyes covered for the next few days,' the surgeon said. 'Just with sunglasses. We don't want to undo all our work now.'

'How long before you know that my sight is restored permanently?' Miller wanted to know.

'That's impossible to say,' Cook told him. 'We'll just have to hope there isn't any kind of reaction, particularly in the left eye. There's always a danger of rejection. That's a consideration in the transplantation of any organ.'

Miller nodded.

'When can I get out of here,' the effects man asked.

'Leave the hospital?' Cook said, almost incredulously. 'I couldn't allow you to leave until we were completely sure there were no adverse reactions to the new eye. It may take a fortnight, perhaps longer.'

'Sorry, Doc,' said Miller defiantly. 'But if you think I'm staying here for another two weeks you can forget it.'

'It doesn't matter whether you want to or not. You have no choice,' the surgeon insisted angrily.

'No, it's *you* who have no choice,' Miller reminded him. 'If I decide to discharge myself there's nothing you can do about it.'

'That would be ridiculous. Without adequate supervision

your condition could deteriorate again. If you leave I can't be responsible for what happens.'

'I'm not asking you to be responsible. When I walk out of here it'll be because I want to.'

Cook shook his head.

'If there was some kind of reaction then you could lose your sight for good and there'd be nothing we could do to help you.'

'Well, that's a chance I'll have to take,' Miller told the surgeon. 'I can see, that's all that matters. I've got you to thank for that and I'm grateful, but I can't stay cooped up in this bloody hospital for two weeks while you watch my progress. I'd go crazy. I realize the implications if I leave and I accept them.'

'As you say, it's your decision,' the surgeon sighed. 'But I wish I could make you change your mind.'

Miller smiled.

'You've done enough. You've restored my sight, that's the most important thing,' he said. 'You and the poor sod who donated his eyes to medicine,' Miller added as an afterthought. 'Who was he?'

Cook swallowed hard.

'I can't disclose details like that,' he said, quickly. Then he shook his head and raised his arms in a gesture which signalled defeat. 'If you choose to leave, that's your decision. My responsibility ends when you walk out of this hospital.'

Miller nodded.

Miller looked across at the clock.

5.35 p.m.

He swung himself out of bed and crossed to the small wardrobe which stood against the far wall. Inside he found his clothes. Rummaging in the pocket of his jacket he discovered what he was looking for.

The hip flask was all but empty. Nevertheless, he hastily unscrewed the cap and swallowed the contents. The whisky tasted slightly warm but it didn't put him off. He wiped his mouth with the back of his hand and replaced the flask in his pocket before closing the wardrobe and wandering across to the window once more.

He looked down at the car park then up at the rain-soaked sky, watching a low-flying plane cutting its way through the clouds.

At first he thought the plane had been swallowed up by the thick banks of grey, but then he realized that the window-frame itself was becoming hazy.

He blinked hard.

His vision was beginning to blur.

Miller closed his eyes for a moment, gripping the window-sill hard.

He opened them again.

Still the haze distorted his vision, like condensation on a car windscreen.

'Come on, come on,' he whispered, squeezing his lids together even more tightly. He stood there like that until his eyes began to ache, then, with almost painful slowness, he opened them.

Shapes and images in the room developed into crystal clarity and Miller breathed an audible sigh of relief.

He was still standing at the window when the door opened and Nurse Brennan entered, followed by an orderly.

Miller watched as the man set down the object he was carrying on the table at the end of the bed.

It was a small portable television.

'We thought you might be getting tired of your own company,' said Nurse Brennan, plugging the set in.

Miller smiled as she switched it on. He watched the shapes take form, delighting in the coloured images as if it was the first time he'd ever seen a TV.

'I'll be back with your dinner in about twenty minutes,' the nurse told him as he lay on the bed, eyes riveted to the set.

As she closed the door, Miller began to laugh.

He was watching an advertisement for spectacles.

Twelve

Miller blinked hard as his vision dissolved once more.

He kept his eyes screwed up, counting to five before he opened them again.

The clarity had returned and he exhaled slowly, resisting the temptation to rub the left eye. There was a maddening itch in the corner of it but he was reluctant to touch the tender orb. He closed his eyes once more, listening to the drone of the TV set at the bottom of his bed. Beside him he could hear the ticking of the clock.

In the corridor outside his room he heard the sound of footsteps coming and going. It was approaching seven-thirty in the evening and visiting hours had brought forth the usual torrent of well-wishers into the wards outside. Miller himself had received a call from Phillip Dickinson asking after his health, and a huge bouquet of flowers had arrived earlier that afternoon with a card signed by everyone on the set. Miller glanced across at the bouquet. Right now he would gladly have exchanged it for just one glass of whisky. His mouth felt dry, his throat parched, but by a thirst which mere water could not satisfy. It wasn't thirst he was experiencing, it was a craving.

He sat up, propping himself up on his pillows, his attention riveted to the screen in an effort to forget the gnawing desire within him. But what he saw did little to engage his mind. It was one of the many vacuous soap operas which proliferated on the networks now. No programme schedule seemed complete without one. Or two. Or three.

Miller reached for the remote control and changed channels.

He flicked through stations as if he were skim-reading a book until finally he found a news programme. Pouring himself another tumbler of water he watched, blinking hard as his vision momentarily blurred again.

'. . . the sixth such murder in the last two months.'

Miller sipped his water, listening as the presenter talked with a photo of a woman projected behind him. The woman was in her early twenties, pretty despite the fact that her front teeth protruded slightly.

'For an up to date report we hand over to Terri Warner,' said the presenter, and the screen was suddenly filled with the face of a dark haired girl in her late twenties. She was dressed in a thick anorak and held her microphone in a gloved hand. The strong wind tossed her hair almost angrily, forcing her, periodically, to brush strands from her face. In the background, Miller could see other shapes moving about. Uniformed shapes. Policemen. Ambulancemen. The reporter was standing in the front garden of a well maintained house in what looked like a residential area. Every now and then Miller saw by-standers gathered close to the fence which overlooked the garden. A uniformed constable was doing his best to move them on but their interest in seeing a corpse was apparently greater than their fear of being arrested for causing an obstruction.

Terri Warner ran a hand through her hair and looked into the camera.

On the screen beneath her, beside the station logo, her name appeared.

'In the house behind me less than thirty minutes ago,' she began, 'the body of a woman was found, and police on the scene are reasonably certain that she was killed by the same person who has so far claimed the lives of five others in the last two months. The woman's body was found by a neighbour who is currently being treated for shock. The victim has been identified as Bernadette Evans, aged twenty-three.'

Miller re-filled his tumbler, then he turned up the sound slightly.

'With me I have the detective in charge of the investigation,' Terri continued. 'Detective Inspector Stuart Gibson.'

Miller smiled thinly as he recognized the policeman.

'Gibson,' he murmured, studying the DI's features.

The two of them had worked together many times when Miller was employed by New Scotland Yard and still met up for the occasional drink. The years, and the job, had woven their own pattern of lines and wrinkles into the face of the policeman. But his blue eyes still sparkled with their customary defiance. Miller smiled again as he saw his former colleague standing agitatedly before the camera. He never had liked the media.

'Is it safe to assume that the latest victim was killed by the same person responsible for the other murders?' Terri asked, pushing the microphone towards the DI.

'It's possible,' Gibson said curtly.

'Was the victim mutilated?'

'No comment.'

'Are you any closer to finding a clue to the killer's identity?'

'No comment,' said the policeman, moving back slightly as if anxious to be away from the probing questions and ever-watchful eye of the camera. 'That's all I've got to say.'

'Is this latest murder motiveless?' Terri persisted, following him a couple of steps.

'No comment,' he said with an air of finality. Then, with one last look at the camera, Gibson moved away.

'So, it would appear that the police are still baffled by this series of murders which has shocked the whole country,' she said. She paused for a moment. 'This is Terri Warner for Independent News.'

Her face disappeared and that of the presenter replaced it.

'There'll be a further report from Terri Warner in our next bulletin later tonight,' he said, moving onto the next story.

Miller turned the sound down once more.

Number six.

He'd read about the murders in the paper and seen Terri herself on the box. She seemed to be making quite a name for herself reporting on the killings. He shook his head wondering how many more would die before the murderer was caught.

His thoughts were interrupted as his sight began to deteriorate once again. This time he could not resist the urge to rub his eyes. Sharp pain shot through him as he did so, but despite the discomfort he was relieved to find that his vision was no longer impaired. He blinked hard a couple of times and wiped some moisture from his lower lid.

As he did so he heard the sound of heavy footsteps outside his room and the voice of Nurse Brennan speaking loudly, almost protestingly. Miller frowned as a second later the door opened.

Miller looked up to see the nurse standing there, her face flushed.

'There's someone to see you, Mr Miller,' she said curtly then stepped back out into the corridor.

Miller gazed at the door waiting for his visitor to enter.

The newcomer appeared and Miller felt the blood draining from his face.

He swallowed hard, his face now pale.

The visitor closed the door behind him and stood looking at Miller.

'What the hell are you doing here?' Miller said, his voice a combination of anger and fear. 'How did you find me?'

Thirteen

For once Detective Inspector Stuart Gibson was grateful for the smell of cigarette smoke.

It masked the stench of blood.

The policeman stood looking down at the body, sucking his teeth in an effort to remove a small fragment of the sandwich he'd eaten earlier.

Beside him Detective Sergeant Chandler took another long drag on the Marlboro and blew out a thin stream of smoke. He too was looking down at the corpse.

Bernadette Evans had been a pretty girl in life, that much they knew from her photo. But not any more.

She lay naked in the sitting room of the house she had shared with two other girls. They were both staying with friends while police investigations were carried out, both had been out when the murder happened. Otherwise, Gibson thought, he might have been looking at a trio of corpses. And at this stage one was bad enough.

The dead girl lay spreadeagled, one hand already beginning to close up as rigor mortis set in. The body was beginning to take on a bluish tinge, mainly due to the massive loss of blood which had occurred. The crimson fluid was splattered all over the carpet and furniture. It looked as if some irate artist had wandered into the sitting room and hurled several tins of thick red paint over everything.

Her head, at least what remained of it, had been pulped almost beyond recognition by several dozen pile-driver blows delivered by an antique brass poker which lay close by. The bone hadn't merely been broken, it had been battered into hundreds of tiny fragments by the deluge of blows. The skull had been completely destroyed, as had most of the other bones and tissue above the lower jaw. A sticky flux of blood, bone and brain-matter was spread out around the pulverized head. A fearful stench rose from the corpse and Gibson coughed slightly as he moved closer, inspecting the damage inflicted on the rest of the body, for, if anything, it was worse than what had been done to her head.

The chest and breasts were relatively untouched, except for three or four minor cuts around the right nipple, one of which had narrowly missed the shrunken bud, though the stomach was a patchwork of gashes and lacerations. In at least two places portions of intestine bulged from the rents, thick with congealed blood. But it was around the girl's vagina that the most horrendous damage had been inflicted. Her mound, hips and inner thighs had been punctured so many times that all the wounds seemed to flow into one massive, reeking crater, bloated with congealing gore. Her outer vaginal lips had been clumsily but effectively sliced away and lay beneath her like strips of bleeding steak, now shrivelled and discoloured. There was no doubt about the knife used to inflict the wounds. It was a broad, razor-sharp kitchen knife.

It was embedded, up to the hilt, in her vagina. Jammed there in a final act of obscene frenzy like a steel penis.

'If it's any consolation,' said Sam Loomis, pulling a sheet over the mangled genital area, 'I'm sure *that* was done after she was dead.' The pathologist looked at Gibson and raised his eyebrows.

'It isn't any consolation,' said the DI quietly. He turned and beckoned two waiting ambulancemen forward, watching as the men carefully lifted the ravaged body onto a stretcher. Through the front room window, Gibson could see the emergency vehicle parked outside, its red lights turning silently in the gloom.

'Six victims, six different MOs,' the DI mused aloud. 'You wouldn't think it was possible, would you?' The question was directed at no one in particular.

'Well, we've got the bodies to prove it,' said Chandler, grinding a piece of fallen ash into the carpet. He took a last suck on his cigarette then stubbed it out in a nearby ashtray, waited a moment and lit another. Gibson regarded him with irritation.

'Is that bloody TV crew still outside?' Gibson called to a uniformed man standing near the front door.

The man looked out and nodded.

'Why don't you speak to that girl?' Chandler said, smiling. 'You'll probably get on the ten o'clock news as well.' He blew a stream of smoke past his superior.

'She's been on this bloody case as long as we have,' Gibson said.

'I wonder if she knows anything we don't. It seems we could do with all the help we can get,' said Chandler bitterly.

'I don't see you coming up with too many clues, Sherlock,' the DI countered, glaring at his colleague.

'I'm as baffled as you,' Chandler admitted. 'But then I don't have as much responsibility as you, do I? I wasn't the one who was promoted.'

'No,' said Gibson, looking at the older man. 'You weren't.'

'I'll let you have my report as soon as I can, Stuart,' Loomis said, trying to interrupt the verbal sparring of the two detectives.

'Cheers, Sam,' Gibson said. 'Look, are you sure this one was done by the same murderer? Like I said, the different MOs . . .'

'I'm sure of it,' Loomis said, cutting him short. 'The wounds on the body were delivered with a strong right hand cut that matches up with the wounds on victim number four, remember?'

'How could I forget,' said Gibson.

The fourth victim, Nicholas Blake, had been found three weeks earlier on a bench in Hyde Park, his throat cut in six places, his head practically severed. No murder weapon had been found. No weapon. No fingerprints. No clues.

There were never any clues.

'Can you be sure there isn't more than one killer, Sam?' Gibson asked the pathologist.

'As I said,' Loomis began, 'the cutting action is the same in two cases. But the fact that all the victims were found in roughly the same prone position shows a certain consistency which also points to a single killer. The first victim was shot while lying on his side, then pushed over onto his back. Maybe the killer wants us to know he's working alone.'

'Why?' Chandler asked.

Loomis shrugged. 'Don't ask me. I'm a pathologist, not a psychiatrist.'

'Oh Christ,' sighed Gibson, seating himself on the arm of the nearby sofa, his eyes fixed on the crimson stain which covered the carpet. 'And I promised my kids I'd spend some time with them tomorrow.'

'Occupational hazard,' said Chandler, matter-of-factly. 'With position comes responsibility.'

Gibson wasn't slow to catch the sarcasm in his colleague's voice. He got to his feet angrily.

'That's right,' he snapped. 'And don't you forget *who's* in charge, Chandler. They promoted *me*. You and all your moaning and groaning won't change that, so why don't you just get on with your job?' The DI headed for the door but turned as he reached it. 'Before they decide to replace you with someone else. Someone younger.'

Chandler's face darkened and he murmured angrily under his breath as his superior left the room.

Someone younger. It was bad enough having to take orders from Gibson, the DS thought. At forty-five he was seven years older than his superior. Seven years more experienced, he thought bitterly. But, when the time had come, it had been the younger man who'd been promoted. He had pondered over and over again why he should have been passed by. Could it have been because he once took back-handers from a video dealer in Soho when he was with the vice squad? No, he reasoned, no one had ever found out about that or he'd have been out on his ear. It was departmental politics, he was sure of that. Gibson was married with a couple of kids while Chandler himself lived alone with only an Alsation for company. Gibson presented a better front to the powers-that-be higher up the ladder. He appeared more settled, more reliable. And, besides that, he'd been instrumental in tracking down the members of an armed gang who'd robbed a security truck of £750,000 six months earlier. They'd cut a hole in the truck with a chainsaw then promptly used the lethal implement on a guard who'd decided to play the hero. One of the other guards had been paralysed for life by a shotgun blast which had blown away part of his spine while the third member of the group had been relatively lucky to escape with only mild brain damage when a pick-axe had been driven through his helmet and into his skull.

Gibson had supervised the hunt for the gang who, it turned out, were a professional team from overseas. However, by sealing off air terminals and ferry routes and confining the search to central London, Gibson and his men had chanced upon some of the money and traced it back to one of the drivers used in the escape. Under interrogation he'd cracked and informed on his companions. Within four days they were all locked up and awaiting trial.

At the time of the raid and the track-down Chandler had been laid up at home with a slipped disc, so he'd missed the operation. Gibson had picked up the praise *and* the promotion.

Chandler took a last drag on his cigarette then dropped it into the ashtray on the table. He wandered outside to see Gibson talking to the TV reporter. She'd been present at every scene ever since the killings began. She ought to keep out of the way, he thought, running appraising eyes up and down her shapely form. The jeans which she wore tucked into a pair of ankle boots clung invitingly to her legs and buttocks. Tight, mused the DS as he passed.

'Look, what can you tell me off the record?' Terri asked the DI.

'Nothing's ever off the record with you lot,' said Gibson, scornfully. 'If I told you anything it'd be the main story in the next bulletin.'

'The public have a right to know what's going on,' the reporter told him. 'If there's a maniac running around butchering people then you shouldn't hide facts from them.'

'When it's time for the public to know all the facts they'll be told by New Scotland Yard not by a bloody TV reporter,' Gibson rasped. 'You must think I'm stupid. You've been on this bloody case from the beginning, I know it's making *you* a household name, no wonder you're interested.'

'I'm only doing my job,' Terri told him.

Gibson nodded. 'Yeah, and it makes great television doesn't it?' he snapped. 'Well I'm trying to do my job too but part of that job doesn't include giving press interviews at the scene of every murder.'

'Do you think there'll be more?' she asked.

Gibson eyed her suspiciously for a moment and thought about walking away but he hesitated, his voice losing some of its harshness.

He shrugged wearily.

'It seems possible considering the type of nutcase we're dealing with.' He fixed her with a cold stare. 'But don't quote me on that.'

Terri smiled and shook her head.

Gibson walked past her, heading for the blue Fiesta which was parked close by the ambulance. Chandler sat in the driving seat, a cigarette dangling from one corner of his mouth. As he clambered inside, Gibson waved a hand in front of him in an effort to disperse the smoke which was rapidly filling the vehicle.

Chandler started the engine as the DI belted himself in.

The car sped away.

Terri watched it go, feeling the first spots of rain on her face. High above her, dark clouds began to fill the sky.

The drive back into central London took less than thirty minutes, but in the uneasy silence which descended between Gibson and Chandler the journey seemed to take an eternity. The DI had his eyes closed, thoughts tumbled through his mind. Every now and then he would look up to see the rain which spattered the windscreen being swept away by the rapidly moving wiper blades. The lights of passing vehicles and neon glow of cinema and theatre hoardings seemed to merge into a liquid mass as the rain poured down the glass of the windows.

Inside, the car smelt of stale cigarettes. Gibson wound down his window slightly to allow the stink to escape. The smell of exhaust fumes flooded in to replace the other odour.

'You shouldn't have spoken to that reporter, you know,' said Chandler.

Gibson opened his eyes slightly and regarded the DS with annoyance.

'Don't tell me how to handle the press, Chandler,' he said, irritably.

'She's good looking though,' the DS said, smiling. 'I wouldn't mind a crack at her.'

'How do you know she goes for older men?' Gibson said, quietly, a slight smile on his lips.

Chandler shot him an acid glance.

'Anyway, we've got more important things on hand than women,' the DI said. 'Did you get the forensic boys to go over the house after we left?'

'Before and after,' Chandler told him. He turned a corner and was forced to brake hard as two pedestrians stepped off the pavement a yard ahead.

'Get out the way,' the DS snarled as he drove past.

Gibson looked at his colleague and frowned disapprovingly.

'We'd better hope forensic find something this time,' Chandler said. 'The longer these killings go on the bolder the killer's likely to get.'

'And if he does he's more likely to make a mistake,' countered Gibson.

'You mean it's just a matter of how many more people have to die before we come up with some ideas?' Chandler said sardonically.

'Like I said, I'm not the only one on this bloody case,' Gibson reminded his colleague.

'No, but you're in charge.'

'That's right. I am,' the DI said flatly. 'And don't you forget it. If you worried about the case more and less about losing your promotion we might all be better off.'

Chandler brought the car to a halt and the DI pushed open the door, stepping out into the rain. His own car was parked on the wet tarmac close by.

'See you tomorrow,' he said perfunctorily, slamming the door behind him.

'Yeah,' hissed Chandler. 'See you.'

He watched his superior clamber into his own car and, deep inside, he felt his anger seething.

Gibson would have to learn that Chandler wasn't going to allow himself to be walked over.

Somehow he would learn.

Obsession

The blood which covered the road was already beginning to congeal. Solidifying beneath the rays of the sun.

The cat had managed to drag itself across the road despite the fact that the car which had hit it had crushed its back legs into pulp. As it crawled it left a trail of blood and pieces of mashed entrails behind until it finally found refuge in a shallow ditch by the roadside. It lay there helplessly, its body twitching as spasms of pain racked it mercilessly.

The child squatted a foot or so away watching the dying feline, running appraising eyes over the shattered body.

The cat had been penned in the back garden to prevent it from getting close to the main road, but somehow it had found a way out and had paid the price. The child watched as blood ran freely from the smashed lower body, gazing with fascination as intestines swelled and bulged from the torn stomach as if they were being pumped up from within. Here and there amongst the crimson mush, pieces of bone gleamed whitely.

The cat had been old, fat and bloated and now it looked as if its body had burst, such had been the impact of the car when it had been struck.

The child watched as half a dozen flies settled on the bleeding remains, feasting like so many gourmets on the reeking banquet. The cat made a low mewling sound and, as it did so, fresh blood ran from its mouth and nose. Its eyes were half-closed and the child realized that the animal was close to death. Did the cat know that it was dying? Did it realize that it was going to lie in this ditch until it stopped twitching and moved no more? The child wondered as it watched, eyes roving up and down the cat's body.

The cat's fur had been ginger but now it was covered by thick, matted gore which stuck to the coat like crimson glue.

The child moved a little closer, watching more intently as the cat continued to utter the low mewling sounds, lifting its head as if soliciting help, but even if it had been able to offer help, the child would not have done so for it watched the dying moments of the creature with fascination.

What kind of pain was it feeling? Could it feel the steaming coils of its own entrails attempting to break free of its torn belly like bloated, bloodied snakes?

The cat's head flopped backwards for a moment and it lay still, only the scarcely perceptible movement of its chest showing that it still lived.

The child reached behind it and found a long branch, fallen from one of the trees that overhung the ditch. Gently, the child prodded the cat with the small branch, watching for any more signs of movement. The animal miaowed loudly, a sound of pain which the child recognized. It discarded the branch for a moment, watching the animal writhing in agony. More flies had joined their companions, some of them actually wandering inside the cat's riven body. The child looked on in wonderment, trying to count the black shapes against the vivid red of the cat's blood.

The movement of the cat's chest was slowing, its final breaths coming in shallower inhalations, as if the mere act of breathing was causing pain.

The child moved a little closer, listening to the rasping sounds that were receding into liquid gurgles.

Blood spilled more copiously from the cat's mouth and its body began to quiver uncontrollably, its forepaws jerking as if suspended by invisible wires. Then its entire body seemed to shudder and its head flopped backwards.

The child watched for any further signs of movement, and when none were forthcoming it reached for the stick again and jabbed gently at the cat's head.

It didn't move.

The child reached out and touched the intestines which bulged from the hideous tear in the animal's belly. They were still warm. The coppery odour of blood was strong in the air and the child *inspected the gore which coated its hand, sniffing it slowly before looking once more at the dead animal.*

One of the flies had crawled inside its blood-filled mouth.

The child looked on, mesmerized.

Fourteen

Frank Miller splashed his face with cold water then stood up, studying his reflection in the mirror. He watched the droplets of moisture dripping from his chin for a second then reached for the towel and dried himself.

'I can't condone your decision, Mr Miller,' said George Cook, watching as Miller ran a hand through his hair. 'As I told you before, if there is any adverse reaction I won't take responsibility.'

'I realize that,' Miller said, pulling on his jeans. As he pulled the dark sweatshirt over his head he noticed several small burn marks, no bigger than pin-heads. They were the result of the sparks from the exploding squibs which had blinded him. He smoothed his hair once more and ran a hand over his heavily stubbled cheeks, listening to the whiskers rasp beneath his fingers.

'I really want to thank you and your staff for what you've done for me, Doctor,' Miller said.

Cook sighed.

'You could show your thanks by staying here under observation for another two weeks,' the surgeon said.

Miller smiled.

'Nice try,' he said, crossing to the wardrobe and his jacket. From one pocket he withdrew an instamatic camera. 'I never go anywhere without it,' he said, his tone softening slightly. 'Look, I know this may sound ridiculous but I was wondering if you'd mind if I took a couple of pictures. You could call it force of habit.'

'You're the celebrity, Mr Miller,' Cook said, smiling. 'It's me

78

who should be taking photos of you.'

The door opened and Nurse Brennan entered.

'Perfect timing,' said Miller, handing her the camera. 'Can you take a picture of Dr Cook and me together, please?'

The nurse nodded and smiled as Miller showed her how to work the camera, then he and the surgeon stood side by side as she focused. Miller winced slightly as the flash went off but he hid his discomfort well and asked Cook to repeat the procedure. Miller snaked his arm around the nurse's waist, smiling as she coloured slightly. The flash glowed once more and Miller took a photo of the surgeon and nurse. That task done he pocketed the camera and pulled on his jacket.

'You promise me that you'll be back in a week for a check-up?' Cook said. 'It could be vital. And if you have any pain or adverse reaction before then you must return immediately. For your own sake.'

Miller smiled and nodded. He stood before the doctor and extended a hand which the surgeon shook warmly.

'Thanks again,' Miller said, then he turned and kissed the nurse lightly on the cheek, watching as she turned a shade of scarlet.

'I'll walk with you to the main doors,' Cook said.

'There's no need.'

'It's hospital rules,' the surgeon said. 'At least do *one* thing you're told.'

Miller nodded and followed the surgeon out of the room.

They rode the lift to the ground floor, Miller resisting the urge to rub his eye as it blurred slightly, but as the doors slid open he could see clearly once more.

As the two men walked slowly up the long, polished corridor which led to the main doors Miller saw two interns hurrying through to casualty, one pushing a gurney, the other carrying two packs of blood for a transfusion. A nurse scuttled behind them.

Outside, the sound of sirens filled the air.

The electronic signal pinned to Cook's lapel began screeching and the doctor sighed.

'I think I've got work to do,' he said, extending his right

hand. Miller gripped it firmly then turned to watch as the surgeon sprinted off back down the corridor. Miller stood alone by the main doors for a moment then stepped out into the sunlight.

He almost shouted aloud in pain as the hot rays hit him. He shielded his eyes and sucked in a painful breath, staggered by the agony which throbbed in his skull. It fell as if someone were trying to pull his eyes free of their sockets with red-hot pincers. He stepped back hurriedly into the welcoming coolness of the entry-way. To his right were three public phones. Miller crossed to one and called a taxi to take him home.

He decided to wait for it inside.

By the time he got home the sun had been swallowed up by rolling banks of cloud drifting in from the west. Miller screwed up his eyes against the natural light but there was no more pain. He fumbled for his key and let himself in, standing in the stillness of the hall for long moments. There was a pile of mail lying on the mat at his feet but he ignored it, walking through into the sitting room instead. He crossed to the drinks cabinet and took out a large glass which he half filled with Haig. He swallowed a sizeable mouthful, wincing as the liquid burned his throat and stomach but then he smiled and held the glass before him.

'Welcome home,' he chuckled.

With his free hand he reached for the nearby phone, jammed the receiver between his ear and shoulder and jabbed out a number. He heard the drone of the ringing tone then a woman's voice at the other end.

'I'd like to speak to Phillip Dickinson,' Miller told her.

Mr Dickinson was busy on the set, he was informed.

'Tell him Frank Miller called. I'll be back at work tomorrow.'

She thanked him for calling and hung up.

Miller poured more whisky into his glass then walked out of the sitting room down a short corridor to another door. He unlocked it and walked in.

It was dark inside the room, the curtains still firmly closed, but Miller stood with his back to the door for a moment, enjoying the enveloping gloom. Finally he reached up and slapped on the light.

The banks of fluorescents in the ceiling sputtered into life bathing the room in a cold white glow.

To his right was a large desk, beyond it stood endless banks of filing cabinets.

Propped up in a metal dish on the closest of these was a severed head.

Miller looked across at the blood-spattered object and smiled.

Fifteen

The corpse was naked.

It sat in a straight-backed chair in one corner of the room, head tilted back slightly to expose the savage gash which had almost parted the head from its body. Blood had poured down the chest and stomach to the ravaged lower body.

Between the legs of the corpse, jutting out like a bloated erection, was a thick worm-like object, sickly white in colour but covered in blood too. Near the head of the object were what looked like two tiny arms, the fingers twisted into hooked claws. Like some kind of bloodless, deformed tadpole, the creature had its mouth open to reveal a row of sharp teeth, pieces of flesh stuck between them from where it had eaten its way free of the host body.

Miller studied the body with justifiable pride. It had been one of the most audacious and effective pieces of work he'd ever undertaken. It had been used in a film he'd worked on almost two years earlier called *Intruder*. When the picture had been released in the States there had been some talk of cutting the scene in which the creature tore its way free of its host while he was making love to his wife. It was then, according to the script, to have disappeared into her vagina where it created similar bloody havoc, but this latter part of the scene was eventually shelved. Even so, due to the other nauseating effects Miller had contrived the picture received an X rating in the US and, consequently, died a death at the box office. But Miller was still pleased with the way his effects had turned out. He gazed admiringly at the body for a moment longer then glanced across at another occupant of the room.

82

It was a woman.

The flesh of her face had been peeled off to reveal a network of muscles and tendons beneath. One eye was missing, dangling half-way down her cheek by the optic nerve. Her mouth was open to reveal the remains of a tongue, severed by a knife. The same knife which had been used to flay her so expertly.

Close to her was a badly burned body.

A severed leg, maggots attached to the stump, stood in a corner like some kind of umbrella stand.

Beside it lay the torso of a man, thick tentacles hanging from the place where his legs should have been. Gripped in those tentacles was the pulped and bloodied body of a child.

Miller smiled as he looked at that particular creation. Each of the tentacles had been worked by a combination of hydraulics and wires and it had taken himself and a team of six other technicians over a week to complete a shot which appeared on screen for less than eight seconds. To this day, when he watched the film, Miller could not see the wires, even though he knew where each one had been. It was another scene he was justifiably proud of.

Seated in another chair was a man with a gaping head wound. Miller had made the head of the replica hollow then filled it with steak, stage blood and sheep's brains. When the time came for the 'victim' to be shot in the head the actor responsible had merely fired a real shotgun blast at the top half of the dummy and half the head had been torn away. After filming had been completed, Miller had brought the dummy home. It now sat staring back at him with one blank, glassy eye.

The effects man sat down at his desk and looked around his workroom. He had converted the study himself shortly after moving into the house. Initially it had been used as a darkroom when he worked as a photographer. It still retained a double sink and the smell of developer hung in the air, mingling with the ever-present odour of rubber. Latex was one of the more popular materials for creating prosthetic effects and Miller had found that it was easy to work with as well as being durable. Some of the monstrosities which shared the room with him looked as fresh as the day they'd been constructed. Miller smiled to himself, remembering how an interviewer from a film magazine had called him a modern day Doctor Frankenstein, surrounding himself with his creations.

As well as the whole replicas there were numerous heads, eyes, skulls and limbs dotted around the room. All had been used in films on which he'd worked. On his desk lay several sketches of the make-up he'd devised for the *Astro-cannibals* and also a number of photos both of the finished product and also make-up in more experimental stages. Miller flipped through the sketches and photos as he seated himself behind the desk, his attention gradually drawn to the wall opposite him.

On it was a huge notice-board and completely covering it were more photos. Only these were not of Miller's creations. They were a legacy of his days as a police and press photographer. Colour and monochrome reminders of the horrors which he had viewed and preserved over the years.

The blood-spattered remains of a pram which had been hit by a drunken driver, the pulverized mess which had been its occupant wedged beneath the car's front wheel. Miller could still remember taking it, the horrified mother screaming behind him. Cars slowing down to get a glimpse of the accident. The blood running into a drain.

Click.

A woman gang-raped by four men and then tied up with electrical flex before a broken bottle was jammed into her vagina.

Click.

Two victims of a gangland reprisal killing, their teeth torn out with pliers before they were both strangled with cheese-wire.

Click.

The suicide who'd decided to take a businessman with him onto the electrified tracks at Knightsbridge.

Click.

A man who'd decided to be a hero and foil an armed post-office raider, lying in the gutter with his genitals blown off, his hands buried deep in the hole where his legs met.

Click. Click. Click.

Miller took another sip of his drink and glanced across at the filing cabinets. They were crammed full of photos too. A storehouse of pain and misery all immortalized by his camera. Laminated horror which he referred to often. But the sights were filed away in a much more complex cabinet too. The memory bank which was his mind. Each vile, repulsive sight gouged across his mind like a scab, never to be erased. Behind him the clock ticked loudly, its rhythmic refrain amplified by the silence inside the room.

Miller sat at his desk, the tumbler of whisky cradled in his hand. He blinked as he felt a slight gnawing pain in his left eye and a second later his vision faltered. It was like looking through a piece of gauze. Miller cursed and rubbed his eyes, gasping in pain as he did so, but when he'd finished his sight was clear again. He downed what was left in the glass and got to his feet, crossing to the bank of filing cabinets. Sliding the closest one open he reached in and pulled out a bottle of Haig. It was already half empty, a testament to his previous visits. He unscrewed the cap and poured a large measure. Then he looked across the room at his monstrous creations and raised the glass in salute.

It was the strident ringing of the phone which woke him.

Miller sat up sharply, a little too sharply, his head throbbing immediately. He managed to glance at his watch before snatching up the receiver.

It was 4.36 p.m.

'Hello. Frank Miller,' he said, massaging the bridge of his nose between his thumb and forefinger.

No answer.

'Hello,' he said, wearily.

Low breathing on the other end.

'You picked the wrong house for an obscene phone call,' he snapped, preparing to slam the phone down.

'Miller.'

The sound of his own name prevented that simple act of retaliation. He pushed the receiver gently against his ear once more.

'Miller, can you hear me?' the voice asked and he knew it instantly.

'What the fuck do *you* want?' Miller said angrily. 'I told you at the hospital not to contact me here. If I need you I'll call you.'

'Just wanted to check that you're back home,' said the voice.

'Get off the line,' he said through clenched teeth.

'See you soon,' said the voice and Miller thought he heard a low chuckle before the line went dead. He slammed the receiver down, pushing the phone away from him as if it had been contaminated. He just sat staring at it.

As if he were afraid it might ring again.

Sixteen

Miller stood in his workroom bathed only in the sickly red light positioned over the work-bench in the corner.

Water was running from the taps of both sinks, washing the developer from the photos he'd removed from his camera. Miller watched as the images formed more clearly and he carefully hung the photos up to dry, smiling as he saw the one of himself and Nurse Brennan. He peered up at the one of Doctor Cook and the nurse.

Miller's smile faded slightly as he studied the picture more closely.

At first he thought that his eyes were playing tricks on him.

He blinked but the photo did not change.

A fault in the film, he thought. It had to be some kind of fault in the film.

Miller checked the photo of himself and Doctor Cook.

Then re-checked it.

In both pictures there appeared to be a faint, almost luminescent outline around the figure of the doctor. As if his body were giving off some kind of aura.

Miller held the photos up to the light and closed his right eye, squinting at the curious haze which surrounded every inch of the doctor's image.

It seemed even more pronounced. He exhaled deeply, a frown creasing his forehead.

He closed his left eye and looked again.

'What?' he murmured. The aura seemed to have disappeared. The photos looked normal.

He tried it again looking through the left eye.

The luminous outer-shadow re-appeared.

Miller chewed his bottom lip contemplatively, aware now that the aura only showed up when viewed through the transplanted eye. He shook his head, puzzled not only by his ability to see the peripheral glow which was apparently radiating from Cook's body, but by the other fact which bothered him.

What the hell was it?

Seventeen

A couple of hijackings, a terrorist bombing in Italy, ever-increasing unemployment and a batch of rapes, muggings and murders.

Just like any other day, thought Miller as he sat watching the news, his glass propped on one arm of the chair. His eyes felt gritty, as if someone had rubbed sand into them and he rubbed the delicate orbs cautiously. The bottle of Scotch beside him was three-quarters empty but Miller was still far from being drunk. In fact, he couldn't remember the last time he'd been really smashed. Perhaps that was something he should remedy now he thought, raising the glass to his lips.

The phone rang.

Miller froze for a moment, listening to the harsh tones. Then he turned in his chair and glanced across the darkened sitting room towards the table where the device was housed.

It was still ringing.

He jabbed the mute button on the remote and the newsreader was transformed into a soundless cipher.

Still the phone rang.

Miller got to his feet and crossed to it, sucking in an anxious breath as he allowed his hand to hover over the cradle.

Not twice in one night, surely, he thought uneasily.

He waited a moment longer then reached for the receiver.

The ringing stopped.

Miller sighed and looked down at the phone, his hand still poised over it.

He drew it away sharply as the strident tone began once more.

This time he snatched the receiver up and pressed it to his ear.

'Miller,' he said, quietly.

'Frank, about time. How are you feeling?' said Phillip Dickinson. 'I'm sorry to bother you so late, but I got your message about coming back to work and I thought I'd better tell you that there's been a change in the shooting schedule. I'm going to need some different props for tomorrow. I know it doesn't give you much time but there's nothing else I can do.'

'What do you need?' Miller asked.

'Well, we're doing the scene where the cannibals break into the orphanage,' said Dickinson.

Miller raised his eyebrows and chuckled to himself.

'It's scene forty-three in the shooting script, if you want to check it out,' the director continued. 'I need a severed arm. The rest of the effects specifications are in the script. I'm sorry it's such short notice, Frank.'

'No sweat,' said Miller, sipping his drink. 'I'll get on to it now.'

They said hasty goodbyes and Miller hung up.

He turned and headed for the hall, not bothering to switch off the TV. Finding a copy of the shooting script in his workroom, he flipped through it until he found the required scene. In the margin, written in red ink he read;

SEVERED ARM
DEAD BABY

Miller checked his watch. It was approaching 11.36 p.m.
He set to work.

1.58 a.m.

Miller ran his index finger slowly around the rim of his glass and looked at the object which lay before him on the work-bench.

The arm had been severed at the shoulder, pieces of bone showing through the pulped mass of flesh. Several deep gashes had also been gouged into it around the wrist. The fingers were splayed wide as if ready to grasp the first object that came within reach.

The effects man looked at his creation with pride. It certainly looked realistic. As good as anything you'd find in a casualty room he thought, chuckling.

The arm was made of rigid foam and covered in rubber to give flexibility. Miller had then sculpted the latex into shape, working quickly and expertly. It had then been baked and painted. The script had called for an articulated arm so that the hacked off appendage could crawl along the floor and grab an actor by the ankle, but with such little time to work in, Miller had been unable to add the hidden motors and mechanical attachments which would give the replica arm a life of its own. The moving arm shot should be relatively simple. An actor would merely put his arm through a hole in the floor, that arm would then be made up to match the fake arm and the action could commence from there. Miller had used the same technique numerous times with decapitations. A dummy head was hacked off then an actor merely put his head through a gap and stage blood and latex flesh were spread around his neck to give the appearance that the severed head was still alive. Simple, he thought, smiling.

He glanced at his watch. Miller re-filled his glass and looked again at his work. Then he looked across at the shooting script, his eyes scanning the crumpled page.

'The cannibals grab a baby and take it into the kitchen,' Miller read aloud, smiling slightly. 'There is a fight between one of them and the cook. The baby . . .' He allowed the sentence to trail off, shaking his head. Someone was actually paying out over four million dollars for shit like this. The film business never ceased to amaze him.

'The baby,' he said, quietly glancing at the red handwriting in the margin.

DEAD BABY

Miller scratched his head. More work? He took a long swallow from his glass then hurriedly re-filled it, his hands shaking slightly.

Miller looked at the phone close by him.

The ticking of the clock was deafening in the silence.

He closed his eyes for a moment as his vision blurred slightly.

When he opened them again he was gazing at the phone. He exhaled deeply and reached for the receiver, hesitating slightly before picking it up.

He held it to his ear, listening to the low monotone buzz for a moment.

He clenched his fist, trying to stop his hand shaking, then, slowly, he relaxed. It had done no good, his fingers still trembled.

Miller gritted his teeth then, finally, he dialled.

Eighteen

The room at New Scotland Yard which had been chosen for the press conference seemed far too small for the purpose.

Gibson counted at least thirty journalists crammed into the small carpeted room which was already hazy with the smoke of many cigarettes. Periodically a flash bulb would explode and the air was alive with the constant clicking of cameras and the murmur of expectant voices. The DI shuffled the sheaf of papers before him as if anxious to find something to do with his hands.

Next to him, seated at the table which took up half the width of the room, the coroner, Sam Loomis, was busily attempting to light his pipe. The older man had practically disappeared inside a fog of smoke and it looked to Gibson as if his colleague was close to combustion himself. His face was red and perspiration had formed in silvery droplets on his bald head.

Next to Loomis sat Lawrence Chapman, the Commissioner of Police. Chapman was a tall, almost painfully thin individual with pinched features and short grey hair. He hardly looked the imposing figure who controlled the City's police force virtually single-handed, but appearances were deceptive. Beneath his harassed look, Chapman was a veritable demon. As a detective, earlier in his career, he'd twice received commendations for bravery, and on the second occasion he'd also received a bullet from a .38 through the shoulder as a more permanent reminder of the hazards of the job.

Beyond him sat DS Chandler, who was picking his teeth with a broken match. He stopped as Chapman threw him an irritable glance.

93

Terri Warner stood close to the table looking at the four men, waiting for her chance. No TV cameras had been allowed into the conference, which had been announced only the previous day. Considering the police apparently had very little to go on, she wondered why they'd gone to the bother of calling a meeting of this kind. As she saw Chapman rise to his feet she hoped she was about to learn the answer.

The commissioner banged hard on the table with the flat of his hand then sat down again, waiting for the babble of conversation to die away. Only the clicking of cameras continued.

'Ladies and Gentlemen, I'd like to get this over with as quickly as possible,' he said. 'After all, we all have jobs to do, don't we?' He smiled humourlessly. 'The reason you were called here is because there have been significant developments in the case we are currently working on. I hesitate to use the term mass murderer, but I can think of no better description. Anyway, I would like to hand you over to the detective in charge of the case.'

Chapman introduced Gibson and then sat back in his seat, hands clasped across his stomach.

The DI coughed self-consciously and looked at the swarm of expectant faces. He spotted Terri at the front and looked away from her.

'As you know, the killer has so far murdered six people,' Gibson began. 'And, up until now, we've not been able to find any clues either to motive or suspects.' He coughed again. 'Yesterday we arrested a suspect. Someone is now helping us with our enquiries.'

The relative silence in the room was suddenly replaced by a barrage of questions and murmurs of surprise, not least from Terri, who saw Gibson glance hastily towards Chapman who merely smiled thinly.

'I thought you had no leads,' said a reporter from the *Express*.

'Don't believe everything you read in the newspapers,' Gibson said, trying to smile at his own joke. 'There are still one or two loose ends we have to tie up, but we are confident that charges will be formally filed very soon.'

'How was this breakthrough made?' a voice near the back shouted.

'We discovered a link between the six victims,' Gibson said, looking down at his notes.

'Can you say what that link is?' Terri persisted.

'Not at present,' Gibson told her. 'All I can say is that we found a number of similarities in the killing methods.'

'What details can you give about the murderer?' Terri asked, noticing that Gibson was glancing towards Chapman once more.

The commissioner shook his head almost imperceptibly.

'None as yet,' Gibson said, wiping a bead of perspiration from his top lip.

'How long will it be before you can give any details?' asked the man from the *Express*.

'No comment,' Gibson said, flatly.

There was another clatter as dozens of cameras were fired off in one noisy barrage.

'Is it true that all the victims were mutilated?' the man standing next to Terri called. He had his notepad open and was scribbling hastily.

'No comment.'

'Was there any form of sexual interference with the female victims?' yelled a *Sun* reporter from the back of the room.

'No comment.'

'Can you give any details at all about the suspect?' Terri demanded, her eyes never leaving Gibson's face. 'Age, sex, background or anything like that?'

'I've already said no,' Gibson responded, his throat feeling dry. He reached for the glass of water before him and took a hefty swallow.

Terri glanced across and saw that Chapman was looking at her. She felt curiously uncomfortable beneath his gaze.

'Has a motive been established?' she persisted.

'No comment,' said Gibson, rather hastily.

'We'd rather not disclose any more details at present,' Chapman suddenly interjected. 'Suffice it to say that an arrest has been made and we'll release a full statement in due course.' He looked across at Gibson and the two men exchanged brief stares. 'That will be all for now,' shouted Chapman as the sound of cameras and the babble of questions grew into one vast crescendo. The press showed no sign of leaving. Only when the policemen rose to their feet and headed towards the door behind them did the reporters begin to file out.

Terri paused for a moment, looking at Gibson and Chapman as they left the room, both of them chatting animatedly. Then the door was closed and both disappeared from view. She sighed and shook her head slowly, her brow wrinkled into a frown.

'They'll never swallow it,' said Gibson anxiously, standing in the annexe behind the conference room.

'Of course they will,' snapped Chapman. 'I think you overestimate the intelligence of the press, Stuart. We told them we'd made an arrest and they believed us. By tomorrow it'll be front page headlines in every paper and main report on every news programme. As far as the press and public are concerned this killer is under arrest.'

'And what if someone finds out the truth?' said Gibson. 'What if they find out we're no closer to finding the bastard than we were after the first killing? What then?'

'It's our job to make sure they *don't* find out,' Chapman told him. 'This conference was set up to give us a little breathing space, you know that. We've got to find this maniac before he kills again.'

Gibson sighed and looked across briefly at Chandler.

In that split second, he was sure the Detective Sergeant was smiling.

Nineteen

They didn't fit.

No matter how many times she re-arranged the pieces in her mind, Terri Warner could not get the pieces of this particular jigsaw to fit.

Less than a week ago the police had been completely baffled by the series of murders, totally clueless. But now, suddenly, they had arrested a suspect. She shook her head slowly as she considered the revelation. No way, it just didn't fit. As the saying went, *'If it don't gel, it ain't aspic.'* This wasn't gelling. She brushed a strand of dark hair from her face, feeling the perspiration on her skin.

It was like an oven inside the car.

Terri glanced down at the broken heater which was blasting out hot air and decided that next time she had a spare moment she'd get it fixed. As the traffic ahead of her slowed up she wound down her side window.

A cloud of exhaust fumes promptly poured in and she hurriedly closed the window again. The heat, she decided, was preferable to the smell. Behind her, the driver of a black Porsche banged hard on his horn. Terri adjusted her rear-view mirror and glanced at the impatient motorist who was tapping his steering wheel agitatedly. He finally revved up his engine, swerved out into the road and shot past her as if he were on the starting grid at a Grand Prix.

Terri smiled to herself, catching a glimpse of her own reflection in the mirror. She clucked her tongue as she saw the beginnings of dark rings beneath her eyes. Too many late nights, what would mother say? she mused. Theresa Nicole

Warner, you should take more care of yourself. She could almost hear her mother's voice inside her head. Both her parents had objected strongly when she'd announced her intentions to leave home seven years earlier. They'd trotted out the usual string of clichés about London being a hotbed of vice and iniquity, with evil people just waiting to get their hands on a naive twenty-year-old girl. The fact that Terri had a job with a large advertising agency already lined up, as well as somewhere to live, didn't seem to hold much water as far as they were concerned. However, she would have been surprised if they hadn't protested and she'd suffered their well-intentioned paranoia happily enough until her mother had tried a new angle of attack. Two weeks before Terri was due to leave, her mother had lapsed into deep depression. A state which rapidly became tiresome, especially when she took to bringing out the old photo albums and complaining that she was losing her only daughter. At first Terri had tried to humour her but then the first barbs had begun to cut her.

'Since Eve died,' her mother had said one evening. 'You're all we've got. *She* wouldn't have wanted you to leave.'

The reference to her dead sister had affected Terri deeply, if only because it was the lowest and most painful ploy her mother had yet tried.

Eve had been a year older than Terri and mention of the other girl had struck a chord deep inside her. She'd died of spinal meningitis when she was twelve and Terri could remember being dressed in her finest clothes and forced to stand for hours on end gazing at the body of her sister which was on display in the sitting room of the house. To begin with she'd stood and wept but, as the ritual was repeated day in, day out, for almost a week, she had gradually come to look at her dead sister with feelings of bewilderment rather than grief. Her mother had even taken photos of the dead girl as she lay in her coffin. Those were included in the photo album as well.

With Eve's death all her parents' smothering love had been transferred to Terri, who grew up feeling suffocated. To this day she wondered how she had ever found the courage within herself to leave home.

But, although her mother had attempted the supreme piece of emotional blackmail towards the end, if anything it had only stiffened Terri's resolve to leave. Her father had done his part too, taking her on one side and reminding her how deeply hurt her mother was going to be by her departure. But even this two-pronged assault on her family loyalty had not dissuaded her. Though, even now, she felt she was entitled to hate them both a little bit for not having been at the station to see her off. In fact they hadn't even been in the country. The week she was to leave they'd conveniently decided to take a week's holiday.

Terri rang them as often as she thought necessary, to let them know how she was keeping and that she still had a job, hadn't yet been gang-raped by hordes of psychopaths and, no, she had no intention of returning home. The hotbed of vice and iniquity was treating her rather well. She hadn't thought it worth mentioning the three or four short-term relationships she'd gone through. They'd meant little to her, why bother her parents with them? Up until recently she had shared a flat in Bloomsbury with another girl, but she'd left a month or two ago to live with her boyfriend, leaving Terri with the flat and two lots of rent. But she coped, her job as TV reporter paid well, and since she began reporting on the murder case she'd been given a rise.

She'd joined the Independent Channel four years earlier as a secretary, worked her way up to become a researcher, then finally been given a break in front of the cameras. Her appearance had swayed the powers-that-be, for not only was she good at her job, she happened to be very attractive too. News always seemed more palatable when it was being presented by a pretty face. Even if that pretty face *was* giving details of the most savage and bizarre string of killings seen for many years.

Terri swung the Mini Clubman into the car park at the rear of the TV studios, found a parking space and drove in. She gathered her handbag from the passenger seat, locked the vehicle and strode across the tarmac towards the glass doors which fronted the entrance.

The figure stood impassively.

Watching her.

Twenty

Terri rode the lift to the fifth floor, smiling self-consciously at two plump cleaning ladies who gazed raptly at her, beaming inanely. The reporter could smell bleach in one of the women's buckets, its pungent odour filling the lift. The two women continued smiling at Terri until she got out at the appointed floor. She heard an excited muttering from behind her.

'It *is* her, the one who's reporting on those murders.'

'I knew it was. Terri something . . .'

The voices were lost as the doors slid shut. Terri made her way down the corridor, her high heels clicking on the recently polished floor. She passed framed photos of staff members, of newsreaders, presenters and the station's controllers. The fifth floor was given over almost entirely to news, while those below housed the nerve-centres for light entertainment, drama and documentaries. The building was vast, but after four years there Terri knew it like the back of her hand.

She turned a corner, exchanging brief greetings with a cameraman she knew then she came to a door marked NEWS EDITOR. Terri pushed it open and walked in.

She was greeted by the clattering of typewriter keys.

Paula Crane looked up and smiled as the reporter entered.

'Morning, Terri,' said the secretary in her broad Cockney accent. 'Bob's in his office,' she continued, inclining her head in the direction of the door behind her. 'Shall I bring you a cup of coffee through?'

'Please, Paula,' Terri said gratefully. 'Is he in a good mood?'

The phone rang and Paula reached for it, raising a hand to silence Terri momentarily.

'Hold up,' she said, raising the receiver.

'Good morning, Bob Johnson's office,' said Paula, her diction perfect, her accent now completely devoid of its East-End twang. 'No, I'm afraid Mr Johnson's busy at the moment. Can I get him to call you back? Thank you.' She put the phone down. 'Bleedin' hell, that phone's been going mad all morning,' she said, slipping back into her usual accent.

Terri laughed and walked through into her boss's office.

Bob Johnson was sitting at a computer console, punching keys, but he looked up as Terri entered.

'What about this?' he said, holding up a computer read-out. 'The latest ratings. Our programme is up by 50,000 since these killings started.' He pushed the read-out towards her. 'That's about 8,000 a victim, isn't it?' he chuckled humourlessly. 'If this nutcase keeps going we'll be bigger than *New at Ten*.'

'Great,' said Terri none too enthusiastically. 'Only if what I heard from New Scotland Yard is right then you'd better start looking for another story, Bob. They reckon they've arrested the murderer.'

Johnson looked round, his forehead wrinkling.

'That's not possible,' he said, quietly, smoothing his black hair back with the palm of one hand. 'They said they had no leads.'

'That's what I thought,' Terri told him.

Paula entered with two mugs of coffee and set them down on Johnson's desk. She took one look at the news editor and hurried out again. He looked at the ratings read-out a moment longer, then dropped it onto his desk.

'Tell me about it,' he said, sitting back in his seat as Terri described what had happened at the press conference less than an hour ago. Johnson listened intently, his eyes never leaving Terri although she was aware that his attention was wandering. For short periods he would pin her gaze to his, but most of the time he seemed to be inspecting the rest of her body.

He studied her finely-chiselled features and her slender neck, framed by that mane of brown hair, before allowing his stare to move to her breasts, the outline of her bra visible beneath her blouse. She had her legs crossed and Johnson looked longingly

101

at her denim-clad limbs wondering how soft the skin beneath the material was.

She sipped her coffee, aware that his gaze was still upon her, only slightly unsettled by his unmasked appreciation of her physical attributes.

Bob Johnson was a powerfully built individual who looked as though he might have been a boxer earlier in life. His face was almost square, his nose flattened against the pitted skin close to his deep-set eyes. He had a scar below his right ear which ran parallel with his jaw until it reached his chin. The shirt which he wore was open at the throat as if to allow his pendulous Adam's apple more room. His hands were broad, his fingers thick despite their length. Beneath his shirt Terri could see well-developed biceps, and his forearms were also thick, covered in black hair. He was, she guessed, five or six years older than herself, but no one seemed to know Johnson's exact age. He'd been the editor and programme director of *News Update* for nearly a decade. And in that time had made it one of the most successful independent news programmes on the air. He was treated with a mixture of respect and fear by his staff and it was a combination of emotions which Johnson was at pains to perpetuate amongst those below him. During his reign as director he had, to Terri's knowledge, sacked at least a dozen people and once, when a cameraman protested too vigorously, Johnson had laid the man out with a left hook.

Now he sat listening as she spoke, seemingly unwilling or unable to tear his gaze from her body.

Terri shuffled uncomfortably under his constant stare and drank some more of her coffee.

Johnson looked at her soft hands as she cradled the mug in her lap, her fingers clasped around the china. He felt the beginnings of an erection growing between his legs and sat forward, leaning on the desk.

'I don't get it,' he said, as Terri finished speaking. 'And the police said that they had a suspect in custody?'

She nodded.

Johnson got to his feet, crossed to his window and looked down into the car park below.

'They can't know,' he said, quietly, his eyes narrowing.

'What do we tell people?' Terri asked. 'The viewers will have to know something. We can't just pass over the sto   all the other news programmes will run it and the daily papers are going to be full of it tomorrow. I got the impression that's what the police wanted.'

Johnson didn't answer, he merely shook his head then said again, 'They can't know.'

Terri gazed at his broad back for a moment longer then got to her feet. Johnson turned.

'We'll have to go with the story,' he said. 'Go into studio three, I want something recorded for the six o'clock bulletin.' He exhaled heavily, watching as she put the mug down.

Terri nodded and left.

Johnson waited a second then moved across to his desk and picked up the mug from which Terri had been drinking. He was breathing heavily as he lifted it to his face, trying to catch a hint of her perfume on it. He pressed it closer to his mouth then, closing his eyes, he sucked gently on the rim of the mug in the place where Terri had been drinking. His tongue flicked hungrily over the china, lapping back a dribble of his own saliva, wishing that it had been hers.

He gripped the mug tightly, his erection throbbing even more strongly.

Exploration

The child knew where to dig.

There was no need to switch on the torch.

Not yet.

Every now and then the small figure would pause and glance around at the house, fifteen or twenty yards up the garden, but there was neither sight nor sound of movement.

The spade sank easily into the wet earth and the child turned the clods with ease, making a small pile of dirt as it dug deeper. From the bushes a few feet away there was a rustling sound and the child paused, squinting through the darkness in an effort to detect the source of the noise. But there was nothing to be seen. The blackness of the night closed around the child like a cloak.

It continued digging until the rustling came again and, this time, the child dropped the spade and picked up the torch, flicking it on, sweeping the powerful beam back and forth.

A hedgehog ambled into view from beneath one of the hedges, saw the light then scuttled away again.

The child extinguished the torch and continued digging until finally the shovel brushed against something soft and pliant. Now was the time to use bare hands. Squatting beside the shallow hole, the child scraped the remaining clods away exposing a torn grey dustbin bag. The child slid a penknife from its pocket and moved closer to the bag, running the blade into the plastic, cutting it open.

An overpowering stench of decay burst forth like the odour wafting from a gangrenous wound. The child coughed but continued cutting the bag, holding the torch in the other hand, shining it on the remains of the mangled cat which had been buried five days earlier in this humble grave.

The carcass was alive with maggots.

Both eye sockets were seething with hundreds of wriggling white forms which twisted and undulated in the light from the torch. Worms, bloated and swollen like tumefied veins, slithered from the nostrils and ears of the dead animal while dozens more had found nourishment in the cavity of the cat's belly. The body seemed to be stuffed with parasites, their appetites for carrion more than satisfied by the feast.

The child prodded the cat's head with the torch, watching as several of the maggots fell into the grave, their bodies standing out in stark contrast to the blackness of the earth. Smaller wounds were filled with freshly hatched flies' eggs, the smaller maggots also busily feeding.

The child sat on the edge of the hole watching intently. So, this was death. Was this how everything placed in the earth ended up? Food for worms and maggots? Was this the fate of human beings who lay in their coffins like carefully prepared meals until the scavengers arrived? The child wondered what it would feel like to lie there in the darkness and to know that thousands of parasites were eating into each eye, into every cut and graze, slithering into each orifice.

Was there a Heaven or a Hell, or was this all that remained? Nothing beyond death except the complete physical destruction of the body. Food for carrion eaters.

The child shone the torch over the dead cat once more and sat staring. The maggots continued to feed.

Twenty-one

The axe must have weighed close to six pounds and the force of its downward arc almost caused Miller to overbalance. He hefted the lethal object before him and smiled thinly.

'You should have been a lumberjack,' Phillip Dickinson told him, peering through a wide-angled lens at the effects man. Miller blinked hard as he felt a slight twinge from his left eye, but the feeling of discomfort rapidly passed and he handed the axe to the waiting actor. Pat Sullivan took it, watching as Miller drank deeply from his hip flask before returning his attention to the business in hand.

Standing close by, attempting to smoke a cigarette, was Kevin Brady. But even that most simple of acts was made almost impossible by the heavy make-up which the actor wore. He'd already been encased in the latex for three hours and it was starting to feel as if someone were crushing his skull inside a vice. He fancied that he could feel his veins swelling up beneath the mask of rubber, threatening to burst if he wasn't soon released from his mobile prison.

Miller beckoned him across and undid the heavy coat which the actor wore. Beneath it, his right arm was strapped across his chest, hidden from view.

'I feel like Nelson,' he mumbled through the make-up.

Miller ignored the remark and reached up to adjust the network of thin rubber tubes which terminated at Brady's shoulder. It was through these that the fake blood was to be pumped.

Miller now turned to the table behind him and pulled the piece of cloth from the object beneath.

106

It was the arm which he'd laboured over the previous night.

Dickinson stepped from behind the camera to look at the imitation appendage, shaking his head in admiration at Miller's prosthetic skills.

As the effects man set about fastening the fake arm to a harness on Brady's shoulder, the director described how he intended shooting the scene.

It took less than five minutes.

Brady, one of the 'astro-cannibals' was to confront Sullivan in the ward of the orphanage and, during the fight, Brady's arm would be lopped off. Dickinson would hold on a one-shot of Sullivan raising and swinging the axe then cut to a shot of the arm apparently being struck by the blade and flying from the shoulder. This illusion was to be completed by carefully concealed wires attached to the arm which two assistants would pull, thereby tugging the fake arm free. Miller had also built three or four blood bags into the stump of the arm which would be detonated by remote-controlled squibs as the stump was exposed to the camera.

'Then we'll cut there,' Dickinson said, smiling. 'If you'll excuse the pun.'

Miller bent close to the arm, swiftly inspecting the squibs, a flicker of concern in his eyes as memories of the accident suddenly came flooding back.

'Set,' he said, stepping back.

'I appreciate you coming back to work so quick, Frank,' Dickinson told him as the cast and crew took up their positions.

Miller merely shrugged, wiping his left eye gently as his vision blurred slightly.

'And I'm sorry I had to call you last night, but these scene changes couldn't be avoided,' the director continued.

'No sweat,' the effects man told him, inspecting the control panel which he held in one hand. In the other he held his hip flask.

'All right,' bellowed Dickinson. 'Everybody ready? Cameras, do we have speed?'

A garbled chorus of affirmatives rumbled around the set.

'All right, turn over,' Dickinson shouted. He prodded Pat

Sullivan forward. 'Action.'

Sullivan approached Brady, who was hunched forward before the camera, arms dangling limply at his sides.

Miller looked on intently, glancing to one side to make sure that the wires attached to the fake arm were not visible. He took a swig from his hip flask, one eye on Sullivan the other on the two men who crouched out of shot to his right.

Sullivan raised the axe.

Brady ran at him.

The blade swung down, the sound slicing through the air as surely as the metal itself.

'Cut,' roared Dickinson and Sullivan stepped back a couple of paces, still gripping the axe. 'Now, camera two, I want a medium shot of Kevin as the arm comes off.'

The lights were dimmed once more, the cameras began to roll and Brady found himself acting alone, feigning agony as the axe supposedly sheared through his arm.

He heard the material of his jacket rip and, a second later, on a signal from Miller, the two assistants tugged hard on the concealed wires, jerking the fake arm free. As it hit the ground Miller pressed the appropriate button on his remote and the blood bags burst with a liquid squelch, spilling their sticky contents around the latex stump. More of the fake fluid spurted from the network of tubes attached to Brady's shoulder and, as instructed, he slapped his free hand to the bogus injury as the fluid ejaculated forth.

'Cut it,' shouted Dickinson and lights once more bathed the set. 'Beautiful,' he said, patting Miller on the shoulder. 'I just want to try the axe-swinging bit from a couple of different angles,' he said to Sullivan.

Miller retrieved the arm as if it were a long-lost treasure wrapping it in the towel on the table behind him.

'Call me when you're ready for the next scene,' he told Dickinson. 'I'll be in the make-up trailer.'

The director nodded and returned to setting up his cameras to re-shoot Sullivan's attack on the 'astro-cannibal'.

Miller wandered away from the set, taking another swig from his hip flask as he reached the door which led off the sound stage. He stepped out into the sunshine, shielding his eyes momentarily against the searing glare of the morning sun. From the back pocket of his jeans he pulled a pair of sunglasses which he slipped on, welcoming the slight respite which the darkened lenses brought him from the ferocity of the glare. He made his way across the car park, feeling the heat through the soles of his shoes as he crossed the tarmac. Still cradling the fake arm he fumbled for the key to the trailer and let himself in. It was cool inside and Miller welcomed the lower temperatures. He laid the arm carefully on a table and sat down on the sofa nearby. He took another sip from his flask then pushed the receptacle into his back pocket.

Beneath the table he glanced at a large black leather hold-all, tightly sealed. Even the zip was secured by a tiny padlock.

Miller could smell the leather as he inhaled.

He gazed at it for what seemed like an eternity then he pulled it towards him and searched for the tiny key which would unlock the fastener. That done he pocketed it and slowly pulled back the zip. It made a low rasping sound as he did so, opening like a metal-edged mouth to reveal its contents.

Inside, like the occupant of a flexible coffin, lay the perfectly-formed body of a baby less than eight months old.

Miller looked in at the motionless form, his own eyes drawn to the hypnotic stare of the small child which looked back blindly through eyes which were balls of glass.

He ran appraising eyes over the inanimate body then, carefully, he drew the zip closed once more.

Picking up the hold-all, Miller made his way back out of the trailer.

'You make sure you get this right first time, Phil?' the effects man said, glancing through the glass door of the microwave oven.

The baby lay curled up inside like the still-born product of some steel womb.

'It's incredible,' said Dickinson. 'So life-like.' He seemed mesmerized by the sight of the tiny creature.

Miller took a hefty swig from his hip flask and ignored the

compliment.

'Let's get on with it eh?' he said, closing the door, watching as the camera moved closer, the man behind it focusing on the occupant of the microwave.

'How are you going to work this, Frank?' Dickinson wanted to know. 'Is the model already wired up with squibs?' He indicated the baby.

Miller nodded almost imperceptibly.

'Just turn up the heat and watch,' he said, swigging from his flask once again. Then he stepped back beside the camera which was aimed at the microwave oven and its occupant like some massive telescopic sight.

'OK,' Dickinson said to the cameraman. 'Turn over.'

'Rolling,' the man said.

Dickinson reached for the temperature control dial on the microwave and, out of shot, he turned it.

Inside the steel coffin, the baby's skin seemed to glow a dull pink.

The director turned the control again.

200 watts.

The heat from the oven could now be felt by those standing within a foot or so of it.

300 watts.

Miller took another swig of whisky and watched as the baby's flesh turned a deeper shade of pink. The searing heat, he realized was working from the inside out.

400 watts.

Two extras, one of them a woman, stood mesmerized as the lifeless shape of the baby suddenly twitched as if it still retained some semblance of life.

500 watts.

Its skin was beginning to pucker now, and as Miller looked on more closely he noticed that the flesh was beginning to undulate almost imperceptibly, as if the internal organs, having disintegrated under the ferocity of the temperature inside the oven were now beginning to boil. The small body seemed to be quivering.

600 watts.

Miller waited.

The baby uncurled inside the oven.

One eye melted in the socket as the temperature soared to incredible levels.

700 watts.

Miller wondered how much longer it would take.

Ten seconds. Twenty.

The baby's body began to shudder even more violently as its skin finally turned a livid red. Its mouth opened as if it were screaming for help, but all that came forth was a foaming flux of dark-brown fluid and bubbling pus which gushed from its throbbing orifices as if it had been some gigantic boil squeezed and milked by invisible fingers.

There was a loud and nauseating plop as the entire body burst like a corpulent balloon, the whole figure exploding in a reeking liquescent welter of corruption. The steaming mess splattered the insides of the oven, and at least one of the watching crewmen turned away in revulsion. Miller kept his eyes on the oven and its churning contents, now reduced to fluid by the incredible heat.

He looked on impassively, not even aware that others were gazing at him.

Some in amazement.

Some in disgust.

The cameraman didn't wait for Dickinson's signal. He merely stopped rolling, his own stomach lurching violently.

'How the hell do you make it look so real?' asked one of the extras, his face pale.

'Trade secret,' Miller told him.

He drank deeply from his hip flask and watched the steam rising from the door of the oven.

The stench was vile.

'Trade secret,' the effects man whispered softly to himself.

Twenty-two

Miller pulled down both sun-visors inside the Granada, but the powerful rays still seemed to find a route to his eyes. He blinked hard, squinting through the dark glasses in an effort to diminish the effects of the blazing orb which hung in the sky above.

As he drove he massaged the bridge of his nose between his thumb and forefinger, trying to stroke away some of the pain which seemed to be building in the centre of his forehead. He glanced down at the dashboard clock and noticed that it was almost two-thirty. He was due at the hospital in another fifteen minutes for his check-up. Miller pressed a little harder on the accelerator, coaxing the car along the nearly deserted road with a little more urgency.

He would not return to work that afternoon he had decided. Dickinson had said that he was going to shoot some interiors and discuss the following day's shoot with his leading actors, so there was nothing for Miller to do anyway. After his visit to the hospital, he would drive home. Before leaving the studio he had cleaned up the microwave, scraping the remains of the baby from the walls of the metal coffin, scooping them into a black bag which he had since disposed of. Miller had declined any offers of help with the cleaning up, preferring to attend to the task himself. Dickinson had told him that he thought the realistic effect had been achieved by placing some kind of heat-sensitive charge inside the replica child which had been activated once a certain temperature was reached.

Miller had smiled thinly and shrugged, content to let the director believe whatever illusion he chose.

Miller wasn't about to tell him the truth.

He slowed down slightly as he came to a bend in the road, muttering under his breath as his vision began to cloud slightly. He drove on, screwing his eyes up briefly in an attempt to clear the mist from his vision. It had descended like a film of gauze wrapped tightly around his head.

He cursed under his breath, his foot easing on the right hand pedal.

'Come on, clear,' he muttered, blinking hard once more.

His eyesight returned quickly and with surprising clarity. Miller smiled and drove on, noticing that a large container-truck was approaching on the other side of the road. Even from a hundred yards away he could hear the roar of its engine as the eighteen-wheeler thundered towards him.

Darkness.

'Oh Jesus,' he gasped.

Sudden, total blackness enveloped him. He was blind.

Unable to see a hand in front of him.

The car skidded wildly as he wrestled with the wheel, aware that the juggernaut was powering towards him. It blasted out a warning on its horn but Miller could only struggle with the wheel, trying to get the car off the road, knowing that the lorry was drawing closer.

Should he hit the brakes?

If he did that he risked sending the car into a spin.

If he could guide it towards the roadside hedge, perhaps the privet would soften the impact.

Provided the lorry didn't flatten him first.

Behind his blank eyes thoughts flashed through his mind and he gripped the steering wheel in blind terror.

Then, suddenly, as quickly as it had vanished, the light returned.

He could see again.

See that the lorry was only yards from him.

See that the massive truck was about to hit the car.

Miller stepped on the accelerator and sent the Granada hurtling across the road into the roadside hedge.

The lorry swept past, missing the tail-end of the vehicle by inches and Miller heard the loud hiss of its air brakes as the massive juggernaut juddered to a stop.

For his own part he stepped hard on the brake, crashing forward into the steering column, the impact winding him. He slumped back in his seat, noticing out of the corner of his eye that the lorry driver was running towards him.

The man reached the car and pulled open Miller's door.

'What the fuck is going on?' he hissed, some of the anger leaving his voice when he saw how pale Miller looked. 'You could have been killed.'

Miller didn't answer, he merely took off his dark glasses and gently rubbed his eyes.

'Are you all right?' the driver wanted to know.

Miller nodded.

'Do you want me to get an ambulance or something?'

The effects man shook his head.

'No,' he said, and as he spoke the lorry driver detected the hint of whisky on his breath.

'Have you been drinking?' he demanded.

'Not so you'd notice,' Miller said. 'Anyway, it wasn't that.'

'Fucking drinking and driving. It's bastards like you that get people killed,' the man rasped.

'I said it wasn't the drink,' Miller hissed, fixing the other man in a piercing stare. His own breath was still coming in short gasps and he found it hard to swallow. He closed his eyes for a moment, frightened to open them in case he'd suffered another loss of vision, but as he allowed his lids to gently part, the light flooded in.

'Are you sure you don't want an ambulance?' the driver persisted.

'I'm all right,' Miller told him, starting his engine again.

The lorry driver stepped back as Miller reversed back onto the road, then he watched as the Granada sped off. Shaking his head he watched it disappear around another bend in the road.

'Bloody maniac,' the driver muttered to himself as he trudged back to his cab.

Miller shook his head and touched two fingers to his left eye. It was throbbing like a sore thumb. Bastard. He swallowed hard, noticing that beads of perspiration had popped onto his

114

face. He wasn't sure if they were a product of the heat or his near miss with the lorry.

Or the realization that blindness could strike again without any warning.

He drove on.

Twenty-three

Doctor George Cook brought the Audi to a halt, switched off the engine and clambered out.

There had been more traffic on the road than he'd expected, the congestion not helped by the fact that a tractor had overturned about a mile down the road and he'd been sitting in a jam for over thirty minutes while someone went for help. His shirt was sticking to him and he shrugged his shoulders in an effort to loosen the clinging material. He decided that the first thing he'd do when he got inside his house was take a shower. There was plenty of time for him to wash and change before he returned to the hospital.

He set off up the gravel driveway, his feet crunching the stones as he walked. In a tree to his right birds were singing, sheltered from the sun by the broad leaves. A tall hedge flanked the driveway and on either side of it were immaculately kept lawns. He paid a man called Doug Walsh to look after the gardens. Cook certainly never had the time himself and his wife, Helen, wasn't the gardening type.

She ran a boutique in the nearby town, but over the past few months she had shown less and less interest in it and had suggested selling her share of the business to her colleague. Cook had asked her what she would do with herself without the shop to go to but she was adamant that she wanted to finish work. Fortunately his salary was more than enough to support both of them and to keep their two children at boarding school.

Cook brushed the back of his hand across his forehead, puffing as he saw that it was stained with perspiration. High above him the sky was cloudless, the only blemishes caused by the vapour trails of a couple of aircraft.

As he approached the front door of his house he glanced up at the ivy which clung to the building, making a mental note to tell the gardener to cut it down. Cook fumbled in his trouser pockets for his keys, looking around as he did so.

The door to the garage was open slightly.

Frowning, he dropped the front door key back into his pocket and wandered across to the garage door to close it. As he reached it he peered inside.

Helen's car was parked inside.

Cook's frown deepened.

She wouldn't be home from work yet, it wasn't even three o'clock. So what was the car doing there? He stepped into the garage, placing one hand on the bonnet as he did so. It was cool. The car obviously hadn't been used that afternoon. The doctor exhaled deeply, feeling a bead of perspiration trickle down his cheek, but he didn't wipe it away, he merely turned and headed for the door which connected the garage to the kitchen.

It was locked.

He hurriedly pulled out his key-ring again, selected the right key and stepped into the welcoming coolness of the kitchen. He stood in the silence, his ears alert for any sound of movement from within the house.

There was none.

He crossed to the kitchen door and then wandered through into the dining room which was also empty. As was the sitting room.

Perhaps the car had failed to start and Helen had taken a cab into work. He decided to phone the shop to check.

It was as he turned towards the phone that he noticed one of her shoes lying beside the sofa.

Cook swallowed hard and crossed to it.

As he picked it up he peered through the half-open hall door and saw the other one lying at the foot of the stairs.

The doctor moved through into the hall, still clutching the first shoe, pausing at the bottom step, looking up towards the top of the flight.

Slowly, he began to climb.

It was as he reached half-way that he heard the first of the sounds.

For a moment he froze as he heard a low rasping exhalation coming from above him but then, moving quickly but stealthily, he climbed the remaining steps until he reached the landing. Once there he stood motionless, leaning against the balustrade.

Listening.

The sound came again but with it came other noises. Soft, slithering sounds suddenly punctuated by a gasp which was unmistakably female.

Cook crossed to the bedroom on the left and stood on the threshold listening, peering through the crack between door and jamb.

His face darkened and he stepped into the room.

They were naked, both of them.

His wife lay on her back, both legs wrapped around the buttocks of Doug Walsh as he thrust smoothly in and out of her. So lost were they in their passion that neither heard or saw Cook standing there clutching his wife's shoe, looking on like some kind of voyeur. He glared at the couple through narrowed eyes, watching as the perspiration glistened on Walsh's back, his muscles tightening with each thrust. Every penetrative movement causing Helen Cook to writhe with renewed pleasure. She was clawing at his back and buttocks, trying to force his erection more deeply into her, trying to heighten what already appeared to be the considerable pleasure they were experiencing. Hers were the soft rasping moans which he'd heard. Walsh seemed to answer her with deeper grunts, each one coinciding with his forceful movements within her.

Cook froze, riveted by the tableau before him.

It seemed an eternity before he finally moved.

As Cook stepped forward, his wife's eyes snapped open and in that brief second she saw him. She opened her mouth in a mixture of surprise and fear but all that emerged from her moistened lips was a gasp which Walsh took to be a further indication of the pleasure she was feeling.

The next thing the younger man felt were strong hands on both of his ankles.

118

He shouted in surprise as Cook gripped him hard and tugged, pulling him off Helen, the force of the wrench sending him sprawling on the floor beside the bed. As he tried to get up, Cook, his face now contorted with rage, swung the shoe he'd been clutching at the younger man. The stiletto heel caught him on the shoulder, breaking the skin and drawing blood. Walsh tried to roll to one side but Cook was too fast for him and he drove a powerful kick into his side, knocking the wind from his adversary.

Helen was sitting up on the bed, her body sheathed in sweat, her nipples still erect from the recent attention lavished on them, her dark hair smeared across her face like sticky tendrils.

'Stop it,' she shouted as her husband seized Walsh by the hair and dragged him upright, jerking his head back. A moment later he drove a powerful left hook into the youth's face, the impact splitting his bottom lip. He fell backwards crashing into a dressing table.

'George, stop it, for God's sake,' Helen sobbed, watching helplessly as her husband dragged Walsh to his feet and punched him twice in the stomach. The youth went down heavily again, and as he rolled onto his back Cook kicked him hard between the legs. This time the younger man let out a high pitched shriek of pain and swiftly drew himself into a foetal position, clutching his throbbing crutch, but Cook hauled him upright and shoved him towards the bedroom door, then across the landing towards the stairs.

'Get out of here,' the doctor rasped, returning to the bedroom briefly to retrieve Walsh's clothes. He rolled them into a ball and hurled them down the steps, pushing Walsh after them. He staggered on the top stair, teetering dangerously for a moment until it seemed as if he would fall, but he clutched the banister and made his way down, one hand clutching his throbbing testicles.

'If I ever see you around here again,' Cook roared at him, 'I'll kill you.'

Walsh paused to pull on his jeans.

'Get out,' bellowed the doctor watching as the younger man staggered out of the front door.

From inside the bedroom Cook could hear his wife sobbing, repeating Walsh's name over and over again. He gripped the balustrade until his knuckles turned white, the veins at both temples pulsing angrily.

'Shut up,' he rasped at her, his breath coming in short gasps. He waited a moment longer then stormed down the stairs into the sitting room. There he pulled open the drinks cabinet and poured himself a large measure of brandy which he downed in one mighty swallow, the liquid burning its way into his stomach. He wiped his mouth with the back of his hand and poured himself another.

A minute or two later Helen appeared in the doorway, a dressing gown wrapped around her. She had wiped her face dry of perspiration but her make-up was smudged, almost washed away by her tears. She ran a quivering hand through her matted hair looking away as Cook glanced angrily at her.

He wanted to say something but he couldn't. Under the circumstances, silence was its own communicator.

'George . . .' Helen Cook began, taking a step towards him.

'Shut up, Helen,' he hissed. 'Don't say anything. Not a word.' He finished what was left in his glass and brought it down on the table with a force that threatened to shatter the delicate crystal.

Then, he turned and headed towards the kitchen and the garage beyond.

She screamed his name but Cook ignored her cries, his jaw clenched tightly, the knot of muscles at the side pulsing madly. He pushed his way through the garage door and out into the sunlight again. The heat met him like a wall and he recoiled for a second, sucking in deep lungfuls of air in an effort to calm down. He wanted to shout, to yell his anger loud but something inside him prevented it, and he stalked down the drive towards his car repeatedly clenching and unclenching his fists. He noticed that he'd taken the skin off two of his knuckles, doubtless when they'd made contact with Walsh's teeth. There was blood on the sleeve of his shirt. Flecks of crimson were soaking into the material.

Cook reached the waiting Audi and slid behind the wheel.

Somewhere in the back of his mind he searched for the reason which had brought him home in the first place. Had it been to look for some notes? To check something in one of his own reference books? He couldn't remember now. All that remained in his mind was the vision of Walsh and Helen locked in their glistening embrace. He could only guess at how many times before such meetings had taken place. How many previous couplings there had been. How many more betrayals.

Cook thumped the steering wheel angrily then he reached forward and twisted the key in the ignition. The engine purred into life and he drove off.

The heat suddenly seemed to be the least of his problems.

Doug Walsh watched the Audi pull away, his eyes narrowed to steely slits.

'Fucking bastard,' he muttered, flicking his tongue over the deep cleft in his bottom lip. He tasted blood and spat out of the open window of the Datsun. Seated behind the wheel in just his jeans he rubbed his side, looking down to see that a violet bruise was already beginning to form.

'Bastard,' he whispered once more.

When he looked up again the Audi was rounding a bend in the road ahead.

Walsh started the engine of his own car, stuck it into gear and drove away.

He kept a safe distance, ensuring that even if Cook should peer into his rear-view mirror, he would be unable to distinguish the face of the man following him.

Walsh gripped the steering wheel tighter and drove on.

Twenty-four

'Follow the light with your eyes.'

In the darkened room the words seemed to come from some intangible source. Miller obeyed nonetheless, watching as the pen-light was guided slowly back and forth by Doctor Simon Thompson.

'The pupillary reaction is good,' said Thompson, aiming the thin beam away from Miller's eyes then directly into each one in turn. 'Have you had any discomfort at all? Any reaction?'

Miller swallowed hard, remembering the attack of blindness he'd suffered only thirty minutes earlier. Then there had been the incident with Cook's photo. The aura . . .

'No reaction,' he lied.

Thompson gently pulled down the lower lid of Miller's left eye, inspecting the conjunctiva, satisfied with its bright red colour. He noticed too that there was a dense network of veins snaking up from the bottom of the eye. The tendril-like lines appeared to be swollen and Thompson peered at them intently.

'Are you sure you've had no pain from this eye?' he persisted.

'Look, I can still see,' Miller said. 'That's all that matters to me. I knew there could be problems but I was ready to take that chance.'

'You said you'd had no problems.'

'I'm fine, Doc. Right?' Miller repeated.

'You know that I was opposed to the operation in the beginning?' he said.

'No I didn't, but it wouldn't have made any difference to me,' Miller told him. 'I was the one who was blind, remember?'

'That eye that we transplanted. . .'

122

Miller cut him short.

'It worked. I cancelled the order for the white stick and besides, guide dogs eat too much,' the effects man said. 'I've got my sight and that's the only thing that counts.'

'It's *your* future, Mr Miller,' said Thompson crossing to the window and opening the curtains.

He didn't see Miller recoil slightly as the sunshine flooded through.

The doctor returned to his desk and it was Miller's turn to wander across to the window. He peered down into the car park.

'What would you have done, if there *had* been any adverse reaction with the transplanted eye?' he wanted to know.

'We'd have removed it,' Thompson told him, flatly.

Miller nodded almost imperceptibly, his eyes still fixed on the tarmac area below.

Geoge Cook brought the Audi to a halt in its appointed place in the hospital car park. He switched off the engine and sat back in his seat, eyes closed for a moment. The surgeon was thankful that he wasn't scheduled for any operations for the rest of the day. His mind was bursting with thoughts and ideas. Anger and recrimination. He looked down at his bloodied knuckles and flexed his fingers rhythmically.

Satisfied that Cook was still unaware of his presence, Doug Walsh guided his Datsun between two parked cars about seventy yards from the surgeon's vehicle. He kept his foot on the accelerator, revving the engine gently as he sat watching.

'I'd appreciate it if you could come back to us for another check-up in a fortnight, Mr Miller,' Thompson said, scribbling some notes on a piece of paper. 'Or, of course, if there are any problems with the eye before that.'

Miller seemed not to hear. His eyes were fixed on the figure of George Cook who he watched as the surgeon locked his car.

'Mr Miller,' Thompson repeated.

'I heard you,' Miller told him, his eyes never leaving Cook as the surgeon strode across the car park towards the main doors of the hospital.

'Now we'll see who's the fucking big-shot,' rasped Doug Walsh as he watched Cook set off across the car park. The younger man jammed the car in gear, gripped the steering wheel tightly and pressed down on the accelerator.

The Datsun shot forward like a bullet, speeding towards its appointed target.

Miller, ten floors up, could only stand and watch as the Datsun bore down on Cook.

And, despite the warmth in the room, he suddenly felt a chill run through him.

He guessed that the car must have been doing almost sixty when it hit Cook.

Twenty-five

George Cook barely had time to turn before the Datsun hit him.

He certainly never had the chance to see Doug Walsh hunched over the wheel, a demonic grin carved across his features.

The car smashed into him with sickening force, the impact flinging him into the air like a rag doll. His body twisted once then crashed down onto the roof of the car and skidded off. He hit the warm tarmac, unconsciousness already closing in around him, but before he blacked out he had time to see the Datsun screech to a halt a few yards away. He had time to see the smoke spinning from the back wheels as it reversed towards him with the same furious intent.

The rear offside wheel rolled over his head, crushing the skull with ease, transforming his face and most of his upper body to crimson porridge. Thick grey slicks of brain matter sprayed out from beneath the churning tyres and, as the car sped backwards, one of Cook's legs was also pulped, the foot nearly severed at the ankle. Blood began to spread in a wide pool around the pulverized surgeon who, fortunately, was beyond pain by the time Walsh drove over him a second time.

The car skidded on the blood but Walsh ensured that he manoeuvred the vehicle so that it rolled across the dead man's spine. There was a loud crack as the vertebrae were splintered and the body, which had been jerking madly suddenly ceased its frenzied movements.

By the time Walsh reversed over it again the corpse had been transformed into little more than a rag. Blood, shattered bone and a reeking spillage of bile and mashed internal organs had now spread for several yards in all directions around the devastated form.

Tyre tracks of blood formed a ragged pattern about the scene.

And now the car park was filled with other sounds.

Shouts. Screams.

A woman fainted, crashing heavily to the ground as her young son stood mesmerized by the grisly tableau before him.

Somewhere inside the building an alarm bell was throbbing with its strident tone.

Ten floors up, Frank Miller looked down on the scene impassively.

Attracted by the noises from below, Thompson joined him, a look of horror crossing his face as he saw the blood and the remains of the dead man lying on the tarmac.

'It's Cook,' Miller told him, flatly.

'What happened?' Thompson wanted to know.

Miller told him briefly then the doctor turned and headed for the door.

'I wouldn't rush,' Miller said. 'They're going to need a bucket, not a stretcher to move him.'

Thompson hesitated a second longer then disappeared, leaving Miller alone in the room, gazing down on the frantic scene. The Datsun had stopped moving now and the effects man watched as two ambulancemen dragged Walsh from inside. He stepped in some of the spilled blood as he stumbled out but it didn't seem to bother him. He merely looked across at the mashed body of Cook and smiled. Miller heard him bellow something at the remains but from his high vantage point he couldn't make out the words. The effects man crossed to his jacket and pulled out the small instamatic camera, complete with telephoto lens, which he always carried. He took three shots of the gathering below him then slipped the camera back into his pocket again. Hooking a thumb inside the collar he slung it over his shoulder and walked out.

The images gradually gained clarity as Miller pulled the photos through the developer using a pair of plastic tongs. He dipped them in fixer then rinsed the residue off, laying the prints on the worktop beside the sink. The pictures of Cook's mashed body were remarkably clear.

Miller shook the last droplets of water from the first picture and studied it more closely, his eyes drawn to the human wreckage which had once been a man. On the left hand side of the picture, almost out of sight, Doug Walsh was standing looking at his dead victim, peering down at the damage he'd done.

Miller looked at the second photo. And the third.

He sighed and shook his head almost imperceptibly then he crossed to his desk and fumbled in the drawer for what he sought.

Seated silently in the chair to his right, the flayed woman watched him with unseeing eyes and Miller noticed his image reflected in those glass orbs as he passed her. The burn victim, his flesh hanging in charred strips, also looked on impassively as his creator busied himself searching the desk.

The effects man finally discovered what he wanted.

He pulled out the photos of himself and George Cook and laid them on the desk.

Miller looked at them carefully for a moment then he covered his left eye and gazed at them.

The images remained the same.

He covered the right eye.

The faint luminescent line around Cook appeared as it had before. As if some kind of vague light were seeping through his skin.

Miller traced the outline of the aura, repeating his actions on the other picture.

It was present there as well.

Miller sighed and shook his head, reaching for the glass of whisky he'd poured for himself. Eyes still riveted to the pictures he swallowed a mouthful of Scotch, feeling it burn its way to his stomach.

The question persisted.

What was the aura?

He'd photographed Cook less than a week earlier and now the man was dead.

Murdered.

He looked across at the first photo of the surgeon who was smiling happily for the camera. Then he glanced at the one he'd taken that afternoon. The dead doctor lying in a pool of his own blood, his body crushed virtually beyond recognition.

He studied them both, his attention returning every time to that curious phosphorescent glow which surrounded Cook.

He shook his head slowly.

Twenty-six

Detective Inspector Stuart Gibson sat back in his seat and rubbed his eyes. He kept them closed for long moments, as if he were hoping that when he opened them again the piles of notes spread out before him would have vanished. It wasn't to be, and Gibson reached wearily for the clipboard on which he'd been scribbling.

On one corner of his desk a photo of his wife and two children gazed at him but the picture seemed in danger of being pushed off the desk by the sheer volume of material which Gibson had laid out for perusal.

He read his notes aloud, his voice sounding flat in the confines of his office.

'Peter Manuel. Executed July 11th 1958. Manuel's trademark was the murders of entire families which he completed by shooting them in the head with a .38 calibre pistol whilst they slept.' Gibson reached for the mug of coffee teetering on a pile of manilla files. He took a sip, wincing when he discovered it was cold.

'Mark Forrester. Shot in the head while he slept. Murder weapon, .38 calibre pistol.'

The date next to the note was July 3rd, just two weeks ago.

Gibson ran one index finger around the rim of the mug and scanned his notes again.

John George Haigh – *The acid bath murderer. Executed August 6th 1948. Dissolved his victims in acid.*

There was a name written opposite that of Haigh, except that this one was a victim, not a killer.

Nicholas Blake – *Battered then attacked with sulphuric acid.*

129

Murdered 5th July this year.

And so it went on, the names of past killers cross-referenced to those of contemporary victims, the catalogue of atrocities written out in Gibson's efficient hand. Each one linked by a red arrow drawn in Biro.

DENIS NILSEN – *arrested February 9th 1983 for the murder, by strangulation, and dismemberment of 15 men.*

William Young – *murdered July 7th. Strangled then dismembered with a meat cleaver.*

JOHN REGINALD HALLIDAY CHRISTIE – *Hanged July 15th 1953 for the murder, by strangulation, of at least six women.*

Angela Grant – *murdered July 11th. Strangled.*

PATRICK DAVID MACKAY – *Arrested 23rd March 1975 for the murder of Father Anthony Crean whom he battered to death with an axe.*

Louise Turner – *murdered July 16th. Beaten to death with a length of lead piping.*

And finally, Gibson wrote:

PETER SUTCLIFFE – *The Yorkshire Ripper. Arrested January 2nd 1981. Second victim stabbed repeatedly in the stomach and genitals.*

Bernadette Evans – *murdered July 20th. Multiple stab wounds to the stomach and genitals.*

Gibson allowed his eyes to skim over what he'd written, convinced now of the links between the killings.

The murderer was imitating the killing methods of some of the most notorious men in criminal history.

The question was, *why?*

But more importantly, could he be stopped before he took his total to seven?

Twenty-seven

She moaned softly in his arms, feeling one of his hands slip inside her dressing gown. There his questing fingers touched her breast, coaxing the nipple to stiffness beneath his expert attentions. She snaked one hand around the back of his neck, drawing him closer as they kissed, her tongue darting into the moist wetness of his mouth. He responded hungrily, the first sign of an erection pressing against his jeans.

They broke apart hurriedly as the trailer was shaken by three loud bangs on the door.

'Shit,' snapped Lisa Richardson, hastily pulling the cord of her dressing gown tight around her waist. She turned away and sat beside the mirror close to her, inspecting her features. At thirty-five she was what is euphemistically described as 'well-preserved'. Fifteen years as one of the country's leading actresses had not manifested itself in the lines of concern which she had seen etched deeply into the faces of other women of her profession. Her body, too, retained that youthful appearance. She was tall, and a little heavy breasted, that fact accentuated by the slimness of her waist and hips. Her finely-shaped features were framed by shoulder-length brown hair which was pinned up, loose strands dangling over her forehead like silky tendrils. Eyes like chips of emerald still glinted with a hidden mischief.

But Lisa Richardson was at a difficult age for an actress. Too young to play character parts and a little too old for the 'dewy eyed innocent' which she had often played earlier in her career. Hence her appearance in films such as *Astro-cannibals*. It was her second film since the beginning of the year, the previous effort having been a third-rate action adventure which had failed miserably in both the States and Europe. She'd done a couple of TV shows in the States but her agent had persuaded her to take the part in this horror picture mainly for the money which, surprisingly enough, was good.

And the film had shown other benefits too.

She sat looking at one of them now.

Colin Robson was four years younger than Lisa, a powerfully-built man who enjoyed the position of responsibility which the post of assistant director gave him. He and Lisa had been lovers for the past six weeks and neither of them made much of an effort to disguise the fact. *He* was unattached and *her* husband was in America. Who the hell cared anyway?

Robson crossed to the trailer door, opened it and looked out to see Frank Miller standing there.

'Well, what a surprise,' said Miller sarcastically. 'Fancy seeing you here and all that.'

'What do you want, Frank?' said Robson, wearily.

'I want the charming Miss Richardson,' Miller told him, clutching a copy of the shooting script in his hand. 'As you're no doubt aware, she is due in front of the cameras this afternoon.' He smiled thinly. 'I suppose that's what you've been doing. Rehearsing.'

Robson stepped back to allow the effects man into the trailer, his eyes narrowing in anger as he looked at Miller's broad back.

'I need you in my trailer, please,' Miller said with as much politeness as he could muster. 'Some of the make-up is pretty complex and I've left my notes there.' He shrugged.

'I told Dickinson I wasn't going to wear that shit on my face,' Lisa said, irritably. 'I don't know why it's necessary.'

'Look, it's in the script, I get paid for creating make-up effects so, if you don't mind I'd like to do my job. On you,' Miller added, his eyes never leaving hers.

'Perhaps we ought to call Phil and check whether or not he really wants the full make-up,' Robson interjected.

Miller turned slightly, a hard edge to his voice when he spoke.

'What is this? A debating society?' he snapped. 'It's in the script. The scene requires make-up, I don't see why we're arguing.' He took a swig from his hip flask.

132

Lisa looked on distastefully.

Miller rounded on her once more, their eyes locking.

'I told Phil that I didn't want that make-up on,' the actress said.

'He never mentioned anything to me,' Miller informed her.

'I think Lisa's got a point,' Robson interrupted.

'What are you, assistant director or fucking script supervisor?' Miller rasped at the other man. 'I came here to do a job. Now, you either want to work or you want to stand around moaning all day.'

'You know, Miller, your attitude might be a little better if you didn't drink so much,' Robson said, indicating the hip flask.

'I don't tell you how to screw the lovely Lisa here,' Miller said acidly. 'So don't tell me about my drinking.'

Lisa coloured and was on her feet.

'Get Dickinson now, I'm not being spoken to by a make-up man this way. Who the hell do you think you are, Miller?' she demanded.

'Don't pull the "star" routine with me,' he said. 'You're not even a has-been. You're a never-was.'

'You bastard,' she hissed, taking a step towards him.

'Get out of here now, Miller,' Robson snarled.

'Are you going to make me?' Miller said defiantly. 'Come on, big shot. Impress your girlfriend.' There was a fury in Miller's voice which was matched by his actions. He snatched up a stool close by him and brandished it like a club. 'I'll kill you.'

'You're crazy,' said Robson, swallowing hard.

'You might just be right,' said Miller.

'Forget it, Colin,' Lisa said. 'You're right, he's crazy. What's more, he's not even very good at what he does. I've worked with better make-up men . . .'

She got no further.

With a roar of rage Miller hefted the stool before him, swung it back over his shoulder and hurled it towards the actress. She screamed and dropped to the floor as the object flew over her head, propelled by the force of Miller's anger. It struck her mirror which promptly exploded in a frenzy of pulverized glass. Long slivers shot out, one of them nicking her left arm, drawing blood. Shards sprayed around the room like crystal shrapnel. Miller picked up one of the longer ones, ignoring the fact that the sharp edge had laid the palm of his hand open. Blood ran from the cut and dripped from his wrist and for brief seconds he could see his own distorted reflection in the length of mirror.

He moved the point slowly back and forth, first to Lisa then to Robson.

'You *are* mad,' said Robson, quietly, one eye on the wickedly gleaming tip of the shard.

'Call the police, Colin,' Lisa said, tearfully, her eyes fixed on Miller.

Robson didn't move, his eyes too were on the glass dagger.

Miller finally hurled it to the floor where it shattered into several dozen more tiny fragments. He pulled a handkerchief from his pocket and wrapped it around his gashed palm, then he turned and headed for the door of the trailer.

'You've never worked with anyone better than me,' he said, his voice low but full of anger. 'And you never will.'

With that he was gone.

Robson crossed to the door and locked it. He looked across at Lisa who had paled visibly. Despite the fact that she was shaking, Robson seemed reluctant to move across to her, as if he were frightened to leave the door. Perhaps fearing that Miller would return. He swallowed hard and wiped a droplet of perspiration from his forehead.

He found that his own hand was shaking.

Twenty-eight

The lift rose slowly, bumping to a halt at the fourth floor. As the doors slid open a red-faced man wearing a safari suit peered in and enquired if the lift was going down.

Ken Rogers smiled politely and shook his head, clutching the gift-wrapped box tightly to his chest as the doors closed once more. He leant back in one corner of the lift, watching as the lights above him lit up in numbered sequence as the car rose higher. It reached the ninth floor and he stepped out into the carpeted corridor, still holding the box beneath his arm.

It had arrived on his night porter's desk about five minutes earlier, appearing as if by magic. He'd nipped off to the toilet and, when he'd returned, the box had been waiting there. The card on it read: *Lisa Richardson*.

That was it. Just her name. No room number, nothing else. Ken had left his cocoa to cool and checked through the register to track down the recipient of the gift and he'd discovered that she was in room 926. As he approached the room he hefted the box before him, inspecting the pretty paper and the carefully tied bow. Someone had told him that the woman in 926 was an actress, so perhaps what he held was a gift of some kind. Maybe from a fan. But who the hell delivered gifts at 12.30 a.m.? He checked his watch against the nearby wall clock as he passed.

Not to worry, he told himself, he was paid to take care of the hotel and its guests from midnight onwards, and if that meant delivering packages then fair enough.

He rounded a corner and approached the door of 926.

Lisa Richardson switched off the shower and stepped out from

135

behind the frosted glass partition. She wrapped one towel around her dripping hair and another around her body, drying her arms and legs swiftly. From the bedroom beyond there came the sound of the TV set. Lisa wandered into the room, adjusting the volume control as she passed. Her companion didn't speak, he merely smiled at her, watching as she sat down at the dressing table and began towelling her hair dry.

There was a knock on the door.

'I'll get it,' Lisa said, standing up, checking that the bath towel was held firmly in place. 'Did you call for anything from room service?' she asked, but her companion merely shook his head.

Lisa opened the door and found Ken standing there, clutching the parcel.

'Miss Richardson?' he said, taking the opportunity to run appraising eyes over her slim legs and the hint of cleavage visible despite the thick folds of the towel. 'This just arrived for you.' He held out the gift-wrapped package. 'I hope I'm not disturbing you?'

She shook her head and took the package from him, frowning when he hesitated, waiting for a tip. She finally said a curt 'goodnight' and closed the door.

'Tight cow,' muttered Ken to the closed door. He turned and made his way back to the lift.

'Looks like I've got a secret admirer,' said Lisa, setting the box down on the dressing table. She inspected the card for a moment but her name was typed. No clues as far as handwriting was concerned. She set to work opening the package.

Her companion swung himself onto the edge of the bed, watching as she unfastened the large red bow then slid her nail beneath the rim of the box lid. It was like a large hat box and Lisa lifted the top excitedly, peering in with all the excited curiosity of a child at Christmas.

There was another slightly smaller box inside.

She lifted it out, noticing for the first time a strange fusty odour which made her recoil slightly. Nevertheless, she pushed the first box to one side and set to work opening the second.

It too was fastened by sellotape but Lisa again used her nail to break the seal. She lifted the lid.

The smell rose like a noxious cloud of gas but, despite that, driven by a morbid compulsion, Lisa reached for the object within.

She was acting instinctively now, her eyes bulging wide, her hands and arms moving as if they had a will of their own. Her mouth dropped open and she made a low croaking sound in the back of her throat.

In her hand she held the severed head of Colin Robson.

Blood dripped from the stump of the neck as the grisly object dangled by its hair, held by Lisa against her will. She stared into the sightless eyes, gazed at the blood which had spattered the face. The mouth was open in a soundless scream, matching her own horrified expression.

Finally, with a shriek of pure terror, she dropped the head which landed on the floor before her, its eyes gazing at her lifelessly.

She screamed again. And again. The sound gradually merging into one high-pitched caterwaul of revulsion and shock. Red fluid began to run from the neck across the dressing table, some of it dripping onto her bare legs and this brought fresh screams from her. Try as she might, she could not tear her horrified stare from the severed head of her lover.

From behind her, the man darted from the bed towards her, his own mouth agape. His own fear and bewilderment now threatening to overwhelm even his sanity.

Colin Robson stood shaking, looking at a mirror image of himself. Staring at the head which was a perfect replica of his own.

Lisa looked at the severed lump then up at Robson and the sight of the two of them sent her into fresh paroxysms of hysteria. She fell away from the dressing table and began crawling towards the bed, trying to wipe the blood from her legs.

Robson reached out and touched the head, feeling the skin, noting how cold it felt. Like frozen rubber.

Rubber.

Latex.

He gritted his teeth and lifted the head up, dropping it back into the box, ignoring the blood which splashed him as it dripped from the tendril-like veins of the neck.

Lisa was still screaming, her body now curled into a foetal position on the floor, the shrieks punctuated by sobs.

Robson looked at her, knowing that there was nothing he could do to comfort her at the moment. He gritted his teeth but his expression this time was one of rage, not horror.

He reached for the phone.

Twenty-nine

Frank Miller inspected his reflection in the bathroom mirror, running his fingers over the stubble on his cheeks. To hell with it, he thought, he wouldn't bother shaving. He splashed his face with cold water, trying to wash some of the sleep from his eyes. He'd slept heavily the previous night, which was unusual for him, now he watched the sink fill with water, studying his own distorted image which rippled on the surface.

He was just wearing jeans and trainers, and as he turned slightly he caught sight of the vicious scars which ran across his lumbar region, legacy of being too close to a football riot which he'd been photographing some years back. One of the thugs had come at him with a Stanley knife, slicing two deep gashes across his back, one of them narrowly missing a kidney. That same day Miller had seen a policeman beaten to death with bricks.

The photos were on the wall of his workroom.

The doorbell sounded and Miller glanced at his watch. He frowned. Eight o'clock in the morning. He wondered who could be calling so early.

Miller yanked the plug from the sink, hauled a sweatshirt over his head and made his way downstairs.

He opened the front door, smiling as he saw his visitor.

'It must be important,' Miller said, 'to bring you to my house at this time in the morning.'

Phillip Dickinson nodded and walked in, following Miller through into the sitting room.

'It *is* important,' the director said. 'It's about Lisa Richardson.'

139

Miller smiled thinly and began filling his hip flask from a bottle of Haig.

'What about her?'

'She's in a London hospital suffering from shock,' Dickinson said. 'And don't ask me what that's got to do with you, Frank. I know about what happened last night. About your little "prank".'

'She had it coming,' said Miller, harshly. 'Her and that tosspot she's hanging around with. She insulted my work, Phil. Nobody does that and gets away with it. Well, now she knows *exactly* how good I am.'

'You're a fucking idiot,' rasped Dickinson.

Miller eyed him malevolently.

'Why couldn't you let it drop?' the director demanded. 'So what if you had a row with her? So what if she's sleeping with Robson? You were hired because of your effects skill not as a fucking morality guide. I've lost my leading actress because of you. You've put back the shoot for at least three days. Jesus, when I rang the hospital this morning they said they had her under sedation. She was practically raving when they took her in last night.'

'If you're waiting for an apology, you can forget it,' Miller said, his voice devoid of any remorse.

'This is more than just revenge, Frank,' Dickinson said. 'It's costing the company money. Every day lost is thousands of bucks down the drain.'

Miller continued filling the flask, trying to ensure that he didn't spill any of the precious fluid.

'Get another actress,' he said. 'The only scenes she had left were ones under make-up. Who the hell would know?'

'That's not the point,' the director snapped. 'I didn't come here to discuss how we could get round the problems of not having a leading actress.'

'So what *did* you come for?'

'I came to tell you that it might be a good idea if you stayed away from the set for a few days,' Dickinson informed him.

'You're firing me?'

'No, I'm asking you to stay away until things cool down.'

Miller took a swig from the whisky bottle, gripping it in one hand.

'This could cause a lot of problems, Frank. I don't know why you couldn't let it go. But no, not you. You always have to have the last word don't you?'

Miller nodded.

'And I'm going to have it now,' he said, his eyes narrowing. 'I'll stay away from the set for a few days. I won't put any more spokes in, Phil. But I'm surprised at you. I never thought you'd let some nothing actress and her boyfriend frighten you. Why didn't you tell *them* to stay away from the set for a few days?'

'*You're* the one who sent her into shock, Frank. I'm just trying to smooth things over.'

'Ever the diplomat eh, Phil?' Miller said. 'Right, you've said your piece, now get out.'

'It's that goddamn temper of yours . . .'

'I don't need a character reference. Just get out.'

'People are frightened of you, Frank,' Dickinson told him. 'You're bad news.'

Miller drew his arm back, the empty whisky bottle still clutched in his fist.

'Get out,' he roared and flung the bottle.

It whistled past Dickinson's head, struck the wall behind him and shattered, spraying glass in all directions.

The older man looked first at the wall where the bottle had struck, then at Miller who was still glaring at him through eyes which were now little more than steely slits. Without a word Dickinson turned, opened the front door and walked out.

Miller took a hefty swig from his hip flask, wiping his mouth with the back of his hand.

'In a state of shock,' he said, a smile beginning to spread across his face.

He chuckled to himself and headed towards his workroom.

Fascination

There were uniforms everywhere.

Policemen. Ambulancemen. Railwaymen.

The child watched the profusion of officials with interest as they swarmed around the edge of the platform close to the front of the train.

The driver had been helped from his cab and was sitting, white-faced, on one of the benches close by. Both hands were pressed to his forehead and he was shaking his head almost imperceptibly. The body lay on the track about twenty feet away and the child stood gazing at the mangled form, watching as two sweating ambulancemen tried to lift the smashed individual free of the lines.

Passengers had spilled from the halted tube train, some gathering on the platform like the child, others only too anxious to be away from the scene of horror. Policemen were doing their best to usher the gathering crowd in the direction of the exits but morbid curiosity had gripped them like some collective fever and each pushed forward in an effort to get a better view than their neighbour. People jostled one another, craning forward to peer at the destruction before them. The child squeezed between the legs of two tall men who were trying to catch sight of the blackened shape being lifted from the rails. The child heard words floating around inside the cavernous platform area. Words like suicide. The victim, a man in his thirties, had apparently waited a few feet from the tunnel entrance, then as the train emerged, had launched himself at it. The damage had been horrific but, unfortunately, not fatal. The man's face had been staved in and, after having been catapulted several feet down the tracks, he had lost one leg, severed at the knee, to the churning wheels of the train. An arm, the fingers still twitching spasmodically, lay

142

near the edge of the platform, blood oozing from the severed arteries.

Someone close by had vomited and the bitter stench mingled with the acrid odour of ozone and seared flesh.

The child moved closer as the ambulancemen lifted the body up onto the platform edge, laying it carefully on a grey blanket which had been spread out by their companions.

Blood from the stump of the victim's leg rapidly began soaking into the thick material. The child watched in fascination as the crimson fluid ran from the remains of the limb.

The policemen were still trying to push the crowd back but few seemed to pay any attention to the men in blue.

The child stared intently at the body which lay on the blanket. At the pulped face, pieces of shattered jaw-bone visible through the torn flesh and muscle. At the blackened skin and the ragged extremities of the leg and arm wounds which dripped blood with a rhythmic pulsing.

The child looked on with fascination at the mangled body, catching the first hint of a more choking stench. The stench of excrement. The contorted face of the man twisted into an even more repulsive visage as he opened his mouth and gasped out something unintelligible. Then, as the child watched, he rolled onto his side and let out a loud moan. A sound torn raw and bloody from the base of his shattered spine. A sound which reverberated in the underground cavern and bounced off the walls of the gaping tunnel. It was a grunting noise, the pained wailing of some great primate in agony. A bellow of unendurable suffering which drummed in the child's ears as it looked on impassively.

Then the sound dissolved into a low grunt, a rumbling like that of a stuttering motor. One filled with blood.

The child watched as the body underwent one final spasm, then the rumbling sound was replaced by the liquid sound of soft excretion as the man's sphincter muscle finally gave out.

One of the watching ambulancemen pulled a blanket over the corpse. The crowd standing nearby began to disperse slowly but the child remained where it was, gazing at the shapeless bundle beneath the blanket. Finally a policeman motioned for the child to leave, but it turned away reluctantly, finally caught up in the mass exodus from the platform.

As it moved away, the child glanced round one final time to see the body being lifted onto a stretcher, and in that moment the sound which the dying man had uttered seemed to echo around the inside of the child's head like some kind of wailing lament.

The child smiled thinly and walked on.

Thirty

Terri Warner nudged the front door of the flat closed using her elbow, almost dropping the armful of library books which she carried. She moved through into the sitting room, dumping the heavy tomes on her desk near the window, then she reached across and pressed the 'rewind' button on the answerphone. While the cassette spun in reverse, Terri wandered into the kitchen and retrieved a can of coke from the fridge. She stared in at the food and sighed softly. She couldn't be bothered to cook now, she thought, pulling the ring on the can. There was plenty of frozen stuff in the freezer. Thank God for convenience food, she thought as she moved back into the sitting room.

Terri kicked off her shoes, massaging her aching feet with one hand, reaching for the 'play' button of the answerphone with the other. There was a high pitched bleep and the first message began:

'. . . I hate talking to these bloody machines,' the voice said and Terri smiled. 'Terri, this is Peter Landon. I don't know if you remember me? We met at the studios about a week ago.'

Terri nodded as she sipped her drink. She did remember him, a tall, well-built man about a year younger than herself. He had been working as a floor director on one of the light entertainment shows which were made in the same building that housed her office. She sat back, listening to the remainder of the message feeling a little sorry for the caller as he muttered on as if racing the thirty-second time-limit which the machine allowed.

'. . . I know we only met once but I was wondering if you might like a drink with me some time. I mean, I'd buy. Or perhaps even lunch, or dinner? If you had the time of course. If

145

you'd like to ring me back I'll give you the number. I know we might bump into each other in the building but I'd better give you the number just to be on the safe side. These bloody machines have a time-limit don't they? Oh shit, sorry.' Terri was giggling by now as she listened to Landon's frantic babblings. 'Look, the number to ring . . .' There was another high pitched bleep. End of message. Terri shook her head and chuckled.

'Hi, Terri, it's Tina. How about coming over to my place on Thursday night. Joe's away for a week so I've only got the dog to talk to. Ring me.'

Another high-pitched bleep.

Tina Kennedy had worked with Terri as a researcher when she'd first joined the independent network but she'd left about a month earlier when she'd discovered she was pregnant. Terri reached for her handbag and pulled her diary out, flipping through the pages. Thursday was fine. She scribbled Tina's name in the appropriate space and made a note to call her back as soon as the messages had finished.

Another bleep.

'Terri, it's me again. Peter Landon.'

She smiled.

'The tape ran out before I had time to give you my number, so here it is.'

Terri dutifully wrote it down in the back of her diary. Landon had seemed like a nice enough man, a little shy, but that was a welcome change in the loud-mouthed, ego-laden world of TV. She took another sip of her drink and wondered if she'd ring him.

Another tone. Another message.

'The police don't know.'

Then silence.

The tape continued running but there were no more messages.

Terri looked at the machine, her brow creasing. She rewound the tape slightly and listened again.

The tone.

'The police don't know.'

146

She put down the can of coke and swung herself around so that she was facing the machine, her attention now riveted by those four words.

She listened again.

And again.

'The police don't know.'

Terri exhaled slowly.

The words were spoken slowly almost as if the caller was choosing each syllable with care, ensuring that the message would not be misheard.

But the voice.

She re-wound the tape.

Listened again.

'The police don't know.'

Terri lost count of the number of times she replayed the message until finally she switched off the machine and reached for the phone.

'The police don't know.'

Bob Johnson stroked his chin thoughtfully and looked first at the answerphone then at Terri. The news editor shifted in his seat as Terri rewound the tape yet again.

'You say you don't recognize the voice?' he said, his eyes never leaving hers.

Terri shook her head.

'With just four words it's not much to go on is it?' she said. 'Do you really think it could be the murderer?'

Johnson shuffled in his seat again and shrugged.

'Everyone knows that you're heavily involved with this case,' he told her. 'If the killer has seen you on TV it's possible he might try to contact you. It *has* been known before. A bloke called Peter Alphon contacted a journalist about the murder that James Hanratty supposedly committed in 1962. Alphon confessed to the killing after Hanratty had been hanged.'

Terri sighed.

'But we can't be sure it's the murderer,' she said. 'It's the first message I've had. What I'd like to know is, how did he get hold of my number? I'm ex-directory.' There was a long silence

147

during which Terri was aware that Johnson was constantly allowing his gaze to travel up and down her body, pausing at her crossed legs and rounded breasts. She began to feel slightly uncomfortable beneath his unrelenting gaze and got to her feet. She asked if he wanted another drink and he did. She poured him another whisky and returned to her seat opposite Johnson who peered at her over the rim of the glass.

'Perhaps I should ring the police,' she said, finally.

'No.'

Johnson sat forward almost spilling his drink.

'Leave the police out of it,' he urged. 'For now at any rate. Firstly, you don't know if it is the murderer, but if it is then perhaps he wants to make contact with you.' Johnson paused for a moment, watching the expression on Terri's face change from one of fear to one of curiosity. 'There could be one hell of a story here, Terri,' he told her. 'Don't fuck it up by calling in the police. And don't destroy that tape, whatever you do.' He motioned towards the cassette. 'Wait and see if he calls again. See what he says.'

She nodded slowly, unable to maintain eye contact with Johnson. Terri felt as if his gaze were boring through her, probing her soul, such was its intensity. After a moment or two she got to her feet and padded through to the bathroom.

Johnson watched her go, sipping slowly at his drink.

He heard the click as the bolt was slid across, then, unhurriedly, he crossed the room and picked up one of Terri's discarded shoes. Gripping it by its long heel he ran his index finger slowly around the inside of the shoe. A feeling of warmth began to spread around his groin, growing more intense as he repeated the procedure with the other shoe, this time bringing it close to his face, sniffing at the leather interior, rubbing the high heel rhythmically. His penis was throbbing now, straining against his trousers and, as he heard the toilet flush he replaced the shoe and walked across to the window, looking out over the street below, trying to hide the bulge between his legs.

Terri seated herself on the sofa once more and looked at Johnson's broad back, watching as he turned slightly, downing what was left in his glass in one mighty gulp. He asked if it was all right to use the toilet and moved quickly from the sitting room, hiding his bulging erection from her.

Once inside the bathroom he bolted the door and stood with his back against it, his breath coming in short gasps, the raging fire in his groin now almost uncontrollable. He fumbled with the zip of his trousers, freeing his rampant organ, massaging the stiff shaft with one hand. He crossed to the lavatory itself, kneeling in front of the porcelain bowl, gazing down at the seat. He reached out with one hand and touched it, feeling the warmth on the plastic, now rapidly fading.

Beside his hand there were two or three tiny, tightly curled pubic hairs.

Johnson picked each one up as if it were a strand of precious silk then he wrapped them carefully in his handkerchief, the black curls standing out starkly against the whiteness of the material. It was as he stood looking at the dark curls that he felt the first drops of thick fluid dribble from the end of his penis. The sensation, pleasurable though it was, startled him and his reaction was sufficient to prevent a full outpouring of his desire. He wiped the end of his organ with a piece of toilet paper then pushed his stiff shaft back inside his trousers, taking several deep breaths before he finally flushed the toilet. That done he folded up his handkerchief and put it in his pocket.

Johnson splashed his face with cold water from the sink and wiped the excess away with his hands before drying them on a towel. Then he slid back the bolt on the door and walked back out, through to the sitting room.

'Let me know if he calls again,' he said, looking down at Terri, who held the tape in her hand. 'But don't get in touch with the police.'

Terri nodded and replaced the tape in the machine.

Johnson announced that he would have to leave and it was with something akin to relief that Terri got to her feet and walked with him to the door. He looked deep into her eyes, allowing his gaze to rest briefly on her breasts. Then he stepped out into the hall.

'Don't let anyone know about the call,' he repeated. 'No one.'

She watched as he turned and headed towards the lift. After a moment Terri closed her door and retreated back into the sitting room where she crossed to the answerphone as if drawn by some powerful magnet. Johnson could be right. If the killer did intend contacting her then she would have a superb story on her hands. What puzzled her at the moment was the voice. She ran the tape again.

'The police don't know.'

Terri shuddered slightly as she realized that there was something vaguely familiar in those words.

She couldn't be sure but she felt she knew that voice.

Thirty-one

The Granada skidded to a halt as Miller stepped a little too hard on the brake. The vehicle narrowly avoided the rear bumper of the car ahead but Miller seemed unconcerned by the possible collision. He switched off his engine then sat back in his seat, catching a glimpse of his reflection in the rear-view mirror.

His hair was uncombed, and even in the harsh glare of neon spilling from the club nearby his face looked pale. Dark rings beneath both his eyes made it look as if some mischievous child had been drawing charcoal clouds on his lower lids. He rubbed the left eye as it blurred momentarily. Then, muttering to himself, he clambered out of the car and locked it.

The drive into Central London had been uneventful. Not much traffic and, fortunately for him, no vigilant policemen to notice that he'd sometimes exceeded the speed limit by five or ten miles an hour. Just as well they hadn't stopped him, Miller thought, catching a whiff of his own whisky-sodden breath. He was drunk and he knew it. What did he care? He could still walk straight, still speak coherently. Still drive. When he passed out, that was when he'd know he'd had enough. He glanced at his watch. Almost 10.30. London's Soho was a blur of neon. A kaleidoscope of colour and sound. Music blasted from the doorways of clubs, here and there Miller heard shouts and laughter from a pub across the street. Men and women, in couples or alone, wandered past, some content merely to glimpse the tableau of activity, others more intent on joining it. Many were doing business.

At the entrance to the club Miller passed a doorman who was busily picking the head from a bulging spot on his chin. He afforded the effects man only a fleeting glance, his attention fixed on the small sore which he was now squeezing between thick fingers. Miller pushed his way through the curtain of plastic strips which served as a doorway and walked into the club.

The club was in semi-darkness, its denizens huddled in corners as if afraid to emerge into the subdued twilight within the room. There was a green strip-light above the bar which gave it the appearance of being covered in mould, but apart from that meagre glow of illumination the only brightly-lit spot was the stage. Miller paused and glanced across at it, leaning against a chair to support himself for a moment.

The stage was little more than a raised platform about twelve feet square. On it two girls were dancing slowly, moving with as much elegance as a couple of drunks. Their choreography left much to be desired, Miller thought, watching as they clumsily danced around each other. The first of them was dressed in a shiny black basque which barely covered her ample breasts. Her legs were sheathed in thigh-length boots. She wore nothing else.

Miller watched as her companion, a black girl with closely cropped hair and a muscular frame, shrugged herself out of the long cape which she wore, exposing her nakedness. The two girls kissed, the contrast in the colours of their skin rapidly lost as the stage was bathed in red light. Then blue, then green. All the colours of the rainbow lit the scene as a crackling p.a. system carried forth a roaring singer's voice and the screech of guitars. A deafening accompaniment to an act which was anything but tender in its execution.

By the time Miller reached the bar the black girl was on her knees before her partner, lips and tongue pressed urgently to the offered vagina.

'. . . *Thrills in the night, far from the light, passion taking over* . . .' roared from the p.a. Miller smiled thinly and managed to attract the attention of the barman who ambled over, his face expressionless. Miller ordered a large Scotch.

As he sat drinking he glanced around the inside of the club, peering at those who frequented it, some looking as if they used it as a refuge. There was a man sitting at the far end of the bar, slumped across the counter, his head in a puddle of spilt beer. Every time he exhaled bubbles formed in the liquid.

At the table to his right three men sat, all in their mid-forties, all of them staring raptly at the stage where both girls were now naked and were busy inserting a selection of dildos and vibrators into each other. The music seemed to grow louder, a growing crescendo which matched the mounting excitement of the performers. They were either acting or very close friends, Miller couldn't figure out which.

In another corner of the club, barely visible beneath the subdued lighting, a couple were kissing feverishly and Miller noticed that the man's hand was well and truly hidden beneath the short skirt which his companion wore. He watched the woman wriggling on her seat as the man's fingers probed between her legs.

Close by them sat a man on his own, his attention divided between the events on stage and those happening much nearer to him. Miller watched as a young woman approached him, seating herself on the chair beside the punter. Miller saw the girl smile and put her hand on the man's leg, but he seemed to shrink away from her. The girl's smile faded but she persevered a moment longer before finally getting to her feet. She tottered somewhat uncertainly on three-inch heels, towards the bar. Towards Miller.

She sat on the bar stool beside him and smiled her practised smile at him.

'My name's Penny,' she informed him, fluffing up her permed hair with both hands. 'I haven't seen you in here before.'

Miller caught a slight Welsh twang in her accent, although it was difficult to hear anything above the pounding music.

'We've both missed a treat then, haven't we?' he replied. Then, draining what was left in his glass he ordered another.

The girl regarded him warily for a moment then her well-rehearsed grin returned once more to lips which carried a cold sore at one corner. She was in her late teens Miller guessed. Heavily made-up. However, the thick layer of foundation she wore was unable to disguise the spots and craters on her cheeks.

False eyelashes curled out from her lids like marauding spiders. She licked habitually at the cold sore before she spoke again.

'Are you going to buy me a drink?' she wanted to know.

Miller looked briefly at her, features distorted by the phosphorescent green glow of the strip light. Her face was drawn and the look in her eyes reminded him of a predatory animal.

'Buy your own,' he said, flatly.

'If it's too noisy for you here you can always come back to my flat,' Penny told him. 'It's not far from here.'

'You want me to buy more than a drink then?'

'That's up to you,' Penny said, raising one eyebrow and smiling. The gesture was all the more repellent because of its artificiality. Miller felt as if that cold sore was winking at him. She flicked her tongue over it once more.

The effects man moved a little closer to her and her smile broadened.

'Do you know what I'd really like?' he began, forced to shout over the thundering rock music.

Penny looked hopeful.

'I'd like you to find some other mug. Leave me alone, will you?'

She frowned as if his words hadn't registered, then she slid from the bar stool and teetered away, her eyes narrowed as she cast him a derisory glance. Miller watched as she approached a balding man in a leather jacket who had just entered the club. In no time she was sitting on his knee. Miller shook his head and finished his drink.

12.36 p.m.

Miller pushed the glass back across the counter and got to his feet, steadying himself against the stool for a second. As he began walking he found that he could accomplish the action with surprising ease and dexterity considering the amount of alcohol he'd consumed in the last forty-five minutes.

Miller glanced at the stage as he made for the exit and noticed that two new girls had taken over. Both were dressed as nurses, one of them lying spreadeagled on a torn leather couch while the

154

other did her best to insert a stethoscope into her companion's vagina.

'Doctor, Doctor' came thundering out of the crackling p.a. system.

As he reached the exit, Miller caught sight of Penny sitting happily on the lap of her customer. The man was sweating profusely, his face only inches from her breasts. Every now and then he would touch the tempting globes only to receive a mock rebuke from the girl. She shot Miller a triumphant glance as he passed. He smiled to himself. Penny had succeeded in the first part of her task, he thought. The pleasure would be short once the business had been done. The predator had hold of its prey.

As he stepped out onto the pavement the smell hit him like a putrid fist. The smell of vomit spilled in the gutter mingled with the ever-present odour of exhaust fumes. Close to his car two men were trying to pull their drunken companion to his feet as he sat heaving mightily in the direction of a drain that was already blocked. All three of them were drunk.

Miller fumbled for his car keys, opened the door and slid behind the steering wheel. He pushed the key into the ignition but didn't turn it. Instead he reached across and pulled something from the glove compartment of the car.

Checking that the camera was loaded, Miller raised it to his right eye and squinted through the view-finder, sighting it on the trio of drunks nearby.

Click.

He chuckled to himself as he thought how unusual it was to be taking photos of living subjects rather than the wasted, bloated or butchered corpses which had been his models for so many years. He saw two men leaving the club.

Click.

A woman walked past and stopped to speak to the club's doorman.

Click.

Miller sighed, smelling his own alcohol-tainted breath inside the car. He took more photos, recorded more of the gutter life which emerged every night like nocturnal prowlers. London was a city of changing moods, inhabited by two different sets of people. Those that did their living during the daylight hours and those who thrived at night. And now was their time.

Miller felt a curious affinity with those who frequented the darker hours. He belonged, he had come to realize over the years, with darkness. Darkness of the mind and the soul.

He looked up and saw Penny emerging from the club, her customer following meekly behind.

Click.

Miller took another shot of her then watched as she and her companion disappeared around the corner.

Miller blinked hard, trying to clear his head as much as his vision. He rubbed his face with one hand, then placed the camera on the passenger seat and started his engine. The Granada burst into life and Miller spun the wheel, guiding it out into the road. As he reached the corner of the street he peered to his right and left and caught sight of Penny and her guest as they entered a tall, three-storey house. Miller drove past, noticing that several windows in the building were lit. Each room, he presumed, had been converted into some form of bed-sit. He slowed down as he passed the building, running appraising eyes over it, wondering which room Penny was in.

The clock on the dashboard glowed 1.09 a.m.

Thirty-two

Paint was peeling off the walls like leprous flesh. Huge soft slivers of yellow which Penny knew she would have to cover somehow.

The flat had always been damp and now the dark stains were beginning to return on the skirting boards and in the cracks of the ceiling. Like gangrene in an open wound the damp seemed to creep insidiously into every crevice in the paintwork. Penny had decorated the place herself shortly after moving in two years before. Prior to that she'd been living in a squat in Wapping with two other girls. It had been one of them who'd persuaded her to go on the game. Penny hadn't liked the idea much to begin with, but as she realized how much money there was to be made out of it, the prospect of spending most of her time being pawed and mauled by strangers didn't seem quite so repellent. She'd had the odd weirdo in her time but never anyone into violence. There'd been one punter who'd asked her to kick him repeatedly in the arse but, when she'd dissolved into fits of laughter he'd refused to pay her. Bastard. That had happened when she was sixteen, a year after she'd first arrived from Cardiff. Now, three years older and wiser, she felt that she could handle anything.

The punter tonight had been easy. He'd asked for a blow job but Penny had refused. In the beginning she would have agreed but what with all this shit like AIDS about, she, like so many other girls she knew, refused to give blow jobs now. And, even for a straight fuck they insisted that the punter wore a rubber. Some worked without, but she didn't intend taking any more risks than she had to.

She'd satisfied her customer easily. He'd been so worked up by the time she'd pulled his pants off that he'd shot his load as she knelt between his legs. Her long bleached hair had brushed the end of his penis and he'd spurted copiously into her crowning glory.

Now she smiled to herself as she stood over the sink, waiting for it to fill, anxious to wash the dried semen from her hair. She tested the water temperature with her fingertips then retrieved some shampoo from the cabinet above. She switched on the portable radio propped up on the bath beside her and bent forward over the sink, using a plastic cup to scoop water over her hair. She began to sing along with the tune on the radio.

For those who know how, slipping a lock is a simple exercise, especially when the lock is old and needs replacing.

The figure that stood outside the door of Penny Steele's flat found that the task was easier than expected.

The door opened a fraction, the intruder slipped inside and hurriedly closed it once more.

From the bathroom came the sound of splashing water and music. And singing.

The intruder stood motionless at the front door for a moment longer, then advanced slowly into the flat, eyes never leaving the door of the bathroom. The figure trod stealthily, silently. Expertly.

Moving quietly, the intruder glided into the small kitchen. Past the stained cooker which still bore an unwashed saucepan. Past the cracked sink to the drawers.

There was a selection of knives inside.

Penny soaked her hair thoroughly then applied the shampoo, still happily singing along to the radio. She stopped abruptly as the sound faded. Batteries must be running low she reasoned, and shook her radio irritably. It crackled, burst into life again then faded just as rapidly.

A floorboard creaked.

Penny tried to rub the soap from her eyes with her fingers but it made them sting even more and she had to reach for the towel.

Hair dripping she stood by the sink, listening.

There was a sudden rattle of sound as the radio started up again and she glared at it a moment longer before bending over the sink once more.

The sound of splashing water and music blotted out all other noises.

Even the sound of footsteps outside the bathroom door.

The intruder paused, peering through the gap in the door. Aware that the sounds of approach had been masked by the water and radio. Now the figure put one hand gently on the door and eased it open a fraction more.

Penny Steele was wearing a thin cotton house-coat, worn at the elbows. Her head was bowed over the sink as if in prayer, her fingers moved slowly and carefully through her hair, massaging the shampoo into every strand.

The figure watched, gripping the largest of the two knives tightly, edging forward an inch or two towards the threshold of the bathroom.

Penny reached for the plastic cup to rinse the shampoo away.

The radio crackled loudly. Almost like a warning.

Then the intruder pushed the door hard.

It swung back on its hinges and banged gently against the wall causing Penny to look up, but soap ran into her eyes again, momentarily blinding her. All she saw was a dark shape before her attacker was upon her.

She opened her mouth to scream, both shocked and frightened by the sudden intrusion, but the sound came out as a strangled gasp as she saw the vicious glint of the first knife.

Penny tried to wipe her eyes so that she could see the attacker, so that she might have some chance of defending herself. Her wet hair flapped around her like dead snakes as she shook her head, then suddenly her assailant lunged forward.

The knife was fully eight inches long and it was wielded with fearsome power.

As the prostitute put up a hand to deflect the blow the blade sheared through her index finger above the knuckle and severed the digit before hacking a bloody swathe through her palm.

Blood began pumping from the ragged wound and the finger fell to the floor.

The second knife powered into her stomach to the left of her navel. The impact winded her and she felt as if she'd been punched with a steel fist. A sudden excruciating pain filled her lower body, and through it all she could feel the coldness of the steel being twisted inside her as the attacker pressed forward, finally knocking her over.

The second blade swept down again, missing Penny's outstretched hand, scything into her shoulder at the point of neck and clavicle. Blood erupted from the wound, spraying over the cracked white tiles on the bathroom wall.

Still unable to see because of the shampoo in her eyes, Penny began to moan loudly, desperate to escape this ferocious onslaught. It was useless. Both knives were brought down simultaneously. The smaller of the two tore through her left breast, bisecting the nipple. The second and longer knife punctured her lung after scraping off a bone. There was a sound like a rapidly deflating tyre and a foul-smelling blast of air escaped via the yawning gash.

Penny tried to draw breath but the effort caused her acute pain. Air whistled coldly through the hole in her lung and she gasped frenziedly, trying to fill her lungs, attempting to ease the growing pressure which she felt inside her head. But the wound prevented her breathing properly and she flailed helplessly with her arms, her pain now tinged with terror as she realized that she was dying. Blood filled her mouth, the bitter taste making her heave, but still her attacker kept up the merciless assault.

With a strength born of desperation, Penny attempted to fight back, throwing herself at her assailant, hands reaching for the twin blades.

The act of self-defence was useless against such a powerful enemy. The intruder merely dodged Penny's despairing lunge, watching as she sprawled face down on the blood-splashed floor of the bathroom. She lay there gasping for breath, feeling her life-fluid draining from her through the cuts and lacerations which disfigured her body. Then finally she began to crawl, her eyes filled with tears of pain and fear, struggling to find the breath to scream. Every time she tried to breathe searing pain enveloped her. She coughed, feeling a torrent of vomit forcing its way up her windpipe, mingling with the blood which was already flowing freely from her open mouth.

The attacker stood silently, watching as Penny crawled away like a crippled child, listening as the air hissed through the sucking wound in the lung. With a deliberation that bordered on fascination, the killer walked slowly behind Penny as she dragged herself from the bathroom, almost straddling her, much as a parent follows its child as the child learns the first rudiments of walking.

The assailant paused a moment longer then suddenly reached down and gripped both of Penny's ankles, dragging her back bodily into the bathroom, rolling her over onto her back. A position she was used to.

The killer knelt between her legs, as if worshipping at a shrine.

Then, the knives descended again.

And again.

And again.

PART TWO

'You give me evil fantasies.
I want to get inside your mind.'

Judas Priest

'Madness need not be all breakdown. It
may also be breakthrough. It is potential
liberation and renewal as well as
enslavement and existential death.'

R.D. Laing

Thirty-three

How he ever got home Miller couldn't work out. He sat at the kitchen table staring at the kettle, waiting for it to boil, wondering how he'd managed to drive the fifteen or so miles from Soho to his house the previous night. What he also wanted to know was who had set the pneumatic drill hammering inside his skull. He cradled his head in his hands, fists pressed to his temples as if that would stop the thudding inside his head. He swallowed two aspirins dry, gagging at the bitter taste as one stuck in his throat.

The kettle began to boil. Miller got to his feet and made coffee. Some of it spilled onto the work-top but he merely wiped the bottom of the mug with his hand and sat down again. He sipped the steaming liquid, wincing as he burned his tongue. Miller cursed under his breath and exhaled wearily. He glanced at his watch and noticed that it was just after seven in the morning. Three or four birds were singing on the branches of the tree outside the window, their dawn chorus irritatingly loud. Miller closed his eyes and took another sip of his coffee. What's the best thing for a hangover? he asked himself. Drinking heavily the night before? Very funny. It wasn't the time for jokes, not even with himself. What the hell was he going to do to stop his skull cracking in pieces? He was sure that if the pounding got any worse his entire cranium would simply explode.

He hadn't been *that* drunk for many years. So drunk that he couldn't remember what time he'd got home or, more to the point, *how* he'd got home. He was amazed at his own instincts, flabbergasted that he hadn't managed to wrap the Granada around a tree on the way back. He remembered nothing. Not the journey, not his arrival home. Nothing. He could vaguely recollect leaving the house the previous evening.

He recalled finishing two bottles of Haig, driving into Soho. Then, nothing.

It was as if his mind was a computer screen and some bastard had erased everything from midnight onwards.

His camera was lying on the table opposite him and the effects man glanced at it, noticing that the case was open. The cyclopean eye of the lens stared blindly at him and he caught a brief glimpse of his own reflection in the glass. It wasn't a pretty sight. After a moment or two Miller got to his feet and picked up the Nikon, noticing that the film was finished. Whatever he'd been doing the previous night, he realized, at least he had some kind of pictorial record of it. Perhaps if he developed the film it might jog something in his mind. Help him to remember what he'd been doing. He wished that there was such an easy remedy for stopping the pounding inside his head.

Miller picked up the camera and headed towards his workroom.

He heard footsteps outside the front door, and a moment later the daily paper was thrust through the letter box. It landed on the mat and Miller stooped to pick it up. He carried it through into the workroom with him, snapping on lights as he closed the door.

He put his coffee down on one of the workbenches, beside a severed hand, then he flicked off the lights once more and carefully removed the film from the camera, his progress lit only by the single red bulb over the double sink before him. He immersed the strip of celluloid in developer and moved it back and forth with a pair of plastic tongs. While he waited for the images to form on the acetate Miller flipped open the paper and glanced at the headline:

PROSTITUTE SAVAGELY MUTILATED AS REIGN OF TERROR CONTINUES

Miller quickly scanned the report, squinting in the dull light, rubbing his left eye once when the clarity of vision faltered slightly. There was a photograph of the dead girl at the top of the page. Police had not released details of her name but he seemed to recognize the long hair, the sallow features, the cold sore on the bottom lip.

Jesus Christ. The realization hit him like a sledgehammer.

He blinked hard, focusing more sharply on the image of the girl in the picture.

All around her he saw a faint, almost imperceptible glow. A barely visible luminosity which surrounded her like a halo.

Miller studied the picture long and hard then glanced at the photographs he himself had taken. He lifted them from the developer, swilled them through fixer, then rinsed them with the swiftly-flowing water from the tap.

He held up the first strip of film.

Three drunks, one of them half lying, half crouching beside a car. Two men leaving a club. A woman speaking to the door-man. Other nondescript images of London's underbelly, not soft and white but moulding and rotten, putrid with misery and corruption both of mind and body. He looked at another of the photos, his hand shaking.

It was a girl. She was leaving the club with a man but it was her face on which Miller concentrated his attention.

The long hair. The sallow features.

The cold sore on her bottom lip.

He looked from his own photo to the one in the paper and he knew that it was the same girl. And in both pictures she carried around her that barely perceptible glow. An outline of vague effulgence much like that given to saints in religious paintings. Only this girl was no saint.

Miller looked at the photos again, closing his left eye.

They appeared normal.

He closed the right eye.

The peripheral glow returned, shrouding the images.

The effects man put down the picture of the girl and hastily crossed to one of his filing cabinets. He withdrew a manilla envelope and pulled out two snapshots. They were both of Doctor George Cook. And they too bore the slight glow around the man's image.

The aura was present on the photos of both victims.
George Cook.
Penny Steele.
Both dead. Both murdered.
Both surrounded by that almost imperceptible aura.
Miller put down the photos and reached for the phone.

Thirty-four

'No way.'

Detective Inspector Stuart Gibson drained what was left in the pint pot and brought the receptacle down so hard on the bar top it almost shattered.

'There is no fucking way that you are getting a look at the files on this case,' the policeman said, forcefully.

Miller eyed his former colleague over the rim of his glass, sipping slowly at the whisky.

'Who'd know?' the effects man asked.

'*I'd* know,' Gibson protested. 'Christ, Frank, you're not even on the force any more. The commissioner would have my bollocks for earrings if he even knew I was talking to you about this case, let alone anything else.'

Miller ordered another round, watching as the DI lit up a cigarette.

'I thought you'd given up,' Miller said.

'I had.' He blew out a stream of smoke and coughed. 'I'm always going on at Chandler to stop smoking and now I'm at it again myself.' Mention of his partner's name seemed to coax a frown from the older man. 'He never lets me forget that I got the job he reckons *he* should have had. You know, sometimes I think the bastard enjoys seeing me come up against brick walls in this case.'

'So you're no nearer to cracking it?' Miller said conversationally.

'You know what it's like, Frank. Sometimes trails just dry up. There wasn't a trail to begin with in this case. Seven people murdered in the space of a month and yet we're no nearer now than we were after the first one. I've had the press calling all bloody morning, the commissioner's been on my back. I wouldn't mind only that phoney news conference was *his* idea. "Stall the media", he said.' The policeman took a hefty gulp of his beer. 'If it gets out that the press conference was a fake then they'll crucify us – well, me anyway. I stood there and told them that the killer had been arrested, and now there's another murder.'

'The victim wasn't named in the papers,' said Miller. 'Who was she?'

'That's classified, Frank.'

'Come on, Stuart, you're not talking to a reporter now. She was a pro. An expendable commodity, what the hell difference does a name make?'

'Why is it so important to you?' Gibson wanted to know.

Miller reached into the inside pocket of his jacket and pulled out two photos. He laid them both on the bar top before the DI who raised his eyes in surprise as he saw the picture of Penny Steele.

'Where did you take that?' he asked, lifting the photo up, inspecting it more closely.

'It was taken last night, it doesn't matter how or why?'

'It might matter,' Gibson said, eyeing Miller suspiciously. 'Who's the other bloke?' He looked at the picture of George Cook.

Miller explained who the surgeon was then laid the photos out again.

'He was murdered about a week ago, run down.'

'So where's the tie-up with the maniac who killed the tart and the other six victims?' Gibson asked.

Miller asked the policeman to look more closely at the photos, to look for anything unusual. He could see nothing.

'There's a kind of aura around both of them,' Miller explained. 'Like some sort of light, it looks as if it radiates from the bodies, forms a kind of halo around them.'

Gibson raised his eyebrows then looked at Miller's empty glass.

'How many of those have you had?' he wanted to know.

'Only *I* can see it,' said Miller. 'Both of those people had that aura around them and both were murdered. I think it was a warning. They didn't know they had it either but it marked them out as victims.'

'Oh come on, Frank,' Gibson said, incredulously. 'I know you like a drink but right now you sound as if you're totally pissed. Are you trying to tell me that you knew these people were going to be murdered?'

'I saw the aura around them but not until it was too late.'

Gibson shook his head.

'Well, I can't see anything. The photos look normal to me.'

'I told you, only I can see the aura. That's why I want to look at the files on the other victims, to see if I'm right. I have to see those files, Stuart.'

'And I told you, no way. What the hell do you think would happen if the commissioner found out? I'd be out on my ear, that's what.'

'And what happens if the press find out that you haven't got a clue who the killer is? That the conference was all bullshit to buy you time? The commissioner isn't going to be very pleased about that either is he?'

Gibson frowned.

'What are you saying?' he muttered, warily.

'That I want to look at those files,' Miller told him, flatly.

'And if I say no?'

Miller shrugged.

'Then I'm going to phone every newspaper and TV station I can and tell them that the press conference was a farce, that you still haven't got a clue who the murderer is.'

Gibson glared long and hard at his former colleague, his eyes narrowing to steely slits.

'That's blackmail,' he hissed. 'Blackmailing a police officer isn't a very good idea, Frank.'

'You'd never prove it,' Miller said smugly. 'Now, do I get to see the files?'

'No,' Gibson said, unhesitatingly.

Miller slid off the stool and made for the phone in the corner of the bar. He'd only taken two steps when Gibson shot out a

171

hand and grabbed him by the arm. Miller looked down at the DI, his face expressionless.

'Wait,' he snapped, his jaws clenched in anger. He released his grip on Miller's arm, watching as the effects man sat down once more. They locked stares for interminable seconds, Miller's face impassive. 'What good can it do? Seeing the files?'

'I need to see the photos of the victims taken *before* they were killed. If I'm right then they'll show the aura too,' the effects man said.

'What is this crap? This rubbish about an aura? What is it?'

'I don't know what it is. That's one of the things I want to find out. I want to understand it. I want to know why it only shows up on photos.' Miller sipped his drink. 'You're the only one with access to those files. Get them.' There was a hard edge to his words.

Gibson sucked in an angry breath.

'And if I don't you'll really go to the media?' he said.

Miller raised his eyebrows.

'You've known me long enough, Stuart,' he said, a slight smile on his lips.

The DI nodded and drained what was left in his glass.

'Yeah. Too long.'

Miller cupped one hand around the cigarette, trying to shield the lighter flame from the icy gusts of wind which periodically swept across the concrete expanse of the underground car park.

The huge subterranean chamber was practically empty of vehicles. Apart from his own Granada, which was parked near the exit, only three cars occupied spaces in the vast arena. The air stank of petrol, the floor was spattered with the dark stains of oil and grease. Close to the pillar against which Miller leant, someone had urinated. Pieces of paper, cartons from a hamburger takeaway and other litter were tossed and blown periodically by the wind as it raced across the underground cavern. Miller leant on the bonnet of his car and waited.

He checked his watch.

11.14 p.m.

From above he heard the sound of movement, the rumble as a

car approached the ramp which led to the bottom level. Miller smiled thinly as he saw Gibson's Astra heading towards him. As the policeman drew closer he flicked off his lights, seeing Miller only as a dark silhouette, illuminated by the cold white light of the fluorescents that lit the car park. The DI brought his own car to a halt about twenty yards away and clambered out. Miller could see that he was carrying a briefcase.

The sound of the policeman's footsteps echoed loudly as he strode towards Miller.

'You've got fifteen minutes,' Gibson said irritably, dumping the case on the bonnet of the Granada.

'I won't need that long,' Miller told him, slipping the catches. He looked inside at the seven manilla files which lay before him, each one marked with a name. Miller removed the first of them.

'I must want my head examined for this,' Gibson observed.

'Better fifteen minutes with me than a grilling by the press and the commissioner,' Miller murmured as he flipped open the first file.

'You really are a bastard, Frank,' his former colleague snarled, and Miller caught the genuine anger in his voice.

He glanced at the first of the files, flipping past the coroner's report, the investigating officer's account of the case, the witnesses' statements, until he found what he sought.

'Mark Forrester,' he read aloud. The photo showed the victim posing with a girl who Miller took to be his fiancée. Both were smiling in the monochrome print.

All around the outline of Forrester's body he saw the aura.

'It's there,' he whispered, reaching for the next file.

'What's there?' Gibson asked, glancing behind him every now and then, checking that they were indeed alone in the car park. The wind wailed mournfully along the ramps on either side of them.

'Nicholas Blake,' Miller read on the second file. He skipped past the photo of Blake's acid-splashed face and found a photo of the young man taken when he'd been in the army cadets.

The faint glow surrounded him too.

As it did Anthony Banks.

And Angela Grant.

The aura was more noticeable around some than others.

It surrounded Louise Turner.

The hellish glow radiated strongly from Bernadette Evans.

Miller reached the last file.

Penny Steele. The latest victim.

He knew, even without looking, that she would bear the mark. The photo in the file proved him right once more.

Every victim killed during the present spate of murders wore the aura like some kind of luminescent shroud.

The effects man dropped the last of the files into the case and handed it back to Gibson who looked surprised.

'And that's it?' the DI said. 'You just wanted to look at the photos?'

Miller nodded slowly, his mind in turmoil. He closed his eyes for a second but it seemed as if the images were planted in his mind, jostling for space with so many others. Portraits of living souls mingling with the memories of those hacked, shot, strangled. Maggot-infested images of death and corruption branded on his mind as if put there with a red hot iron. Never to be erased.

'I can *see* murder victims,' he said, quietly. 'By looking at someone's photo I can tell whether or not they're going to die violently. All murder victims have this aura.'

Gibson shook his head and snapped the clasps of the case shut.

'Before I thought you were drunk,' he said. 'Now I think you're off your head.'

'I can spot potential murder victims,' Miller insisted.

'So what are you going to do? Run round taking everyone's photograph?' He snatched up the case and turned. 'And I risked my position for you to tell me that?' The DI opened the door of the Astra and tossed the briefcase onto the passenger seat. He slid behind the wheel and started the engine which roared into life, the noise amplified by the cavernous subterranean car park.

'Go back to the booze, Frank,' Gibson shouted. 'It's where you belong.'

He jammed the car in gear and drove off, the tyres spinning momentarily on the concrete. Miller watched as the car disappeared up the exit ramp.

Miller stood alone in the darkened arena, collar turned up to protect him against the cold wind. He shuddered as he opened the door of his own car and slid behind the wheel. Even inside it felt cold.

The ability to pick out a murder victim. The thought carried with it a strange feeling of power, almost of life and death. *He* knew who would die.

What he didn't know was when and how.

He started his engine, suddenly anxious to be away from the semi-darkness of the underground car park.

Gibson didn't believe him. But Miller didn't care.

He knew someone who would be more than interested.

Thirty-five

He sat naked before the TV screen. Legs crossed, buddha-like, in a posture that was intended for repose yet every muscle in his body was tense and throbbing.

The spools of the video recorder purred quietly as images were regurgitated and he sat as if mesmerized by the figure before him.

Bob Johnson sucked in a deep breath through flared nostrils and gazed at the screen, watching the image of Terri Warner. He had the sound turned off, able only to see her, not to hear the words she spoke. But words were not his concern. His eyes flickered over her slim form, his gaze travelling from her face to her breasts then back again. The erection had grown harder and he allowed his right hand to envelope it, squeezing the flesh hard until he began a rhythmic pumping action. His breathing became heavier and he shuffled closer to the TV screen, still in his cross-legged position, hand now clamped firmly around his stiff shaft.

The picture on the video shifted, broke up momentarily then settled once again.

Terri appeared on the screen again, in different clothes. It was a different report. Different location. Recorded over two years ago. Johnson had all the interviews she'd done on tape, all the reports. Each one copied from the master tape which he had access to.

He gazed at her face, his own features tightening as the feeling of warmth spread across his belly and thighs. His hand began to move more rapidly. He watched her lips moving soundlessly, wondering what it would be like to feel his own against them, to push his tongue into the welcoming wetness of her mouth. He began breathing through his mouth, the sound loud and rasping.

His body tensed, muscles swelling. Johnson was aware of the strength within his own body and that knowledge seemed to please him. His right hand continued to pump unfalteringly on his penis as he drew himself to his knees only inches from the screen.

Inches from her.

From that mouth.

That body.

'Terri,' he whispered her name softly, then with increasing volume, thrusting his hips towards the screen as the camera moved in for a close up of her face, her mouth opening and closing as if in slow motion.

He wanted to be inside that velvet cavern, to feel the softness of her tongue and lips.

He wanted to be.

He needed to be.

He would be.

With a final grunt of satisfaction he ejaculated copiously, the thick fluid spattering the TV screen, one long strand of it briefly connecting the end of his throbbing organ to the face of Terri Warner like some kind of fluid umbilicus.

They were joined.

She would be his.

Thirty-six

Miller took another swig from his hip flask and drummed slowly on the steering wheel with the fingers of his free hand. The effects man kept his eyes fixed on the doors of the building ahead of him, breaking his steady gaze only to look at the dashboard clock which told him it was approaching noon. He blinked hard to clear the fuzziness from his left eye then resumed his vigil.

He'd been there for over an hour with only the smell of his whisky and the inane ramblings of the radio for company. But now, finally, the one he sought emerged into the car park.

'At last,' murmured Miller, taking a final sip of whisky.

He watched as Terri Warner pushed open the double doors, then immediately looked up at the banks of dark cloud moving in from the west. Large spots of rain had already begun to fall, a portent of what was to come, and Terri quickened her pace as she headed for her car which was parked close to Miller's.

He waited until she was less than ten feet away then pushed open his own door and clambered out.

'It is Terri Warner isn't it?' he said, although it came out more as a statement than a question.

She nodded slowly, running appraising eyes over this newcomer. He didn't look like an autograph hunter, she mused. She smelt the whisky on his breath as he stepped closer and felt compelled to take a step back.

Miller extended his hand and introduced himself.

Terri shook the offered appendage, feeling the strength in his grip.

'I need to talk to you, Miss Warner,' he said. 'It's important.'

'I'm busy right now,' she said, still unsure of this man. 'Perhaps if you gave me a number I could call you . . .'

Miller interrupted her.

'It's about this series of killings,' he said. 'You could say we both have an interest in it.'

Terri frowned.

'In what way?'

'I've seen your reports, watched you on the TV,' he told her. 'You've made quite a name for yourself out of this case.'

'Look, I'm just doing my job. If you want to criticize –'

He cut her short once again. 'I don't want to criticize, I want to help,' he told her. 'I think I might have some information you may find interesting.'

The rain, which had been falling in isolated droplets, suddenly decided to begin lashing down.

'I didn't really want to stand here discussing all this,' Miller told her. 'There's a pub nearby. Follow me.' He slid behind the wheel and started his engine, swinging the Granada out of its parking spot. In his rear-view mirror he saw Terri start up her Mini and follow. Miller smiled. He flicked on his windscreen wipers, watching as the slim rubber arms struggled to brush away the torrent of rain which was pelting down furiously. He signalled left and Terri followed, her eyes on his tail-lights as he braked to avoid a pedestrian.

Who the hell was this man, she wondered? She knew his name but that was all. And what was his interest in the case? She shuddered involuntarily and, for reasons which she herself found inexplicable, she heard the voice on her answerphone echoing inside her head.

'The police don't know.'

Was there something familiar there? Questions tumbled through her mind, all without answers. The main one being, if she was so wary of this man why was she now following him? Curiosity could kill more than cats, she told herself. But, nevertheless, she followed.

Other eyes had seen her go.

Had seen her standing, speaking to Miller.

As he saw the two cars disappear into the main stream of traffic Bob Johnson clenched his fists angrily.

'Bitch,' he murmured.

Thirty-seven

The lounge bar of The Phoenix was crowded and noisy and it smelled of damp clothes. People had bolted into the pub with the sudden onslaught from above and now stood drinking and talking while their clothes dried on them. The carpeted floor was sodden and Miller fancied that he heard it squelching beneath his feet as he returned to the table where Terri sat waiting for him.

Two youths with short haircuts and paint-spattered denim jackets were talking loudly close to him, jostling one another around the fruit machine. The taller of the two bumped into Miller, almost causing him to spill the drinks he was carrying. The youth laughed until he saw the look which Miller shot him, his eyes blazing.

'Get out the fucking way,' Miller hissed, pushing past the youth, who suddenly seemed to have lost his bravado. He raised two fingers to Miller's back then returned to his antics with the fruit machine.

The effects man put down the drinks and slid into the seat opposite Terri.

She smiled thinly, still unsure of this man and even more unsure of why she had agreed to come to this place with him.

'I realize that you don't know me from Adam,' he said, sipping his drink. 'But I had to talk to you about these murders.'

'So talk, Mr Miller,' she said, reaching for her own glass.

'Frank,' he said. 'We don't have to be *that* formal.'

She nodded but didn't relax.

'I know that you must be wondering what the hell I'm up to.'

'It had crossed my mind,' Terri confessed.

'What I'm going to tell you might sound crazy. In fact, maybe it was me who made the mistake bringing you here.' He shook his head and downed a mouthful of whisky.

Miller had played his trump card. The bait was there.

'I think it might be a good idea if I left. I'm sorry,' he said.

'No, don't go,' Terri said, sitting forward. 'Let me hear what you've got to say.'

Miller hid his smile. She'd bitten. He had her hooked.

'You're wondering whether or not to trust me,' he said. 'Well, the feeling's mutual.'

Terri sighed.

'This is all very vague, Mr Miller,' she said. 'Sorry – *Frank*. How do I know what I can or can't be trusted with until you tell me what the hell it is you're going on about? If you're going to confess to these murders then maybe you should have picked one of the newspapers –'

He cut her short. 'Were you at a press conference at New Scotland Yard about ten days ago?' he asked.

She nodded.

'The police told you that they had arrested the murderer, and before you say anything, yes I know it was on TV and in all the papers so I'm not telling you anything you don't know. That entire conference was a sham.'

'I had my suspicions. How do you know?'

'Because the head of the investigation told me himself. The police still haven't got a clue who they're looking for.'

'Why would anyone from New Scotland Yard tell *you* something like that?'

'Let's just say I used my influence. I used to work for them. Detective Inspector Gibson and I are close friends. Or at least we used to be.'

'I still don't see your interest in the case,' Terri told him.

'The seven people who've been murdered were destined to be victims. I could see that when I looked at their photos.'

Terri frowned, not sure whether to laugh, get up and leave or continue listening.

'*Destined*?' she said. 'This is beginning to sound a little bit melodramatic.'

182

'Every murder victim gives off some kind of aura, I don't know what else to call it,' Miller said irritably, realizing that his revelations were indeed beginning to sound ridiculous, knowing that even should he show Terri the photos of Penny Steele and George Cook *she* would be unable to see the aura. 'I can see that aura. But only in photos.'

'Are you telling me you've seen pictures of the murder victims in this case?' she said, her interest suddenly rekindled. 'But they're supposed to be closed files. How the hell did you get access to them?'

'That's *my* business. Anyway, I'm talking about photos of the victims *before* they were killed. That's when the aura is present.'

Terri sipped her drink, regarding Miller over the rim. Finally she put down the glass, toying with the stem.

'Why me? Why choose me to tell your secrets to?' she wanted to know.

'Because I think I can trust you not to repeat them. If there's one thing in this world I hate it's having to trust someone, but you seemed like one of the better choices. Now, what do you know about these killings?'

'Why should I tell you?'

He shrugged.

'Don't tell me if you don't want to, I probably know more than you anyway. I thought we might be able to help each other. Maybe you were right though, perhaps I should go to a newspaper.' He got to his feet but Terri shot out a hand to restrain him.

'All the victims were murdered by different methods,' she said. 'You probably already know that much. But the most interesting thing is that the MO in every case has been copied from a case in the past. Whoever is doing the murders has more than a passing knowledge of criminal history. The latest victim was killed and mutilated in much the same way as the victims of Gordon Cummins. They called him the Ripper of the Blitz. He murdered four women in four days in 1942, two of them prostitutes. The latest victim was a prostitute.'

'How do you know all this?' Miller asked, his eyes never leaving hers.

'After the second murder I got a call from someone claiming he was a member of the murder squad investigating this particular case. He told me he had information for me, about the killings. I thought it was just some joker after publicity, but what he told me was too detailed to be known by an outsider. He's called after every murder since then. But I don't know his name or his position.'

'An informer inside Scotland Yard?' said Miller, stroking his chin, thoughtfully, Gibson's words floating back to him;

Sometimes I think Chandler enjoys seeing me come up against brick walls . . .

'You said whoever was doing the killings had more than a passing knowledge of criminal history?' he muttered.

Terri nodded.

Bent copper? Miller wondered. One with an axe to grind?

Chandler certainly fitted the bill.

There was a long silence finally broken by Terri.

'He called me,' she said, quietly. 'The killer. A few days ago. I didn't go to the police, I thought he might try and contact me again but so far he hasn't.'

'You think he might?' Miller wanted to know.

'Who knows? I can't even be sure it *was* the killer.' She shrugged. 'It might just be someone with a sick sense of humour.'

'Sick enough to kill seven people seven different ways,' Miller muttered. 'Why didn't you tell the police? They could have bugged your phone.'

'It wasn't my idea to keep the call a secret,' she confessed. 'The guy I work for, Bob Johnson, he thought it might make a good story if *I* could find the killer, contact him.'

'Even though it means risking your life?' Miller said, flatly.

'It's a chance I'm willing to take.' She drained what was left in her glass and pushed the empty receptacle away from her. Miller offered her another and, after a moment's hesitation, she agreed. She watched him as he made his way to the bar, wondering why she found this stranger so captivating. Was that the word to describe him? He was attractive, there was no denying that, but Terri sensed a darker side to him, a bitterness which seemed to cling around him like a cloak. When he spoke there was a weariness in his voice usually reserved for men twice his age, as if he were tired of everything around him. His tone, at times, carried something akin to contempt for what he spoke of. Yet somewhere deep inside her she felt drawn to him, or at least to what he had to say and the way he said it. Her musings were interrupted as he returned.

'You seem to know a lot more about me than I know about you,' she said. 'I don't even know what you do for a living.'

Miller smiled thinly.

'I'm a prosthetic make-up artist and visual effects man with a film company that's shooting a picture about ten miles outside London.' He went on to explain briefly his spells as both press and police photographer.

'You must have seen some awful things,' she said, quietly.

'After a while you learn to respect it,' he said.

She looked at him quizzically.

'Death. You come to respect death. How it comes in so many different guises. Some of them inventive, some of them plain bloody stupid. But you also learn that there's no such thing as death with dignity.' He ran his index finger around the rim of his glass. 'I've seen it all. Bodies hanging from trees, lying on railway lines, packed in concrete. Decapitated, gutted, dismembered. Swollen, black, putrid, crawling with maggots.' His eyes were no longer on her but looking past, staring blankly at the back of the seat on which she sat. 'Men, women, kids, babies. Sometimes alone, sometimes in groups. All stinking with that smell of death. It smells like bad eggs and it never leaves you. It gets into your clothes. Your pores. It even gets into your mind.' He swallowed a sizeable gulp of whisky. 'It gets to be like an old friend after a time,' Miller concluded.

'Friends like that I can do without,' Terri told him, smiling. 'Look, this business about the aura around murder victims, how is it you can see it but no one else can?'

He explained about the accident. The operation. The eye transplant.

'I can't think of any other solution,' Miller told her. 'It has to be the eye because I can only see the aura through my left eye.'

'And only on photos?'

He nodded.

'What would *you* think if someone came to *you* claiming that they could spot potential murder victims by looking at their photos?'

'I'd probably tell them they were mad,' Miller replied.

'Journalists and media people are supposed to be hard-headed cynics,' Terri said. 'I must be even crazier for believing you.'

Miller's face showed only a flicker of emotion.

'But keep this to yourself,' he said. 'I said I didn't like trusting people. I took a chance with you. It might just pay off.'

They both drank.

'Are you going to wait and see if you hear from the murderer again?' he asked.

She shrugged.

'I might as well. The police seem powerless to do anything anyway. If only I could build up some kind of rapport with him . . .' She allowed the sentence to trail off. 'I know it's dangerous, but it might get him caught.'

'It also might get you killed,' said Miller flatly.

'I don't think that would bother Bob Johnson, as long as he got good ratings out of it. That's all he seems to care about. This case isn't about people being killed as far as he's concerned. It's about angles, getting people to watch the programme. I think he'll be disappointed when the police eventually catch this maniac.'

'*If* they do,' Miller said, quietly.

'You sound as if you have your doubts, Frank,' she observed, again feeling the power of his stare upon her, but this time not feeling so uncomfortable beneath it.

Miller didn't answer. He merely watched as she got to her feet and manoeuvred herself past the stools next to the table.

'I've got to go,' she told him. 'I've got to work to do.'

Miller got to his feet and shook hands with her. He thanked her for listening to him. She took a piece of paper from her handbag and scribbled her phone number on it. Miller did likewise with his own.

'I'll be in touch, Miss Warner,' he said.

186

'Terri,' she told him.

They locked stares for brief seconds then she was gone. Miller sat down and finished his drink, pushing the empty glass away. He looked at the piece of paper she'd given him before folding it up and sticking it inside his jacket pocket.

It nestled between the photos of George Cook and Penny Steele.

He had her phone number now.

He had a way of getting closer.

Thirty-eight

The rain which had been falling heavily all through the day showed no sign of stopping. Against the black backdrop of darkness, storm clouds moved in rolling banks until the city was shrouded by the oppressive swirling shapes. So thick were the clouds that even the wind seemed powerless to move them. They unfolded, emptying their load on the buildings below.

Like distant cannons, thunder rumbled in the canopy of grey and black, the ever-present roar punctuated occasionally by a whiplash crack of lightning.

Terri Warner muttered to herself as the picture on the TV screen broke up again due to the massive amount of static in the air. She jabbed the buttons of the remote control but every channel was the same. Only a patchwork of broken lines and fizzing white dots. The picture returned briefly, then there was another almighty crack of lightning and the screen went completely blank. Terri switched the set off and wandered into the kitchen to make herself a cup of coffee.

She had barely filled the kettle when the phone rang.

Terri padded back into the sitting room and picked up the receiver, glancing out of the open curtains at the electrical storm which was slicing open the clouds.

'Hello, Terri Warner,' she said, her eyes still on the explosion of celestial fireworks.

There was no answer. Only the hiss of static.

'Hello.'

At the other end the receiver was put down, the click strangely loud in the stillness of the flat. Terri shrugged and replaced the receiver.

She had reached the door to the kitchen when it rang again.

She turned and, once more, picked it up.

Again there was only silence at the other end.

Silence.

But something else.

Breathing?

She pressed the phone closer to her ear, trying to make out the low rasping noise which barely filtered through the crackling which distorted the line.

'Who is that?' she asked, trying to sound calm. 'I think you've got the wrong number.'

Terri suddenly thought of the answerphone. She fumbled to reach the 'record' button. Pressed it.

'Right number.'

The words startled her. So much so that she almost dropped the phone.

'Who is that?' she demanded, her own voice now sounding strained.

Outside there was a deafening clap of thunder.

'Talk to me,' she rasped, anger and fear now shaping her tone in equal measures.

'I'm watching.'

Terri tried to swallow but her throat felt as if someone had filled it with chalk. Yet through her fear she tried to find something familiar in that voice, tried to pick out anything discernible from the brief words.

'This phone is tapped,' she blurted. 'I had it done after the last time you called.'

Silence at the other end.

Breathing.

Or something like it.

The phone went dead.

She dropped it back on the cradle, stepping away from it as if it were some venomous reptile.

For what seemed like an eternity she stood there, watching the phone. Waiting for it to ring again.

Outside, the storm grew in fury.

Thirty-nine

The call had come at about seven thirty that morning, rousing Miller from his slumbers. He'd woken up to find himself sprawled across the desk in his workroom, a bottle of Haig standing half-empty at one corner. He'd taken the call, his senses still dulled from the previous night, not even recognizing the voice at the other end for long moments. Then, finally, the caller had identified himself. Phillip Dickinson. The director sounded almost apologetic for disturbing Miller but, he'd told him, he had good news for him.

They needed the effects man back at the shoot, Dickinson had told him. Miller had asked about the row with Lisa Richardson, the macabre practical joke.

Lisa had walked out on them, Dickinson had informed him. Colin Robson had been fired after a series of rows. Miller was needed again. They'd replaced Lisa with another actress.

Miller had listened to the developments with ill-disguised glee, and for a moment he'd thought about telling Dickinson to find himself another effects man but then thought better of it. Yes, he'd come back and yes, he'd be on the set by nine that morning.

As he pulled the Granada into the car park behind the sound stage Miller felt strangely elated. He was back where he belonged. Working. And if it was amidst blood and violence then so be it. At least *this* blood could be washed off at the end of the day.

He had already seen too much of the real stuff.

As he clambered out of his car he felt the spots of rain splattering his skin. The savagery of the storm the previous night had given way to a mournful cascade of rain which fell from a sky the colour of wet concrete. Miller glanced up at it as he made his way to the door of the sound stage. As he reached it he looked across at the make-up trailer. His own private kingdom.

He was home again.

'Like you said before, there's no problem with bringing in a new actress,' Phillip Dickinson said. 'In the remaining scenes she'll be in make-up anyway. Nobody will know the difference.'

Miller nodded and took a swig from his hip flask.

'I hope you haven't picked another prima donna to take that other stupid cow's place,' the effects man said.

'I'll introduce you,' the director said.

Miller sat gazing down at the sketches before him while Dickinson picked his way through the crowded canteen in search of the one he sought. He returned to the table a moment later, this time with a companion.

'Frank, this is Susan Lewis,' the director said and Miller turned to see the actress standing close by him. He stood up and shook hands with her, running appraising eyes over her slim form. She was in her late twenties, pretty, wearing no make-up. Her long black hair was uncombed and she ran a hand through it as Miller looked at her. She smiled warmly and he noticed how her face seemed to light up with the gesture.

'Frank Miller, our make-up and effects supervisor,' Dickinson announced.

'You've got no objections to wearing make-up I hope,' Miller said. 'Prosthetics I mean, nct eye-liner and lipstick.'

'I've worn it before. It doesn't bother me,' she told him.

Miller seemed uncharacteristically fascinated by her face. By her high cheekbones, the way her chin came to a smooth point.

'You look more like a model,' he told her. 'It seems a pity to cover up that face with latex.' He managed a grin.

'I would have been a model but I was too short,' she told him.

'You're very pretty,' he told her.

'That's about as close to a compliment as you're likely to get out of him,' Dickinson told the actress and she chuckled.

Miller smiled back at her. She was indeed a very pretty young woman.

'I wanted to shoot one of Susan's scenes this afternoon if possible, Frank,' the director told him. 'How long will the make-up take to apply?'

Miller shrugged.

'Two hours, maybe more. I'll need to take some photos and maybe even some facial casts before I start.'

'I'm ready when you are,' Susan told the effects man.

Miller took a swig from his hip flask. Then he led her out of the canteen and across the tarmac towards the make-up trailer.

'I heard that you didn't get on with Lisa Richardson,' Susan said.

'Does that bother you?'

'No, I just heard rumours.'

'Whatever you heard, it was probably right.'

'I also heard that you can be a bit of a bastard.'

Miller stopped as he reached the steps up to the trailer door. He looked at Susan and smiled.

'Is that true as well?' she persisted.

'You'll find out,' he told her. 'If people think I'm a bastard that's usually because they disagree with me. I'm an exception in the film business, I'm one of the few people who actually cares about what they do. I couldn't really give a toss what the film turns out like, that's Phil Dickinson's problem. All I'm interested in is that my effects look good.' He shrugged and opened the trailer door, ushering her in. Miller slapped on lights and motioned for Susan to be seated before the mirror in one corner of the trailer. Then, from a cupboard nearby, he retrieved a polaroid camera.

'I saw some of the work you did on this film, Phillip showed me some rushes,' Susan told him. 'I thought it was great.'

'The sycophantic approach, eh?' said Miller.

Her smile faded, to be replaced by an expression which combined anger and disappointment.

'It looks like the rumours were true,' she told him. 'You can be a bastard. I meant what I said, your work looked great.'

'Thanks for the vote of confidence.'

'Did Lisa Richardson leave because of you?'

192

'Does it matter?'

'I was just curious. You don't strike me as the easiest man in the world to work with.'

'We had our differences.' He checked the camera, satisfied that all was ready. 'Now, can you and I get down to work?' He snapped the first shot, pulling the picture free as the camera rolled it out. He laid it on the table to develop fully then took another shot from the left hand side. Another from the right.

The trio of prints began to darken, images started to form as Miller took another couple of pictures.

'Do you suffer from any skin allergies?' he asked, sounding more like a doctor. 'The make-up can sometimes affect people with sensitive skin.'

Susan shook her head.

'I learned at the beginning that you need thick skin in this business.' She smiled at her own joke.

Miller nodded and turned to look at the pictures. They were still developing. He picked one up and waved it in the air, trying to speed the drying process. The image was practically clear now.

Miller studied the print.

The face of Susan Lewis was surrounded by the aura.

Framed by the luminescent glow.

The effects man clenched his teeth, the knot of muscles at the side of his jaw throbbing powerfully.

'Are the pictures all right?' Susan asked, wondering why Miller had suddenly fallen silent.

'What?' he asked, abstractedly.

'The pictures.'

'Yeah, they're fine,' he lied, his eyes drawn to that rim of light which framed her face like a halo. For interminable seconds he stood gazing at the pictures then Miller turned and headed for the door of the trailer.

'What about the make-up?' Susan called.

'It'll wait,' Miller said.

Then he was gone.

There was a phone in the portakabin near the studio entrance.

Miller told the security man on duty that he needed to use it and the man stepped outside while Miller hastily jabbed out the number he needed. He tapped impatiently on the desk as he waited for the receiver to be picked up.

'New Scotland Yard,' said the voice at the other end.

'I want to speak to Stuart Gibson, he's on extension twenty-two,' Miller said then he waited once more, listening to a succession of pops and clicks as he was re-connected. The extension line was ringing.

And ringing.

'Come on,' Miller hissed.

He finally heard the click as the receiver was picked up.

'Detective Inspector Gibson's office,' the voice said.

Miller recognized the voice.

'Stuart, it's Frank Miller.'

There was a moment of silence then the policeman spoke, the iciness in his tone unmistakable.

'I think we said all we had to say to each other the other day.'

'This is important. You know I told you about the aura around potential murder victims? Well, I've seen it again.'

'Look, Frank why don't you find someone else to pester, I told you, I'm not interested.'

'You'll be interested when she's killed though, won't you?' Miller snapped.

'Who is this *she* you're talking about?'

Miller explained.

'I'm telling you, Stuart. The aura is there on the photos. Just like it was on the pictures of the other victims. She's going to be killed. I'd bet money on it.'

'Then maybe you should have rung Ladbrokes instead of me,' the DI said sarcastically. 'Look Frank, I'm busy. I've got enough to contend with now with *one* nutcase running round, don't add to my problems with more of your hare-brained ideas.'

'What's it going to take to convince you?' snarled Miller.

'More than the word of an alcoholic with an over-active imagination and bad eyesight,' snapped the policeman venomously. 'Now get off the line will you?'

'At least put a tail on her, watch her house or something,' he said angrily. 'You can't just dismiss what I've told you. She's going to be murdered, I'm telling you.'

'Goodbye, Frank,' said Gibson and put down the phone.

'Bastard!' roared Miller and hurled the receiver down. He barged out of the Portakabin, almost colliding with the security man who had heard the raised voices and was making his way back inside. He opened his mouth to speak but Miller had already set off back towards the make-up trailer. The security man shook his head and disappeared back inside the little hut.

As Miller made his way across the tarmac towards the trailer he saw Susan Lewis standing in the doorway waiting for him.

Miller shuddered involuntarily as he glanced at the actress, the vision of her face suffused with the aura still strong in his mind.

Could he be wrong about the strange light? Had the other killings been a mere coincidence? He doubted it, but he prayed that this time he *had* made a mistake.

The shooting went as planned.

Susan Lewis performed well beneath the grotesque prosthetic make-up which Miller had created for her. He had applied it carefully, almost lovingly. Like some insane plastic surgeon, shaping and carving the latex, creating something of horror from what was formerly beauty.

And all through shooting he stood by the camera watching the actress. He stood, sipping from his hip flask and he watched. Haunted by the thought of what he'd seen in the photos. Aware that she carried the aura around her like a beacon. But one that only he could see.

It was approaching seven-fifteen when Dickinson finally called a halt to the day's proceedings, muttering something about the camera crew and lighting riggers wanting overtime. Miller ignored the director's remarks and stood waiting for Susan Lewis to come off-set. She was unable to speak because of the constrictions of the make-up and Miller found that he himself had very little inclination to talk, so once back in the trailer, the make-up was removed in relative silence. She pulled the last few pieces off herself, peeling the latex away as if it were sloughed skin.

As she splashed her face with warm water from the basin in one corner of the trailer she was aware of Miller looking at her.

'Is something wrong?' Susan asked him.

Miller shook his head and took a swig from his hip flask.

The polaroids of Susan nestled inside his jacket pocket. Like silent warnings.

'How are you getting home?' he asked her.

'I don't live far from here, I'm driving,' she told him. 'It should only take me about thirty minutes.'

The effects man nodded slowly.

He told her what time he wanted her at the set the following morning in order to apply the make-up, then he watched as she left the caravan and wandered across the tarmac towards her waiting car. Miller chewed his bottom lip contemplatively, watching as she swung the vehicle out of its space. He waited a moment longer, then pulled the trailer door shut behind him, locked it and sprinted across to his own car. Miller started up the engine and flicked on his lights at half-beam. The approaching evening loomed dull and grey and he needed the extra light as he drove.

At first he thought he'd lost Susan Lewis, but as he swung the car out into the main road he caught sight of her car idling behind a slow-moving lorry. Miller slipped into the stream of traffic four cars behind.

She drove on.

He followed, one hand on the wheel, the other gripping the hip flask, his eyes never leaving Susan Lewis's car.

So, Gibson wouldn't put a tail on her, Miller thought. Well, fuck him. He'd seen the aura around her. He knew she was in danger.

If he had to sit watching her all night he would.

He drove on.

Forty

'Miserable bastard,' shouted Mike Hamilton as the car sped past him and disappeared around a bend in the road. He jabbed a 'V' sign into the air and muttered to himself, gazing into the darkness, waiting for the approach of another vehicle. Maybe a van or small truck would come by, he thought, guys like that were usually amenable to hitch-hikers, and Mike was getting sick of standing by the roadside with his thumb out like a mannequin, relying on the generosity of some passing motorist. He fumbled in his coat pocket and found a roll-up but he was out of matches. Maybe whoever picked him up would have a light. *If* anyone ever picked him up. He stepped back from the roadside and sat down on his rucksack, manoeuvring himself into a more comfortable position.

He glanced up at the dark sky, hoping that the rain would hold off until someone picked him up. His parents would be furious if they knew he was hitching. They'd given him fifty pounds when he left home in Hull two days earlier, more than enough to cover his train fare back from London.

They'd be even more furious if they knew he'd spent more than half the money on drugs. That was why he was reduced to hitching. He'd been smoking the stuff for ten years, ever since his fifteenth birthday party when during a pub crawl a couple of mates had offered him a joint. Where was the harm in it? he asked himself. He hadn't felt the need to move on to the hard stuff, although he'd seen plenty of others who had. He had his own little habit well under control. So well under control, in fact, that he planned to sell some of his stash when he got to London. The trip, ostensibly, had been to visit his older sister who'd left the North to marry two years ago, but Mike was beginning to wonder if he was ever going to get there, despite the fact that he was only twenty miles from the centre of the capital.

He shifted position on his rucksack. If it hadn't been for the ridiculously intolerant attitudes of his parents he would have been driven down from Hull in their car, but his father had vowed that he never wanted anything more to do with his only daughter. Not after she'd married a black man. As far as he was concerned he no longer had a daughter. He'd made a pretty good job of ignoring his half-caste grandson too. Mike felt sorry for his mother, but she hadn't the guts or the inclination to defy her husband and visit her only daughter. Besides, she'd shown as much resistance to the marriage as her husband. So, Mike was the only one who visited his sister, Shelly. He didn't care what colour her husband was. He'd always got on with Roy. If he'd been a six-headed Martian with a lisp Mike would have got on with him. Why create problems in life when they could be avoided, he had always thought. After a couple of joints, nothing really seemed *that* important anyway. He smiled to himself and looked up as another car came towards him, its headlights cutting through the darkness.

Mike got to his feet, thumb hooked in the familiar gesture.

The car sped past and he was left cursing once more.

He felt the first drops of rain and groaned aloud, pulling the hood of his parka up to protect himself from the imminent deluge. The trees and bushes at the roadside grew thickly so Mike retreated towards them, seeking the added shelter. If the worse came to the worst he could always sleep on the roadside, or in one of the fields beyond the boundary of trees and bushes. It wouldn't be the first time he'd slept with the sky for an eiderdown. Every year after the rock gigs at Donington he slept on one of the nearby hillsides where the smoke from the fires still reached up into the blackness. He'd done the same at Reading five years earlier. But tonight, with the rain beginning to fall more heavily, he didn't fancy sleeping under the stars.

More headlights were approaching and, again, Mike stepped forward hopefully.

He smiled broadly as he saw the car slowing down. It came to a halt about twenty yards further up the road and he stood for long moments, as if waiting for it to reverse, watching the taillights glowing in the night. Then he snatched up his rucksack and ran after the stationary vehicle.

The door on the passenger side was pushed open for him and Mike slid gratefully into the seat, tossing his rucksack into the rear of the vehicle.

'Thanks,' he said, not yet looking at the driver. 'I've been out there for hours. I thought I was going to get soaked.' He slammed the door and turned. 'If you're going into London . . .'

He got no further.

There wasn't much room in the car but the driver found sufficient space to bring the hammer down with devastating force.

It struck Mike on the right temple, staving in part of his skull which shattered with a sickening crack.

Searing white hot pain shot through him and he fell back, nausea beginning to bubble in his belly. He slumped against the car door, one hand fumbling uselessly for the handle as he struggled to retain a grip on consciousness.

The hammer swung round once more, wielded with incredible power and expertise within the confines of the car.

The second blow broke Mike's lower jaw close to his left ear, tugging the mandible from its socket. He felt two teeth splinter inside his mouth and blood began to run down his throat. He choked on the crimson flow, only the pain keeping him conscious. Mike Hamilton slipped from the seat, lifting both hands in a reflex action to protect the top of his head.

The hammer swung down and crushed his right thumb as he lay, face buried in the passenger seat.

The blow to the back of his skull opened a small hole through which blood began to pump thickly, matting his hair together. His body shuddered violently as if he were very cold and, somewhere through the agonizing pain which filled his head, he was aware that the car was moving once more. How far it moved he didn't know, he was only barely clinging to consciousness as he sensed rather than saw the driver clamber out once the

199

vehicle had finally stopped. His eyes were clouded with pain, the raging agony making it feel as if his head were on the point of bursting. He heard the passenger-side door open, felt arms dragging him from the car. Then he lay on wet earth, water running into his mouth to join the blood already spilling over his lips. His stomach contracted violently and he felt hot bile clawing its way up from his belly, filling his mouth for a second before oozing down his shattered chin. He moaned, the sudden racking movement causing even greater pain from his smashed jaw and holed skull.

Mike was dimly aware of being rolled over onto his back but the face of the driver who looked down at him was invisible in the gloom. Had the youth been in any state to notice he would have seen that the driver had guided the car off the main road onto a dirt track flanked by high hedges which completely concealed the vehicle from any eyes capable of penetrating the darkness from the main road.

They might as well have been down an empty mine shaft so total was the seclusion.

Mike moaned gutturally and tried to crawl away from the car, white lights dancing before his eyes, his head still throbbing with a pain unlike anything he'd ever known before. It felt as if someone was massaging boiling oil into his scalp and brain with iron fingers and he burbled incoherently as he crawled, his movements slow.

A kick was driven into his side and, once again, he rolled over onto his back, this time unable to move.

The rain had stopped but he felt liquid spattering him.

Thick reeking liquid.

It took him only a few seconds to realize that it was petrol.

Even through his pain he flapped helplessly at his assailant as more of the stinking fluid rained down on him, some of it filling his mouth, making him retch with even greater ferocity. More petrol trickled up his nostrils, the stench unbearable as he writhed around on his back like a fish out of water, terror now filtering through the haze of pain which covered him.

He was drenched, soaked from head to foot in the fuel.

All he could do was lie and watch as the match was struck.

The driver held it above him for agonizing seconds then flicked it.

The moment it hit Mike's body there was a dull *whoosh* as his clothes ignited.

He tried to scream as the flames ate away at his flesh, searing the hair from his scalp before devouring the soft, bloodied flesh beneath, lapping around the hole in his skull, sometimes probing blazing fingers into the puncture until Mike began to pray for death. Anything to end the excruciating agony. He tried to roll over, to extinguish the flames in the wet grass, but it was useless. He felt his blood boiling in his veins, pieces of blackened flesh fell from his hands like flaming slime. His body began to swell up as the fire enveloped it. Fire ate away at his genitals and legs and he found that he was trying to fight the flames with little more than blackened charred stumps where his hands had already been eaten away by the staggering heat.

He tried to scream but his broken jaw prevented even that final act. His eyes dissolved into bubbling mush and, briefly, he smelt the stench of his own incinerated flesh.

The driver of the car stood back, watching the blazing torch which had once been a man. Then quickly, but without undue haste, slipped back into the car, reversed down the dirt track onto the road and drove off.

It was another ten minutes before a passing car spotted the flames twenty or thirty yards off the road. Another thirty before the police arrived.

By that time, the body of Mike Hamilton resembled a spent match.

Forty-one

The blanket was pulled carefully over the blackened remains of Mike Hamilton, hiding the charred corpse from view. The acrid stench of burned flesh still hung in the air and DI Gibson waved a hand in front of his nose as if to dispel the noxious odour.

'How long's he been dead?' asked the policeman.

'It's impossible to say,' Loomis told him, wiping his hands on a piece of tissue. 'Until I've done the autopsy.' He looked down at the grass around the area where the body had been lying. 'It can't have been more than an hour, the poor sod was still warm. Very warm.'

'Any ID on him?' Gibson asked a uniformed man.

'If there was it went up in smoke, sir.'

'Just like *he* did,' Chandler interjected, sucking his teeth and nodding towards the incinerated body.

They all watched as it was lifted carefully into the back of the waiting ambulance. The blue lights were turning silently in the darkness.

'I want footprint casts made and casts of the wheel marks,' said Gibson, sucking on his cigarette. He glanced across at the group of newsmen and women standing behind a cordon of uniformed officers about twenty yards away. 'And I'd like to know where that fucking lot came from? We arrived half an hour ago and they turn up within five minutes. How did they know what had happened and where?' There was anger in his voice. 'If I didn't know better I'd say they'd been tipped off.' He cast a sideways glance at Chandler, who shrugged.

The policemen made their way down the dirt track towards the eager press who moved forward en masse in their efforts to reach the two detectives.

'Who is the victim?'

' . . . has identification been made yet?'

' . . . is it the same killer?'

Questions came drifting through the night and Gibson merely pulled up the collar of his coat and headed for the waiting car.

'No comment,' he called, loudly.

A TV camera was pushed close to him and the DI shoved it away angrily.

' . . . are you treating this as the latest in the series of murders?'

'No comment.'

'You said that you had the killer in custody,' said a fresh voice.

Gibson paused at this latest barb, searching for its source. He spotted Terri Warner almost immediately.

'At the press conference you said that a suspect was under arrest,' she said. 'And yet, two more murders have been committed since then.'

Gibson glared at her for a moment then walked on.

'When are you going to arrest the real killer?' Terri called after him.

'No comment,' Gibson shouted back without looking round.

She watched as the DI and his assistant slid into the Astra and pulled away.

'Some bastard tipped them off,' he said. 'I know it.'

'Maybe the same guy who rang us, the one who found the body,' Chandler offered.

Gibson shook his head.

'He was in a state of shock. He's hardly likely to have informed the media, is he?' There was a note of agitation in the DI's voice.

They rode a long way in silence then Chandler said, 'That's eight he's chalked up now.'

'Thanks for the reminder but I *can* count,' Gibson hissed.

'And still no closer to finding him,' Chandler chided.

'You're enjoying this aren't you?'

'I don't know what you're talking about.'

'*I'm* in charge of the investigation. If the bastard isn't caught it's me who gets it in the neck, from the Commissioner, the media and anyone else with an axe to grind.'

'That's one of the hazards of the job isn't it, Chief?' said Chandler. 'If you crack it you get the credit, if you mess up you get the sharp end of the stick. With position comes responsibility,' he said scornfully.

'I don't need *you* to tell me my responsibilities, Chandler. But *I'll* tell *you* something. If we don't catch him, and I go down, I'll make sure I take you with me. We're in this together, it doesn't matter that I'm in charge. You're on the case too, it's as much your problem as mine.'

'But I'm not in charge, am I?'

'No, that's right. And if I'm replaced do you think *you'll* be offered my position?'

Chandler didn't answer.

'Do you?' Gibson pressed.

'I should have had it in the beginning,' the DS said, venomously.

Gibson laughed humourlessly.

'That's it isn't it? That's been it all along. You don't want the killer caught, do you? Because as long as the bastard's free, the more people he kills, the more it discredits me.'

Chandler shot his superior an angry glance.

'You won't catch him,' he said with an air of conviction which annoyed Gibson.

'I'll get him. With or without your help. And like I said, if I don't, then I'll make sure *you* never get my position. We're in this together, Chandler. It's time we started working together. Before anyone else dies.'

The words hung ominously in the air. Like the smell of burned flesh.

Forty-two

Had he been wrong?

Miller drained the last drops from the hip flask and asked himself that question once more.

He'd followed Susan Lewis to the block of flats where she lived and he'd sat outside in his car all night. Drinking, watching.

Drinking.

Christ, he must have got through more than he'd first thought. Most of the early hours were a blur, scarcely remembered. He could recall dozing periodically, waking suddenly to gaze up at her window again, but other than that the hours between midnight and four a.m. were vague. Now he sat in the driveway of his own house looking down at the dashboard clock which told him it was almost five-thirty. Dawn had risen grey and dirty on the horizon, like a rancid floor cloth stretched across the sky. Miller sighed and swung himself out of the car, not even bothering to lock it.

He fumbled for his house keys and prepared to let himself in. He'd have the chance for a shower and a cup of coffee before he had to leave for the studio. He wondered if he should mention his vigil to Susan Lewis when he saw her. He thought better of it. She'd either laugh in his face or call the police. He grunted. Not that that would do her much good.

Maybe he *had* been wrong.

He found his key and inserted it in the lock.

The door swung back a few inches.

Miller froze momentarily, withdrawing the key as if he'd received an electric shock.

He pushed the door and stepped into the hall, looking round warily. The house was cloaked in silence, an almost conspiratorial solitude which wrapped itself around Miller like invisible mist. He turned briefly and checked the lock. It hadn't been forced. Whoever had entered the house had slipped it.

Whoever had entered had known what they were doing.

There was soil leading out of the hall and towards the stairs to his left. Miller followed the trail slowly, pausing at the bottom of the steps to glance up.

It was only at that moment he realized that whoever had broken in could well still be in the house.

The thought hit him like a sledgehammer and suddenly from his befuddled state his mind seemed to clear. His actions sharpened as he sensed danger.

He began climbing the stairs, quietly but quickly, his eyes never leaving the landing above him, only occasionally glancing at the closed doors which faced him. He stopped on the top step, listening for the slightest sounds of movement.

There was none.

He tried to control his breathing, to slow the pace of his heart which was thudding so loud in his chest he feared that the intruder might hear it.

If *he* was listening out for the intruder then the other was probably listening for *him*.

Miller moved more slowly across the landing, picking up a long, thin glass vase from a cabinet as he did so. At least now he had some kind of weapon.

He pushed open the first of the doors and looked into the room.

Empty.

The door of his own bedroom was ajar.

Miller paused on the threshold, taking a firmer grip on the vase.

He pushed the door, stepping into the room.

Empty.

He swallowed hard and backed out onto the landing again.

There was a noise from downstairs. Miller spun round and walked to the landing, peering over the banister down into the hall.

He listened intently, trying to pinpoint the location of the sound but only silence greeted him this time. He made for the stairs, his heart now thumping madly against his ribs.

As he reached the foot of the stairs he heard the sound again.

It came from his right. From the kitchen.

There was a large window in that room, perhaps the intruder was attempting to clamber out, to get away before Miller got to him. Miller quickly turned over the alternatives in his mind. Should he let the man go? Perhaps he should call the police now. Or tackle the intruder himself?

And yet there was something odd about the entire tableau. If the invader *was* a burglar then why was nothing missing. As far as Miller could see everything was still in its place.

He made his way towards the kitchen as silence descended again.

He was only a couple of feet from the door now, his hand extended towards the knob, the vase gripped more tightly in his fist.

Miller closed his hand around the knob and steadied himself.

He almost shouted aloud when it turned in his grip.

The door was pulled open, the effects man overbalancing, sprawling on the floor of the kitchen.

He dropped the vase, which shattered.

As he struggled to get up he heard a low guttural laugh and looked up to see the intruder standing before him.

'Jesus Christ,' murmured Miller, transfixed by the sight before him.

The intruder smiled.

'I've been waiting for you.'

Forty-three

'What the hell do you want?' Miller rasped angrily.

John Ryker leant back against one of the kitchen worktops, arms folded across his broad chest. The smile had faded from his face and he regarded Miller impassively. Ryker was in his early forties, a tall, powerfully-built man with jet-black hair untouched by even the hint of grey. It looked as if someone had carefully painted each strand of hair with pitch. His forehead was heavy and densely lined, its prominence making it look as though his eyes were little more than small holes punched into his face. His lips were thin, almost bloodless, slashed across his mouth like a thin wound. When he spoke his voice was low but full of menace, and Miller could sense the pent up aggression in each syllable. It was like talking to a human firework. The fuse was lit but he was never quite sure if Ryker was going to explode.

'That's not much of a greeting is it, Frank?' Ryker said. 'I mean, I did take the trouble to visit you in hospital, too. How are you feeling now?'

'Since when has my bloody health been any concern of yours?' Miller snapped, brushing past the bigger man and making for the sink. He spun the cold tap and filled a plastic beaker with water, downing it in two huge gulps.

'Not on the wagon are you?' Ryker asked. 'By the way, I helped myself to a drink when I arrived.' He chuckled. 'You've got some good old malt whisky in your drinks cabinet.'

'Look, Ryker, I told you never to come here. That was the understanding right from the beginning,' Miller said angrily.

'We've got business to discuss. You owe me money.'

'You were paid for the last job.'

Ryker shook his head.

'Yeah, but not enough.' The older man's tone darkened and he took a step towards Miller. 'Listen, I was nearly caught last time. I think some bastard saw me. I'm not going to carry on doing these "little jobs" for you for what you're paying me now, got it? If the law get hold of me they'll throw away the fucking key. Especially with my record.'

Ryker had been in and out of prison for most of his life. A two year stretch for assault, swiftly followed by another for GBH. Then, as he'd got older, he'd graduated to bigger things. His part in a raid on a post office in Lambeth had earned him six years in the Scrubs. Less than two months after his release he was inside again, this time for aggravated assault. He'd been ejected from a pub for harassing customers and had returned the following evening to vent his rage on the landlord with the aid of a baseball bat.

It was during that eighteen-month period that he'd first met Miller. At that time the effects man had been working for the police and he'd been called to Wormwood Scrubs to take photos of a prisoner who was in for child molesting. Somehow, three of the other inmates had managed to corner the man in the showers and had succeeded in first hanging him with nylon string then slicing off his penis with a razor-blade. He'd bled to death.

Ryker had supplied the razor blade.

Miller knew exactly what this big man was capable of and he swallowed hard as Ryker now advanced another step towards him.

'I think it might be an idea to lay off for a while,' said Miller. 'Either that or be more careful.'

'I didn't expect anyone to see me,' Ryker countered angrily. 'Anyway, what the hell do you care? You're only worried in case you go down with me. The prosecution would have a field day with a "celebrity" in the dock. It's in your interests to protect our little business enterprise, and you can protect it by paying me more fucking money.'

'I can't pay you now, I haven't got money on me. Not the amount you're asking for,' Miller told him.

'You haven't heard my new rates yet,' Ryker chuckled. Then, just as quickly, the smile vanished. 'For the next job I want five thousand.'

'No chance,' Miller said, defiantly.

Ryker crossed the room in two giant strides, one powerful hand grabbing Miller by the collar.

'Don't fuck around with me, Miller. Five grand for the next job.'

'And what if there isn't a "next job"?' Miller snarled, pulling away from the older man, his unease temporarily replaced by rage.

'You still owe me more for the last one, I told you, I was lucky to get away. Say two thousand and we'll call it square.'

'You can *say* two thousand but you won't get it,' Miller informed him.

Ryker stepped back, releasing his grip on the other man.

'Two thousand,' he repeated. 'In the next week.'

Miller didn't answer. They merely locked stares for what seemed like an age, then, finally, Ryker turned and headed for the door.

'I'll be in touch, Frank,' he said, smiling. 'You need me.'

Then he was gone.

Miller let out a deep breath, aware that he was trembling slightly.

'Bastard,' he murmured under his breath, the anger boiling within him, but part of that anger was because of his own stupidity. *He* had been the one who'd contacted Ryker in the first place, *he* had offered to pay the man for his services. Miller slammed his fist down on the worktop, realizing that Ryker was right.

If the police were to catch the older man then both he and Miller would be put away.

Something would have to be done.

Forty-four

He'd taken five photos of Susan Lewis on the set that day, discarding the polaroid for a Nikon. Now, as the hands of the clock crawled round to 9.36 p.m., Miller stood in the darkness of his workroom watching as the images gradually formed on the acetate. He swirled it through the developer, the pungent smell filling his nostrils.

With his free hand he held a bottle of Haig which he drank from occasionally, lifting the photos into the tray of fixer. Then, finally he rinsed them with water.

Miller closed his right eye and looked closely at the photos, studying each one in turn.

The aura was present on every one.

But stronger than before, more piercingly bright. It radiated a full inch from all around her face.

Miller rinsed his hands beneath the running tap then flicked on the light, gazing at the pictures. He hadn't mentioned the aura to Susan, nor his long vigil outside her flat the previous night. He had asked her if she lived alone and he'd been informed that she shared a flat with her boyfriend, an out of work actor. She'd been pleasantly surprised by his interest in her private life, if a little puzzled by his incessant questions about her relationship with her boyfriend. Did they row very often? Did it bother him that she was working and he wasn't? Did he ever get violent? Miller himself had finally clammed up, worried that Susan was going to ask why her private life was so important to him.

He looked at the photos once more, tracing the outline of the aura with his index finger.

The loud banging on the front door broke his concentration. He turned, putting down the whisky bottle, wiping his hands on a nearby towel as he headed out of the workroom towards the door, wondering who could be calling on him at this time in the evening. He slowed his pace as he reached the hall.

Could it be Ryker?

No, he reasoned. He wouldn't need to knock. If he wanted to get in he could slip one of the door or window locks.

The knocking continued.

Miller pulled the front door open, his eyes widening in surprise as he saw who his visitor was.

'I'm sorry to call on you so late,' Terri Warner apologized, 'but there's something I think you should know.'

Miller nodded, attempted a smile, then thought better of it. He beckoned her inside, motioned her through into the sitting room. Miller joined her, seating himself in a chair opposite where she sat. He offered her a drink which she accepted.

'I'm sorry if I'm interrupting, I know you're busy working on this film, but it's about the murder last night. You have heard?'

Miller sat forward in his chair.

'I haven't seen a paper today, or heard the radio,' he told her.

She explained about the murder of Mike Hamilton.

'Jesus,' Miller muttered as she gave him the details. 'Did your informant tip you off again?'

She nodded.

'Was the murder another copy-cat killing?' he wanted to know.

'Yes,' she told him. 'The victim was a hitch-hiker as far as anyone can tell. He was battered then burned, just like the victim of Alfred Arthur Rouse. He picked up a hitch-hiker and killed him for no apparent reason. Rouse was hanged in 1931.'

Miller shook his head.

'Why the imitations?' he mused. 'I know the different MOs make it more difficult for the police, but it seems so elaborate. And why more than one murderer? Why not stick to imitating just one killer?'

'Let's just hope he doesn't decide to have a crack at imitating Charles Whitman,' she said, cryptically, expanding when she noticed Miller's vague expression. 'He was an American, obsessed with guns. He climbed to the top of a water tower one morning and shot eighteen people in ninety minutes.'

'Great,' said Miller humourlessly.

Terri rummaged in her handbag and pulled out the tape. She held it before her then tossed it to Miller, who caught it with one hand and looked at her, a puzzled frown on his face.

'Play it,' she told him.

He didn't argue but merely got to his feet, crossed to the stereo and slipped the cassette into the machine. Terri took a hefty swig from her glass as she listened to the messages yet again. Miller looked at her in bewilderment.

'It's the killer,' she told him as he re-wound the tape and played it once more.

'How can you be sure?' he asked.

She didn't like the note of scepticism in Miller's voice.

'The same way you can be sure that you've got the ability to see the aura around a murder victim,' she said challengingly.

Miller smiled thinly and ejected the tape.

'Do you recognize the voice?' he asked.

'There's something familiar about it . . .' She allowed the sentence to trail off.

'What have the police said?'

'I still haven't told them. My boss at the TV station wants me to try and keep in contact with the killer if possible. To let him keep phoning. He thinks he may try to meet me eventually.'

'And then what?' said Miller, tossing the tape back to her. 'Corpse number nine?'

'I don't know,' she said softly, slipping the cassette back into her handbag. There was a long silence finally broken by Terri. 'Look, I think I'd better go now,' she said, getting to her feet. 'I'm sorry if I disturbed you but I wanted you to hear that tape.'

The effects man nodded as he walked to the door with her. They exchanged brief farewells and he watched her as she walked across to her car.

He stood silhouetted in the doorway as she drove off.

But his were not the only eyes that watched.

Terri parked her car beside the lift entrance in the underground car park and allowed her head to loll back against the top of the driver's seat. She closed her eyes for a moment, listening to the sound of her engine dying away within the cavernous confines of the subterranean chamber, then she swung herself out of the car and locked it.

Her heels clicked loudly on the stained concrete of the car park, the sound echoing around her. She reached the lift and jabbed the call button watching as the numbers above her lit up and it descended from the ninth floor of the block. It stopped at eight. Again at six. Terri rubbed her eyes wearily as she waited in the oppressive silence.

From behind her she heard the sounds of movement.

Footsteps. Scraping on the concrete.

She spun round, her eyes searching the poorly-lit area for the source of the noise.

She saw nothing, only the white light of the fluorescents reflecting off the bonnets and roofs of parked cars.

The lift continued to descend.

Terri glanced up at the numbers again, feeling curiously vulnerable. Her heart was thudding hard against her ribs.

The lift was still making its tortuous way down.

Fourth floor.

Third.

She heard more movement. Closer to her this time.

Second floor.

She stood with her back to the lift doors, pressed against them, wondering who the hell was down in this gloomy chamber with her. Why they were so silent.

Why they were drawing closer.

First floor.

She could hear breathing, faint but guttural breathing, and she guessed that it must be coming from behind the stone pillar less than ten yards from her.

The lift had reached the ground floor.

She fixed her eyes on that pillar, watching for any sign of movement, her hands clenched into fists, nails digging into her palms.

Could it be some kids, she asked herself? Just trying to scare her. All part of the game.

The breathing slowed, the silence became unendurable.

She chanced a look at the lift indicator and the blasted thing was finally descending towards the basement, towards *her*.

Terri saw movement behind the pillar.

She stifled a moan of terror as a dark shape seemed to detach itself from the concrete and move into view.

She tried to make out the face but it was impossible.

The figure took a step towards her.

The lift doors suddenly slid open and she almost fell in, jabbing the button which would close them. Jabbing it so hard she nearly broke her nail.

The figure remained motionless, finally disappearing from sight as the lift door shut.

Terri let out a long sigh of relief and pushed the button for two floors above her own. If someone was watching her then she wasn't going to make life that easy for him.

Was her imagination running wild? she wondered.

She had seen the figure there. Why hadn't the newcomer approached her rather than skulk behind the pillar? Why, unless he didn't want to be seen.

She reached the floor and stepped out of the lift, hurried to the stairs and descended the two storeys to her flat. Her hands were shaking as she found her key and unlocked the door.

She stepped on the note.

It lay just inside the threshold.

Terri slapped on the lights, anxious to be surrounded by brightness again, then in the glow of the lamp she looked at the note.

It was on a piece of typing paper, folded in half, the letters cut carefully from a book. The letters weren't taken from a newspaper. The print was most definitely from a paperback, that much she could tell from the quality of the paper itself. Each small letter had been painstakingly cut out and stuck together on the sheet of A4.

i hAvE watcHEd yOu I wanT to MEeT yOU now

I WiLl conTaCT You AGain Do Not teLL thE pOLicE
I aM WatCHinG

She held the note before her, unable to prevent her hands trembling.

When the phone rang she almost shouted aloud.

For what seemed like an eternity she stood staring at it, finally crossing and picking up the receiver, trying to control the fear in her voice.

There was only silence at the other end.

'Who is this?' she snapped, her voice low.

Breathing. Softly.

'I know you're there you bastard,' she hissed. 'Talk to me.'

'Sleep well,' said the voice. Then a chuckle which raised the hairs on the back of her neck.

The line went dead.

Terri slammed the receiver down and backed away from it.

She sat down in the chair opposite the phone, her eyes never leaving it, one hand still gripping the note.

It was warm inside the flat but Terri felt as if she had been wrapped in a freezing blanket.

She looked at the note again.

And she waited for the phone to ring.

Forty-five

Susan Lewis leant back against the headboard, the shooting script held across her lap. As she did so, the sheet slipped from her upper body exposing her breasts. She made to replace it but a hand reached up from beside her and pulled the sheet down once more. Susan chuckled and glanced quickly at Steve Bailey, who was lying on his side looking up at her. He smiled and she sighed when she felt his free hand brush against her knee as it moved steadily higher, stroking the inside of her thigh.

She parted her legs slightly, allowing him easier access, squirming as his eager fingers finally came to rest in the softly curled hair between her legs. Susan didn't stop reading, although little of what she saw was registering now. All that she was aware of was the growing feeling of warmth between her legs, spreading up her body until, as Bailey began tracing the outline of her mound, she also felt her nipples stiffen in anticipation.

He continued his expert manipulations beneath the sheets, his own excitement growing, his penis stiffening as he felt the moistness between Susan's legs.

He knew where to touch her. And how. They had lived together for the past two years, ever since they'd met while making a low budget six-part series for the BBC. Since then, neither of them had been inundated with offers of work. Bailey himself had only managed to land parts in commercials and a walk-on part in the last series of *Minder*. His agent had found him work modelling clothes for catalogues, but it certainly wasn't the big time. Susan, on the other hand, had at least worked steadily albeit unspectacularly. A succession of small parts in series and films and now the part in *Astro-cannibals*. It was her money that was keeping them and that was something which Bailey didn't like. At thirty-one, three years older than Susan, he felt that it was about time *he* broke through. He wasn't asking for the lead in the next Spielberg movie. Not just yet anyway. But he deserved more than he was getting.

He brushed a strand of his long brown hair from his face then resumed his explorations beneath the sheets.

Susan lay back further, the script still gripped in both hands, allowing him to stroke her pubic hair with his index finger, pausing occasionally to glide along the outside of her swelling lips. She drew in a long breath as he disappeared beneath the sheets, his tongue flicking across her pelvic bone then down into the valley between her lips, anxious to taste her wetness.

She made a show of continuing to read, but as his lips fastened around her clitoris she finally gave up and surrendered to his attentions. She felt his tongue glide expertly over her distended lips, outlining each fold and crease, adding his own saliva to the slippery juices between her legs. He coaxed some of that moisture onto his fingertips, rubbing it softly into the tops of her thighs, trickling the slippery digits down her legs and back again until finally he began to probe at the pink mouth of her vagina, his tongue slipping inside for precious seconds before flicking up to gently lash her throbbing clitoris.

He clambered between her legs, rising before her, ready to slide his own rock-hard member into that beckoning cleft.

She shook her head and held his shoulders, keeping him away. Ensuring that he didn't penetrate her.

'Not tonight,' she whispered. 'Carry on doing what you were doing,' she sighed, leaning forward, licking some of her own juices from his lips.

Bailey looked disappointed and rolled from between her legs, laying on his back, his erection poking up at her. She squeezed his penis gently but he knocked her hand away.

'What's wrong, Steve?' she asked, recognizing the look of irritation on his face.

'*Not tonight*,' he said acidly, mimicking her soft plea. 'I'm surprised you've got time for anything these days, not since you started working on this film.' He picked up the script and glanced at it. 'It's a piece of shit, Sue.'

'It's work,' she protested. 'And one of us has got to earn some money.'

Bailey regarded her angrily for a moment.

'Why the hell are you studying the script, you don't have to speak anyway. When the film's released no one's even going to see your face. You'll be covered in make-up.'

'This part might not be much, but the director was saying that he's going back to the States as soon as he's finished to make another film and he's asked me to go over and audition for one of the leading parts.'

'Great,' said Bailey, irritably.

'I thought you'd be pleased for me. For both of us.'

'Why? So I can carry on lazing around while you pay the fucking bills. Do you know how that makes me feel, Sue?' he demanded.

'For Christ's sake, what does it matter as long as one of us is working? I didn't think all this macho bullshit bothered you, or do you think that you should be earning more because you're the man?' There was scorn in her words.

'So you're off to the States eh?' he said. 'For how long?'

'I don't know. It depends whether I get the part or not,' she told him.

'And if you do I'll be lucky if I see you again.'

'What's got into you?' she demanded. 'I tell you a piece of good news and you act like it's an announcement for a funeral. I didn't realize that you were so jealous.' She swung herself out of bed but Bailey caught her by the arm and pulled her back. She shook loose of his grip, angry when she saw the red marks on her forearm.

'I think it'd be a good idea if I slept in the spare room tonight,' she told him. 'I don't think there's enough room in bed for me *and* your ego.'

'Are you sure that the director only wants you to test for a part out there?' Bailey said.

'What's that supposed to mean?' she demanded.

'Well, a big star like you,' his voice was heavy with scorn.

'You're bound to be in demand.'

She shook her head and reached for the script.

'I think I'll come back when you're in a better mood, Steve,' Susan said, picking up the slim folder.

Bailey knocked it from her grasp, the pages scattering over both the floor and the bed.

'You idiot,' she snapped, retrieving some of them.

'Leave them,' he snarled, gripping her wrist hard.

She tried to pull away but he held firm, squeezing so tightly that she was afraid he would break her wrist.

'Get off me,' she yelled and lashed out at him, her nails raking his face, drawing blood as they gouged the flesh just below his right eye.

'You cow,' he hissed, seeing the crimson fluid on his finger-tips. He leapt off the bed and struck her hard across the face with the back of his hand, a blow which sent her reeling. As she fell to the floor of the bedroom, Bailey advanced upon her, fists clenched. She waited until he was within striking distance then lashed out with her bare foot, kicking him hard in the groin. He let out a strangled cry and clutched at his testicles, his rage now reaching even greater heights as she tried to scuttle from the room. He grabbed her by the hair, his hand slipping, ripping her dressing gown so that she too was naked.

He pulled her to the floor, pinning her beneath him.

'Get off,' she screamed and spat in his face but Bailey seemed not to notice. As the long streamer of sputum hung from his cheek like a mucoid tear he fastened his hands around her throat and squeezed.

Susan felt a twinge of fear as Bailey's thumbs gouged her windpipe and she beat even more frenziedly at his powerful arms, but the effort was useless. There was a rage in his eyes. Blind, uncontrollable rage which seemed to add strength to his grip. He straddled her, his erection sticking up between her breasts, his knees pinning her arms. Susan wanted to cry out but the vice-like grip around her throat prevented her doing so. She felt as if someone was pumping her head full of air, as if her skull was expanding and she fought to catch her breath, aware now of white stars dancing before her eyes.

Bailey raised her head a few inches then slammed it back down onto the ground, sending a fresh jolt of pain through her head. He repeated the action, never once loosening his hold on her throat. Susan struggled more forlornly now, making a last desperate attempt to push him off. If only she could weaken his hold for a second, get away from him, lock him in the bedroom. If only . . .

She felt waves of unconsciousness sweeping over her as he slammed her head down once more, and this time there was a dull crack as the impact broke bone. Susan knew that she was not going to be able to fight back now, the effort seemed too great, the pain too intense and Bailey still leered above her, his teeth clenched, lips drawn back in a snarl of rage.

She managed to pull one arm free, but Bailey hardly felt the blow she dealt him. The power, the life, was draining rapidly from her now.

She tasted blood in her mouth but didn't even realize that she'd bitten her tongue. The crimson fluid ran in a thin stream from one corner of her mouth as she gasped for air.

Her body began to spasm wildly and she groaned as the final shrouds of blackness began to envelop her. For in those final seconds she realized that she was dying. She tried to pray but soon all thoughts of God were forgotten. Only the fear remained. The awful certainty that in a moment or two she would be dead.

Bailey lifted her head once more, staring deep into her glazed eyes for endless seconds before smashing her head down with even greater force. A force which finally caused her to black out and which also opened a large gash at the back of her skull. Blood began to soak into the carpet and he loosened his hold on her throat as the muscular jerks grew in intensity. Her legs stiffened for precious seconds, the muscles bulging, toes twisted upwards, and he actually felt himself lifted by the sudden rigidity which filled her body. Then it merely collapsed and he heard the soft hiss as her sphincter muscle opened.

The pungent stench of excrement filled the air as Bailey finally released his grip on Susan Lewis. He stepped back, his eyes riveted to the body which lay before him like some kind of discarded mannequin.

For what seemed like an eternity he stared at it, then, with as much speed as he could muster, he began to gather up his clothes.

Forty-six

'Still no answer,' the girl shouted. 'Do you want me to keep trying?'

Phillip Dickinson looked across at his assistant and nodded.

'Give it another five minutes, then forget it,' he called back, glancing at his watch.

'It's nice to work with reliable people isn't it, Phil?' Miller said sarcastically.

'Fuck you, Frank, it's too early in the morning,' the director snapped irritably. 'She's probably on her way here now.' He looked at his watch again, wondering why Susan Lewis was almost an hour late arriving at the studio.

It was Miller who first noticed Detective Inspector Gibson as the policeman entered the sound stage, glancing around him at the sets. The effects man frowned and pocketed his hip flask, surprised by the appearance of the policeman. He saw a stage-hand approach the DI, saw Gibson flip open the slim leather wallet which carried his identification. The stage-hand nodded in the direction of Dickinson and stepped back.

As Gibson drew closer he and Miller exchanged glances and the effects man turned to move away.

'Stay, Frank,' Gibson said. 'I need to talk to you.'

Dickinson looked bemused as the DI finally introduced himself.

'What can I do for you?' the director asked.

Gibson told him about the murder of Susan Lewis.

'We picked up her boyfriend about two hours later,' the DI concluded. 'He confessed to it, told us everything that happened.'

Miller swallowed hard, his mind suddenly filled with the vision of those photos he'd taken of Susan Lewis. Of the aura.

Dickinson could only shake his head.

Gibson looked at Miller.

'I want to talk to you, Frank,' he said. 'In private.'

Miller motioned for the policeman to follow him and they walked together through the maze of props and cameras set up all around the sound stage. Technicians glanced at them as they passed. Miller finally led the policeman out of the studio towards the make-up trailer. He fumbled in his pocket for the keys as they walked.

'I thought you weren't bothered whether you ever saw me again,' he said.

'This isn't a social call, Frank,' Gibson told him. He jabbed a finger in the direction of a waiting Fiesta and Miller looked over to see DS Chandler scramble out of the vehicle. He was carrying an attaché case. As Miller opened the door of the trailer, he joined them.

'I could say I told you so,' Miller said smugly. 'About Susan Lewis. But I'll resist the temptation.'

'Very funny,' Gibson said, taking the case from Chandler. He flipped it open and Miller saw a pile of photos inside, some of them yellowed and curled at the corners. 'I want to know more about this so called aura around murder victims.'

'Why the sudden interest?' Miller demanded.

'Look, stop messing about and tell me what you know,' the DI hissed.

'I took some photos, you know that,' the effects man began. 'The three people I photographed all had a kind of aura around them when the prints were developed. All three have since been murdered. I think that I can spot potential murder victims from their photos.'

'This is bullshit,' said Chandler, shaking his head.

Gibson shot him an acid glance then returned his attention to Miller.

'That applies to *all* murder victims?' he asked. 'If you see the photos, you can pick them out?'

Miller nodded.

'Convince me,' said Gibson and dumped the pile of pictures on the table in front of him. 'There are twenty pictures there, some of them are murder victims, some aren't. All the photos were taken *before* the victims were killed. Go on, Frank. Impress me.' Gibson stepped back, watching as Miller picked up the first of the photos. He closed his right eye and scrutinized the print. It was a woman, late twenties, pretty. The photo was old.

'Victim,' he said unhesitatingly, his eye picking out the aura which surrounded her.

He began working his way through the pile.

A man in his fifties, balding, eyes deep-set.

'Victim,' Miller pronounced.

Another young woman.

He shook his head and placed the photo on a different pile before continuing.

An old photo. An older woman. She carried the aura.

'Victim.'

It took him less than five minutes to complete the task. There were five photos on the pile he had designated as victims.

'Well,' he said, sipping from his hip flask. 'Do I win a prize?'

'I still say this is bullshit,' Chandler interjected, his comment now directed at Gibson. 'He could have recognized the victims from books or newspaper articles.'

'Do you know any of them, Frank?' Gibson asked. 'Have you ever seen any of the faces before?'

Miller shook his head.

'Just tell me who they are?' he said.

Gibson sighed and held up the photos one at a time. As he did so, Miller saw the aura around each one again.

'Margery Gardner, murdered by Neville Heath in 1946. Jack McVittie, stabbed to death by Reggie Kray in 1967.' The list went on. 'Ruth Fuerst, murdered by John Christie in 1943.' And on. 'John Kilbride, victim of the Moors Murderers.' He held up the final picture. 'Donald Skepper, killed by The Black Panther in February 1974.' There was one last photo. One which the policeman had taken not from the attaché case but from his inside pocket. He handed it to Miller.

'Susan Lewis,' he said. 'Murdered last night.'

Miller drank from his hip flask, glancing again at the photos, each victim surrounded by that infernal aura.

'Now will you believe me?' he asked.

Gibson didn't answer, he merely gathered up the photos and put them back into the case which he then handed to Chandler.

'He guessed,' the DS said, scornfully.

'He was right,' Gibson snapped.

'You're more stupid than I thought if you believe that,' said the older man.

'Wait for me in the car,' Gibson told his assistant.

Chandler hesitated.

'Leave us alone.' The DI inclined his head towards the door. 'Go on.'

The DS left reluctantly, glaring first at Miller then his own superior.

'You're still no use to me, Frank, even if I do believe you. Jesus, if the commissioner thought that I believed what you'd told me he'd have me pounding a bloody beat again.'

The two men regarded each other in silence for long moments then Gibson finally spoke again.

'If you get any more information like this, about possible victims, let me know,' he said, wearily, heading for the trailer door.

'Can I give you some advice, Stuart?' Miller said. 'Watch Chandler.'

The DI nodded almost imperceptibly then left, closing the door behind him. Miller was left alone in the trailer.

Alone with just his thoughts.

And fears.

Forty-seven

He had taken the photograph from Terri's flat during his first visit, pocketing it while she was out of the room with all the speed and assurance of a thief.

The picture had been taken, Miller guessed, three or four years ago. Her hair was shorter, her face a little fatter. But the feature which remained constant was the almost hypnotic perfection of her eyes. Miller had studied those eyes. He had studied the entire photo carefully. For it was not Terri's beauty which had caused him to steal the photograph, it was his need to know the answer to a question which had plagued him since they met.

He had to know whether or not she carried the aura.

'I think it's time you told the police,' said Miller, holding the note before him.

Terri, legs curled beneath her on the sofa, merely looked at him as he sat forward in the chair, the whisky tumbler gripped in his free hand.

'I think he was here the other night when I got back from your house,' she told him, recounting the episode in the underground car park. Miller listened intently, his eyes never leaving Terri as she told him of the man in the shadows who had merely stood watching her in that forbidding subterranean chamber. Even in the comfort and light of her flat she felt a shiver of fear ripple up her spine at the recollection. Miller waited until she'd finished speaking then got to his feet and crossed to the large picture window in the sitting room. He looked out into the night, peering at lights which glimmered in other flats and houses

227

nearby or at the headlights of vehicles below as they pierced the gloom. The sky was mottled grey with rain clouds, the odd drop pattering the glass as if to give warning of what was to come.

'He says he's watching you,' Miller muttered. 'That must mean he's pretty close.'

'Thanks for reassuring me,' Terri said.

'Or he's bluffing. He wants you to *think* that he's watching you.' He took a swig from his glass. 'Either way, I think you should call the police in. This has gone far enough.'

'My boss isn't going to be very pleased. It'll blow the story wide open.'

'Fuck him, it's not him who's being threatened.'

'That's the point, whoever is sending these messages *hasn't* threatened me. Not once. I think he *wants* to make contact. If I go to the police now then I'll lose him.'

'Or he'll take his story to another TV station or newspaper,' Miller said sarcastically. 'That's your real worry, isn't it? You're as concerned about ratings as your bloody boss. You've made a name for yourself reporting these murders and you don't want to blow your chances of wrapping up the story by frightening the killer off. It'll make a great headline though, Terri. "Woman reporter murdered by maniac she hoped to interview".' He shook his head.

'I suppose I could ask what business it was of yours if I want to risk my life for a story. Couldn't I?'

'You could also tell me to get out of your flat.'

She nodded.

'You're probably right, Frank,' she sighed. 'Maybe it *is* time that I called in the police, but I should tell my boss about the note. He has a right to know. He's the one who assigned me to this job in the first place.' She was already on her feet and heading for the phone. Miller watched as she dialled, then he returned to gazing out into the night.

Terri could get no answer at Bob Johnson's home number so she tried the studio. It was snatched up on the third ring.

'News Update, Bob Johnson speaking.'

'Bob, it's Terri. Listen.' She quickly relayed the news of what had happened and Miller listened idly as she spoke, his back to her. Every now and then he would hear Johnson's raised voice on the other end of the line.

'I think it would be better if we let the police handle it from here,' Terri said.

'No way,' Johnson snapped. 'We agreed that you wouldn't involve the police.'

'Unless it was absolutely necessary,' she reminded him.

'But you said yourself that he hasn't made threats.'

'Look, Bob, the phone calls are bad enough but when it comes to finding notes pushed under my door . . .' She let the sentence trail off.

'The minute he gets an idea the police are on to him you can kiss the story goodbye,' Johnson snapped.

'Well, I'm going to have to take that chance. I've been discussing it with Frank and . . .'

Johnson cut her short, his voice low but seething with anger.

'Who?' he demanded. 'You've been talking about this to someone else?'

'It's a free country, Bob. I needed some advice.'

'What was wrong with asking me?' he demanded, and Terri moved the phone away from her ear slightly, surprised at the vehemence in his voice. 'Who the hell is Frank, anyway?' he demanded.

Terri frowned.

'Look, we were discussing the murderer, not my private life. What the hell does it matter who Frank is?'

Miller turned slightly at the mention of his name. He saw the anger on Terri's face, heard Johnson's voice, even louder now.

'Did *he* tell you to call the police?' Johnson demanded.

'No one *told* me. We were discussing it, and I think that it might be a good idea if they knew what was happening and what's been going on with the phone calls. They might be able to trace the voice. Voice-print it.'

There was an angry silence at the other end of the line. Terri was aware only of Johnson's breathing.

She was about to speak again when she heard his voice. Flat and cold as steel.

'Do it then,' he hissed. 'Do as your *friend* tells you.'

Terri stepped back in surprise as the receiver was slammed down. She looked across at Miller and shrugged.

'What is it with him?' Miller asked.

Terri could only shake her head. She seated herself once more, running the index finger of one hand around the rim of her glass.

Bob Johnson sat at his desk and glared at the phone, the knot of muscles at the side of his jaw pulsing angrily.

For what seemed like an eternity he remained in that position, fists clenched, his body shaking with suppressed rage. Then, with a roar of fury, he brought one fist crashing down on the desk top.

'Bitch,' he hissed. 'Fucking bitch.'

How dare she go to the police? They had agreed that the law were not to be involved. This was her story.

Their story.

No one must be allowed to come between Terri and this story.

No one must be allowed to come between him and Terri.

There must be no interference. No police. No outsiders.

He could not, *would* not, permit it.

Forty-eight

As he climbed into his car Miller had no idea he was being watched.

The effects man guided the Granada up the ramp, out of the underground car park.

The driver of the pursuing vehicle kept a respectable distance, eyes never leaving the Granada. As if joined by some invisible tow-rope, the two cars threaded their way through traffic.

It had been a couple of minutes after eleven when Miller finally left Terri's flat. The drive back to his own house, he estimated, would take less than thirty minutes. He pulled up at a set of traffic lights, tapping gently on the wheel as he waited for them to change to green.

Behind him, the other vehicle also waited.

The driver watched Miller's car, coaxing the following car into pursuit once more as Miller moved off.

As he drove, Miller thought back to his conversation with Gibson and the incident with the photos. It had been no accident that he'd recognized each victim, every one of them marked out by the glowing aura. He knew now that the ability was his alone. He grunted. Ability? Was that the word?

Gift, maybe? Or curse?

Was it some kind of second sight, he wondered? But then quickly dismissed his own idea. No, there was nothing psychic involved. The answer lay in celluloid, emulsion and his own transplanted eye. He could *see* the victims.

Behind him, the other car kept up its steady pursuit.

Miller was less than half a mile from his home when the vehicle that had been following him began to accelerate.

At first Miller thought that the car was going to overtake, and he slowed down to allow it free passage. However, he frowned when he realized that the driver had no intention of passing by. The car bumped Miller's Granada gently and stayed where it was.

'What the . . .' Miller hissed, glancing round at the other driver, but the blinding light from the pursuing vehicle's headlamps made it impossible to see inside the other car.

Miller could see the outline of a Capri but that was all.

The pursuing car accelerated and once again Miller felt the slight impact as his bumper was nudged.

'Bloody idiot,' he snarled and put his foot on the gas, pulling away from the other car. Whoever was driving was probably drunk, he reasoned. Either that or they'd mistaken him for someone else.

Miller drove on.

The Capri kept coming.

Just what was this clown playing at, Miller wondered, staring into his rear-view mirror. The other car was speeding up once more, swerving out from behind the Granada this time, pulling up alongside it.

Miller wound down his window, preparing to shout some abuse at the other driver, when the Capri suddenly swerved across the path of the Granada.

Miller slammed his foot down hard on the brake, the front wheels locking as the car skidded three or four yards. His seat-belt gripped him hard, flinging him back against his seat, knocking the wind from him. He sucked in a deep lungful of air, his head spinning.

The Capri was parked about ten yards ahead, its tail-lights winking impishly, as if challenging Miller to get out. He wasn't slow to rise to that challenge. He flung open his door and strode towards the other vehicle.

As he reached the Capri he saw the driver clamber out.

Miller froze, looking into the face of John Ryker.

The older man was smiling.

'I reckon I should have been a private eye,' he said. 'I've been following you for half an hour and you never twigged.'

'What do you want, Ryker?' the effects man snapped. 'I thought we'd said all we had to say to one another.'

A car sped past, its headlamps momentarily illuminating Ryker's features.

'I told you the other night, we've still got business to attend to. You owe me money. Two thousand quid, and I want it before the end of the week.'

'And I told you that's impossible,' Miller hissed, turning away.

He saw nothing.

He felt Ryker's strong hand grip his shoulder then, in the stillness of the night, he heard the familiar *swish-click* of a flick knife. Before he knew what was happening the point was pressed beneath his chin.

'Go on then, kill me,' Miller said, defiantly. 'That's not going to get you your money, is it?' He swallowed hard, feeling the point of the blade against his Adam's apple as he did so.

Ryker pressed harder.

'There are worse things I can do than kill you,' he said softly and released his grip.

Another car passed and the two men locked stares. Then all was darkness again.

Ryker began walking towards his car.

'There are worse things than death,' he said and chuckled.

The sound raised the hairs at the back of Miller's neck. He stood immobile as the older man slid behind the wheel of the Capri and started up the engine. He spun the wheel and screeched away past Miller, who watched the tail-lights of the car disappear into the night. He stood there a moment longer, massaging the soft skin beneath his chin, feeling the warm blood where the blade had nicked him.

He shuddered and clambered into his own car.

Another ten minutes and he was home.

In the gloom of his workroom, lit only by the red light, everything looked as though it had been soaked in blood.

The burn victim stared sightlessly at his creator.

On the walls, hundreds of dead eyes seemed to gleam from the photos which recorded their deaths. As Miller glanced at them he could see the aura around those who had met their ends at the hands of others.

Photos of George Cook and Penny Steele now hung there with the other celluloid nightmares.

There were three pictures of Susan Lewis.

Smiling. Attractive. Dead.

From a nearby drawer, Miller took the photo of Terri Warner.

He held it before him, closed his right eye, and gazed at it.

Forty-nine

'You found this note this morning?'

Detective Inspector Stuart Gibson held the piece of paper before him like an accusation, glancing first at Terri then at the words on the note.

As before, they had been cut from a book, each letter methodically attached to the A4 sheet.

I aM stILl watChINg i wiLL cONtaCt yOU sooN

The GAmE iS NeArlY oVeR I will CaLl yOu

No pOliCE

Gibson handed the note to Chandler who scanned it briefly and nodded.

'Did you call us as soon as you found it?' he asked Terri.

She nodded.

'Does anyone else know about it?' the Detective Sergeant persisted.

'Like who?' she snapped.

'Boyfriend. Lover . . .'

She cut him short. 'No one.'

Chandler looked at her warily for a moment then crossed the room to the phone. A man dressed in an immaculately-pressed blue suit had the device in pieces and was attaching a small microphone to the earpiece. Chandler watched the man at work.

'Why didn't you notify us earlier?' Gibson wanted to know. 'About the phone calls and the other note? We could have tapped your phone. We might even have caught the bastard by now.'

Terri ran a hand through her hair and padded through into the kitchen, Gibson followed, watching as she poured herself a cup of coffee. She offered him one and he joined her, pushing the kitchen door closed, shutting out Chandler and the surveillance man.

'I didn't want to get in touch with you,' Terri told the policeman. 'I probably wouldn't have done this time, but to be quite honest, I'm scared.'

Gibson sipped his coffee and looked at the TV reporter.

'Why do you think he picked you?' he asked. 'Out of all the newspaper and TV people he could have chosen. Why you?'

'That's what Frank Miller said . . .' Terri smiled humourlessly, but the expression faded rapidly as she saw the policeman's reaction.

'Do you know Frank Miller?' he asked suspiciously.

She nodded.

'How is he involved in this?' Gibson wanted to know.

'He approached *me*. You could say we exchanged ideas about this case.'

'How much does Miller know about the killings and what's been going on?'

Terri frowned, surprised at the harshness of tone in Gibson's voice.

'Does it really matter?' she asked. 'You ought to be grateful to him, if not for his prompting I probably wouldn't have got in touch with you. He advised me to call in the law.' She took a sip of her coffee. She went on to explain about the possibility of making a story out of the calls, of finally meeting the killer.

'That wouldn't be a good idea, Miss Warner,' Gibson told her. 'Just leave it in our hands now.'

'I'm not dropping this here,' Terri said defiantly. 'I called you lot in for protection, but I still intend meeting the killer.'

'Not a chance,' Gibson told her. 'I told you, this is our concern now. You take the calls if he rings again, but nothing more.'

Terri didn't answer.

'I'm going to set up a twenty-four-hour surveillance team around this building. If he comes anywhere near then we'll get him.' The DI took another swig of coffee, warming his hands around the mug.

'There's another thing,' he said. 'I'd like you to give us a spare key to your flat. If he should break in for any reason or try to leave any more messages I'd like one of my men on the spot. You don't have to agree to *that* stipulation of course.'

Terri shrugged, got to her feet and crossed to one of the kitchen cabinets. She opened it and produced a key from a small dish.

'My spare,' she told Gibson, handing him the object.

They both turned as there was a knock on the door.

Chandler walked in.

'Sorry to interrupt,' he said sarcastically. 'Surveillance are finished.'

Gibson got to his feet, following his assistant through into the sitting room.

'If he calls,' he told Terri, 'try and keep him on the line as long as possible so we can get a trace going. There'll be men nearby at all times.'

'I hope they're discreet,' she said, smiling.

Gibson nodded then he and his two colleagues left, the DI pausing momentarily at the door.

'There's nothing more you can do now,' he said. 'Just wait for him to call.'

Terri nodded and closed the door behind her. She stood against it for a moment then crossed to the large picture window in the sitting room and gazed out at the other flats and houses which surrounded her. She shuddered involuntarily, wondering if at this moment someone was out there.

Watching.

Waiting.

The lift descended slowly from the fifth floor on its way to the basement car park.

Chandler lit up a cigarette, the smoke wafting in Gibson's direction. The DI coughed and waved a hand in front of him.

'How many men are you putting on her?' Chandler asked.

'It depends how many I can spare,' Gibson told him, glancing

237

up as the lift passed the second floor.

'What if you frighten the killer off?'

'It's going to take more than a couple of plain-clothes men to frighten *this* bugger off,' Gibson said. He turned to look at his colleague as the lift reached the basement. 'You did surveillance work for the Vice Squad, didn't you?'

'So?'

'So, I need an experienced man. You just got yourself a job, Chandler,' Gibson chuckled. He reached into his pocket and handed the DS the key to Terri's flat. 'In case she's not in when you need to get inside.'

Chandler looked at the key then closed his fist around it.

Fifty

The street was almost deserted.

The figure walked slowly along the carefully-tended path, past immaculately kept hedges and fences, the boundaries of gardens lovingly cared for. Apart from the car which the figure had clambered out of there were only two vehicles parked in the street. Neither attended.

It was almost 2.30 p.m. Another hour and the children would be leaving school. As it was, mothers were out and about taking advantage of the respite, shopping or chatting or perhaps even tending gardens that looked as if they'd been lifted straight from the pages of a magazine.

The figure glanced from side to side every now and then but saw only one other moving occupant of the street. A woman dressed in a blue jogging suit was pulling some weeds from the front of her carefully-tended hedge. She had her back to the figure.

She never saw the stranger pass her on the opposite side of the road.

The figure paused, glancing across at the woman for a few seconds, then continued, finally reaching the front of the house which it was looking for.

Frank Miller's house, like most of the other dwellings along the road, was protected from prying eyes by a high fence, but the gate was open and the figure slipped through, glancing back briefly to check that the woman in the blue jogging suit had not seen, but she was still preoccupied with her weeds. The figure approached the house unchallenged, noticing that the garage door was also open. There was no sign of Miller's car. He would be at the studio.

That was how it was meant to be.

The figure moved with disquieting ease and speed around the side of the house, finding shelter in the shadows cast by tall trees.

There, surrounded by the stillness, the figure stood gazing at the small window before it. The tree and fence acted as a perfect barrier from the prying eyes of any neighbours who might be at home, but the figure worked quickly and assuredly on the window, sliding a short-bladed knife between the frame and the jamb, working away expertly until the lock was broken. The window swung inwards a couple of inches and the figure hauled itself through the gap, pushing the glass partition back further until it was possible to slide right through.

Inside the house it was deathly silent.

Particles of dust twisted and fell in the thin shafts of light which had forced their way past the curtains. The figure got up and turned to the left, towards the sitting room. The door was open, the contents of the room exposed.

The figure stood in the doorway for a moment then advanced into the room, towards the standard lamp which stood behind one chair.

The intruder gripped the lamp by its wooden shaft, wielding it like a club, raising it into the air. It stood for a moment, then brought the lamp crashing down on top of the TV set, cracking the cabinet. The second blow shattered the screen and glass sprayed into the room. From the mantlepiece vases were sent flying into the air, one of them smashing against a wall, the other exploding into a dozen pieces before it even hit the ground. A mirror above the fireplace was brought down with a fearsome crash, huge shards of glass breaking away from the reflective oval.

The intruder turned, pushing over the sofa, kicking a small cabinet until the door came off. Bottles spilled out from within, each one then dutifully smashed. Liquor of all colours and varieties spilled across the carpet.

The figure overturned the two chairs in the room then tossed the standard lamp aside, watching as it crashed into the electric fire. Satisfied with the destruction in the sitting room, the intruder headed for the kitchen.

There it pulled out drawers, scattering cutlery all over the floor. Plates were sent crashing to the ground until the lino resembled crazy paving. Glasses were swept from cabinets to shatter amidst the other debris. Once the cabinets were empty the intruder tugged on the doors, finally ripping them from their hinges, tossing the broken partitions about like matchwood.

The orgy of destruction continued upstairs.

Clothes were torn from hangers and shredded by the short-bladed knife. Pillows were ripped and slashed by the steel until feathers filled the air like snow. The bed itself was torn and gouged with a ferocity that made even the intruder pant heavily. The smell of sweat began to fill the air as the figure ventured downstairs again towards the one room which had so far escaped such awesomely destructive attention.

The intruder found the door of Miller's workroom locked but it was only a momentary inconvenience. The lock was picked with the blade and the figure kicked open the door, advancing into the room with an eagerness bordering on glee. As if it were drunk with its own ability to create damage, intoxicated by the ferocious rampage which it had enjoyed.

But now, inside the workroom, the intruder found that it was engulfed by new feelings.

The walls, bedecked with a legacy of death and suffering, seemed to close in on the intruder as surely as if they'd been pushed forward. The endless array of photos. The catalogue of black and white horror which decorated the room like some kind of vile wallpaper caused the figure to freeze. Mesmerized, the intruder looked slowly around.

Sightless eyes glared back accusingly.

The corpse with the head wound looked on impassively, mouth open in silent reproach.

The flayed woman sat immobile, body exposed to the gaze of this newcomer.

The burn victim, face a contorted blackened mess, looked on blindly with one gleaming eye.

The intruder crossed to the flayed woman and slowly reached out a hand to touch the synthetic flesh. It was as cold and clammy as death but the intruder moved an inquisitory hand further up the bloodied arm to the shoulder and then across to the breast. To the latex, prosthetic mound lined with fake veins and raw with nauseatingly realistic blood. The hand of the figure closed around that cold lump, savouring the feel of the imitation flesh.

The smell of latex was strong.

The intruder touched the hair, feeling the softness of the willowy strands even though they were nylon. Half of the rubber scalp was bald, burned black and hairless, modelled to perfection.

The breathing of the figure slowed as it moved away from the flayed woman to the burn victim, running shaking finger-tips over each twisted knot of fake flesh, every ragged scar and seared disfigurement.

Dear God, there was beauty in those abominations.

The intruder leaned close to the gunshot victim, pushing an index finger into the bullet hole itself, marvelling at the feel of the rubberized flesh. How cold yet pliant it felt.

How real.

The back of the head was open, the hair ripped away to expose what was meant to be the exit wound. And through that could be seen the greyish-red mess which represented the brain. This brain was hard rubber, yet it felt gloriously real. The intruder cupped the back of the model's head with one hand and gently toyed with the flaps of fake skin around the exit hole.

The severed head, propped up in a dish on top of a filing cabinet, looked on silently.

From the models, the intruder looked at the photos which covered the walls. The endless shots of death, pain and mutilation. A testament to the ultimate horror which faces everyone. Violent death.

Stabbings. Shootings. Burnings.

Every twisted deviation in human imagination was there, immortalized on shiny ten-by-eight.

Decapitation. Dismemberment. Evisceration.

The invention was endless.

But it was the figures which the intruder finally returned its attention to. Those life-size monuments to a mind on the verge of breakdown.

All thoughts of destruction passed from the mind of the intruder. These models were not to be destroyed.

The intruder moved close to the flayed woman again and stroked her bloodied cheek, enjoying the coldness of her artificial body.

Such beauty.

Fifty-one

The phone was about the only thing undamaged and Miller sat for what seemed like hours in the remains of his sitting room with the device cradled in his lap.

He had checked upstairs, checked the kitchen, and had found the terrible destruction everywhere except the workroom, but now he sat alone in the lounge, surrounded by debris, his face pale. Twice he raised the phone, ready to call the police, and twice he replaced the receiver, allowing himself a moment or two for thought.

The house was a shambles. Whoever had wrought the destruction had been thorough. The bastard. But why had they not wrecked the workroom? The question plagued Miller's mind. The things he valued most were in there, and yet it had remained untouched.

Almost.

He raised the receiver and punched out three nines, asking for the police when the voice at the other end enquired which service he required, but before he could give his name and address he pressed his fingers down on the cradle, cutting off the call. No, he told himself, this was no emergency. Besides, he wanted someone on the job he knew.

He jabbed out the digits which made up DI Stuart Gibson's number, waiting patiently for the phone to be picked up, gazing around at the wreckage in his sitting room. Finally, he heard Gibson's voice.

Miller told him what he had discovered, what had been done to his house. The extent of the damage.

Gibson said that he would be there as quickly as he could.

Miller hung up, then got to his feet and wandered down the corridor to his workroom, still puzzled that the intruder should have left his inner sanctum in such good order.

If it hadn't been for the fact that he knew he'd left the door locked, Miller might not even have known that anyone had been in there.

The rest of the house had been destroyed. Not ransacked, not searched. There had been no theft. Destruction had been the sole motive.

The effects man massaged his chin slowly.

But if that was so, why had the model of the flayed woman been taken?

'You're sure that's all that's gone?'

Gibson looked at his former colleague who was staring at the chair where the model had previously been sitting.

'There was seventy pounds upstairs in my bedroom,' Miller said. 'It wasn't touched. The figure was the only thing stolen.'

Around them, fingerprints men were busily dusting for any clues.

Miller wandered out of the room, back towards the lounge where more plain-clothes men were examining the wreckage, hoping to find even a strand of stray hair or a particle of material.

'I'd ask you to take a seat,' said Miller, 'but, as you can see, there aren't any.' He smiled thinly and took a swig from his hip flask.

'Can you think of anyone who might have done this, Frank?' Gibson wanted to know.

'No,' Miller lied, turning away from the DI. 'Look, Stuart, I don't care about the damage, I just want that mannequin back.'

'Why the hell is that so important. Your house is wrecked and all you're bothered about is some dummy.' He exhaled wearily. There was a long silence between the two men, finally broken by the policeman. 'How well do you know Terri Warner?'

Miller looked at Gibson warily.

'Do you know her as a friend? A boyfriend? A lover?' the DI persisted.

'What difference does it make *how* I know her? She's got

245

nothing to do with what happened here,' Miller said, gesturing around him.

'We've got her flat under surveillance and her phone's tapped. She said it was *you* who advised her to call us in.'

'That's right. I thought she needed protection. Whether your boys will be able to give it to her is another matter.'

'I've put Chandler on it. At least it keeps him out of *my* hair.' There was another long silence then the policeman continued. 'Do you know of anyone who might not want you to see her, Frank? I'm just wondering if whoever broke in here today was trying to warn you off. Maybe there's a boyfriend somewhere she hasn't told you about, somebody who fancies her and feels threatened by you.'

'You tell me, Stuart, you're the policeman. Like I said, I can live with this damage, but I want that fucking model found.' There was a hard edge to Miller's words that Gibson wasn't slow to pick up.

'What's so special about it?' he asked.

'All my work means a lot to me. The models that I keep here are particularly special.' He took another swig from his hip flask.

'I'd just like to know who would want to steal something like that,' Gibson said, bemused.

Miller didn't answer.

Fifty-two

DS Alan Chandler glanced at the clock on the dashboard and grunted irritably.

Nearly eight o'clock and still no sign of Terri Warner. He reached into his jacket pocket and pulled out a pack of Rothmans, lighting one. His companion, Sergeant Derek Grant, glanced across at his superior then returned his attention to the flats across the road. Grant was in his late thirties, on the thin side of slim, his closely-cropped hair making his head look a little too large. As he sat behind the wheel of the Astra he pulled absent mindedly at the hairs which sprouted from the large wart beneath his chin.

As if doubting the accuracy of the Astra's clock, Chandler looked at his own watch. It was almost eight. He muttered something under his breath. Either together or one at a time, he and Grant had been sitting watching the TV reporter's flat for the last eight hours. Every now and then they would drive to another position so as not to make it too obvious that they had the building under surveillance, but they always ensured that they could see at least one of the entrances. Every person who entered or left was noted at arrival and departure, but apart from the other residents of the small block few people had either visited or left.

Chandler chewed on his cigarette, winding down his window to allow some of the smoke to escape. Beside him he heard the slow, rhythmic breathing of his companion. They had exchanged scarcely a dozen words all day. Chandler knew why he had been assigned to this task. He knew that Gibson wanted him out of the way. But if Gibson thought that he was going to give up that easily then he was in for a shock. Eight killings and still his superior was no closer to pinning down the murderer. Chandler smiled. It could only be a matter of time before the DI was removed. He sucked hard on his cigarette and glanced up at the window of the flat once more. There were still no lights. No sign of movement. Where had she got to? He fumbled in his jacket pocket and pulled out the key to Terri's flat.

'Go and check it out,' he told Grant. 'See if there's been anyone about up there. She might even be back by now. She could have used the other entrance.'

Grant nodded and took the key.

Chandler watched as the tall sergeant made his way across the street to the building, disappearing through the main entrance. The DS waited a moment longer, then he too swung himself out of the car. He stretched, hearing his joints pop. The wind ruffled his hair and almost blew the cigarette from his mouth. He re-lit it then dug his hands in his pockets. To hell with this, he thought, he was going for a walk. He'd been sitting for most of the day, it was time he stretched his legs.

Sergeant Grant jabbed the '5' button and stepped into the lift as the doors slid open. He rode the car to the required floor, still holding the key to Terri's flat as he approached the door. He knocked twice, waiting, in case she had returned. But when he got no answer he gently inserted the key in the lock and turned it, easing the door open slowly. He called her name quietly as he entered. After all, he reasoned, she could be in the bath and not able to answer the door, but no, the flat was in darkness. The wind whistled loudly outside, rattling the windows in their frames. Grant thought about putting the light on but found that he could see adequately enough as he moved through the flat. He wandered around the sitting room, not quite sure what he was looking for. It was obvious that no one had broken into the flat, the door showed no sign of forced entry and it had still been securely locked when Grant entered.

He moved through into the kitchen.

A couple of mugs left in the sink to be washed up. But nothing out of place.

The sergeant moved back through the sitting room and checked the bathroom.

Outside, from the lobby, the lift began to rise.

First floor.

Second floor.

Grant pulled the cord which set the fluorescent in the bathroom flickering. He peered inside.

Third floor.

Fourth floor.

There was a short blue bathrobe hanging behind the door, still damp. Nothing else out of place. He decided to try the bedroom then make his way back down to the car.

The lift stopped at the fifth floor and the doors slid back silently, allowing the occupant to step out.

Grant decided to take his time returning to the car. He was certainly in no hurry to be back in Chandler's company. Grant had been on surveillance duty before. It was boring at the best of times, but this stint with Chandler was almost unbearable. He'd tried to make conversation with his superior, but the older man seemed uninterested in contact of any kind. Well, Grant decided, he was a policeman, not a public relations officer, if he didn't want to talk he didn't have to.

Grant never heard the footsteps outside the door of the flat.

He cast appraising eyes over the bedroom. At the nightdress which lay discarded on the duvet, the comb and brush on the bedside table along with a thick paperback.

The wardrobe door which was slightly ajar. The key lay on the carpet nearby.

Grant frowned and crossed to it wondering if Terri had merely forgotten to lock it or whether someone had indeed been inside the flat that day. Perhaps they had been searching for something in the wardrobe. The sergeant opened the door a little further and peered inside, squinting in the gloom.

The door of the flat opened and the newcomer slipped inside silently, crossing the sitting room to the kitchen, moving swiftly in the darkness.

Grant heard nothing, he was too engrossed in the contents of the wardrobe. He looked at the clothes which hung there, smelled the delicate scent of perfume on some of them. He opened the door a little wider.

The intruder gripped the skewer tightly and advanced stealthily back through the sitting room towards the bedroom.

A floorboard creaked.

Grant spun round, his heart beating a little faster. He stood in the silence a moment longer then turned back to the wardrobe, his eye caught by an object which lay in the bottom amongst the rows of shoes and boots. A small innocuous object but conspicuous by its presence. He bent to pick it up.

The intruder moved into the bedroom as silently as a panther stalking its prey, the skewer gripped in one fist, the other hand extended towards Grant's head.

The sergeant frowned as he looked at the cassette which he'd found in the bottom of the wardrobe. As he held it in his hand he noticed that there was a small cardboard box pushed into one corner of the unit. It was full of cassettes, some in their plastic cases, others loose.

Each one was marked with a number.

Grant drew one thumbnail across his forehead, his head tilted downward as if in prayer.

He was still in that position when the skewer was driven forward.

Powered with demonic force it pierced his left ear, the needle-sharp point searching out his brain as it was pushed deeper. His attacker's free hand clamped over his mouth, preventing him from uttering the cries of agony which he longed to give vent to. He struggled in the powerful grip, one hand grasping feebly for the steel prong which was embedded in his skull. He felt searing white-hot pain fill his head as the skewer was twisted madly, boring as deeply as if it had been attached to a drill bit. He felt blood oozing from his ear, running down the side of his neck to stain his shirt, and now his struggles became less frenzied. He uttered a low growl, deep in his throat, as the skewer was wrenched free, only to be rammed in again with even greater ferocity. Yet still there was surprisingly little blood. The second thrust, however, tore his ear lobe and more of the crimson fluid came from that fleshy bud than from his punctured brain. A mixture of glutinous clear fluid and watery blood dribbled from his ear. His body began to spasm uncontrollably as the skewer was driven in as far as the hook at its end. Seven inches of steel had transfixed the policeman's skull and the soft brain within.

His attacker stepped back, watching as he shuddered and writhed like an eel on a hot skillet, listening to the soft sputter as his body voided itself and the stench of excrement filled the room. Grant's eyelids fluttered wildly, flapping up and down with dizzying speed but the eyes behind them were already blind. Already beginning to glaze.

For what seemed like an eternity the intruder stood, watching fascinatedly as Grant died in agony, then the figure stepped over the prostrate body, picked up the cassette which Grant had been holding and tossed it back into the box.

That done, the figure turned and slipped out as easily as it had entered.

Terri Warner balanced the bag of groceries on the crook of one arm as she fumbled for her key with her free hand. She found it and pushed it into the lock.

The door swung open before she could turn the key.

Terri stepped back in surprise, almost dropping the carrier bag.

Should she enter? The darkness inside the flat looked forbidding. Maybe she should go back downstairs and fetch one of the men who were watching her. But when she'd pulled up a couple of minutes earlier she'd noticed that the Astra was empty. Neither of the policemen was in evidence.

Terri swallowed hard and reached inside the door, slapping on the light. She ventured inside a foot or two, aware of a pungent odour. A cloying stench which made her gag. She put down the groceries, trying to figure out where the smell was coming from. It took her just a few seconds to realize that its source was her bedroom. She paused for a moment, listening for any sounds of movement in the flat, but all she heard was the rushing of blood in her own ears.

She drew closer to the bedroom, pushing the door open.

'Oh God,' she murmured, gazing at the body of Sergeant

Grant, his eyes bulging wide as if registering his horror at his own sudden and painful death.

Terri took a step backwards, her eyes never leaving the corpse, her hand fumbling for the door knob, anxious to be out of the flat.

When she felt her hand touch flesh she turned and screamed.

Detective Sergeant Alan Chandler stood in the doorway, staring at her as she shrieked in horror, the sound reverberating off the walls.

It was then that the phone rang.

Fifty-three

'Don't speak. Just listen. I know this phone is bugged. I know the police are listening to this message and I know that they are watching. But so am I. I said that there were to be no police involved but you disobeyed. By the way, don't waste your time trying to trace this call. You won't be able to.

'Now listen to me. I want to meet the girl but I want to meet her alone. It's the girl that I want. Are you listening to me, Terri? It's you I want. You must meet me.

'I want Terri to go to the public phones at Hammersmith Tube station tomorrow night at ten o'clock. You'll be given instructions there on where to meet me. And remember, I'll be watching. The game is nearly over.

'I won't call again.'

Fifty-four

Commissioner Lawrence Chapman leaned forward and switched off the tape. A heavy silence descended, broken only by the occasional cough. DI Gibson rubbed his stomach self-consciously as he heard it rumble protestingly. A thin mist of cigarette smoke drifted lazily across the room adding to the claustrophobic atmosphere. It was as if the walls were gradually moving in, inch by inch, threatening to finally crush the large table which occupied the centre of the room.

Seated around it were Chapman, Gibson, Chandler, two other murder squad detectives and Sam Loomis. The balding pathologist was busy extracting particles of dirt from beneath his thumb-nail and seemed quite oblivious to what was happening around him. The policemen sat quietly, Gibson gritting his teeth as his stomach rumbled noisily once again. He glanced across at Chandler who was in the process of lighting up another cigarette.

'Has this been checked out?' Lawrence asked, holding up the cassette.

'The lab boys ran a voice-print on it. It doesn't match anything in our files,' Gibson told him. 'They did say that whoever made the tape had some knowledge of electronics and access to specialized equipment.'

Lawrence looked puzzled, his brow wrinkling.

'That message was recorded at half-speed then played back through some kind of distortion device.'

'What do you mean "played back",' Lawrence asked.

'When the message came through on Miss Warner's answer-phone we assumed it was the killer speaking directly, but it wasn't. He was playing a tape of his voice straight down the phone.'

'Well, it beats putting a hankie over the mouthpiece,' said Chandler flippantly.

Chapman shot him a warning glance.

'What I'd also like to know is why the killer wasn't seen either entering or leaving Miss Warner's flat,' he snapped. 'Chandler, you were supposed to be keeping a watch on the place.'

'It was impossible to cover both entrances at one time, sir,' the DS said, moving uncomfortably in his seat.

Gibson looked on with ill-concealed glee.

'Why did you go up to the flat when Sergeant Grant had already gone to investigate?'

'I thought that Grant was taking too long.'

'You left both entrances unguarded,' Chapman rasped.

'DI Gibson only assigned two of us to surveillance, sir,' Chandler countered, looking at his superior with a sly smirk.

'Why only two men, Gibson?'

'I felt that there was a danger the killer might break off contact if Miss Warner was being too heavily guarded or watched,' the DI said, glaring at Chandler for fleeting moments.

Chapman nodded, his eyes still on the cassette. 'So it was the same killer who murdered Sergeant Grant?' the commissioner said, looking this time at Loomis.

'I have no reason to suppose otherwise,' the pathologist told him. 'The killer was right-handed, that's consistent with the other victims, and what's more he was very careful. Grant was killed quickly, he died almost instantly but he was stabbed so the murderer didn't end up covered in blood. Inserting the skewer through the ear would have caused maximum damage but with minimum blood-loss, otherwise the killer would have been forced to leave the building drenched.'

'Bastard,' muttered one of the other detectives. 'I knew Grant, his wife was expecting a kiddie any time.'

Chapman ignored the remark, content to tap his nails on the table-top.

'I think we should let the girl make the rendezvous, sir,' said Gibson. 'Let her meet him.'

Chapman looked at the DI aghast.

'You're mad,' the older man said, flatly. 'He'll kill her.'

'It might be our only chance of catching him. She could be tailed.'

'You heard the message. He wants her alone.' The commissioner made a hopeless gesture with his hands.

'I'm not talking about our blokes tailing her,' the DI announced. 'She's pretty close to a guy called Frank Miller and she might feel safer if she was being tailed by someone she trusted. He used to work for the Yard as a photographer a couple of years back. I want Miller to do the tailing.'

Chandler grunted indignantly but Gibson ignored him and continued.

'We wire Miss Warner with a microphone so she can talk to Miller. We give *him* a two-way and he relays information to *us*. Miller follows *her*. We follow *him*.'

'Will Miller do it?' Chapman wanted to know.

'Yes, I already asked him.'

'That's two people's lives we're risking now, Gibson. This had better work, because I'll tell you now, if anything goes wrong I'm holding you responsible. Understood?'

The DI nodded.

'Does Miller know how to use a gun?' asked Chapman. 'If not, show him. It's best to be prepared for every eventuality. And I want the back-up team armed too.' He glanced at his watch. 'It's four o'clock now. We've got six hours before the killer contacts her again.'

The weapon felt surprisingly light in his hand as Miller hefted the Smith and Wesson .38 before him. He thumbed back the hammer, listening to the metallic click, watching as the cylinder revolved to bring a shell beneath the firing pin. He raised it towards the target, closing one eye, squinting down the foresight in an effort to draw a bead on the man-shaped figure. He pulled the trigger.

The .38 slammed back against the heel of his hand, the vibration travelling up his arm with a ferocity that hurt his shoulder. The bang was deafening and his nostrils were immediately assailed by the pungent odour of cordite. The bullet powered into the sandbags behind the target.

Beside him, Gibson chuckled.

'It's not like it is in films, Frank,' he said. 'These are real guns. Real noise and a hell of a recoil. Try steadying your firing hand with your free hand. And squeeze the trigger, don't jerk it.'

Miller braced himself and fired again.

The bullet missed again.

He squeezed the trigger once more.

'Aim for the broadest part of the body,' shouted Gibson above the roar of the pistol.

The next shot clipped the shoulder of the cut-out.

The fourth one hit the leg.

The fifth blasted a fist-sized hole in the stomach of the figure.

Miller squeezed again but the hammer slammed down on an empty chamber. He pushed the cylinder release, flipped it out and ejected the spent cartridge cases before re-loading.

'Remember, Frank, you're only to use that gun if you've absolutely no choice, we want him alive if possible. Only use it if you or Miss Warner are in danger, if your lives are threatened. You never know, he might even chicken out if he sees a gun.'

Miller raised his eyebrows.

'And he might have one of his own,' he replied, firing off another round at the target. It hit home in the chest area. So did the second shot. And the third.

Miller paused, his hand aching, his ears ringing.

'Just make sure I've got plenty of ammunition,' Miller said.

He fired off the remaining two rounds and re-loaded.

Twenty minutes later he was still there.

It was 5.39 p.m.

Fifty-five

Terri Warner lifted her arms as the surveillance man wound the
piece of thin cable around her torso, apologizing whenever he
got too close to her breasts. By the time he'd finished his face
was bright red and he kept his gaze lowered as he attached the
tiny microphone to the lapel of her jacket.

Sitting on the bed in the hotel room, Miller watched as the
policeman completed his task then stepped back almost thank-
fully. He handed Miller an earpiece which the effects man
pushed into position.

'Say something,' he instructed Terri.

'Like what?' she said and Miller grunted in pain, clapping one
hand to his ear.

'That's enough,' he said, smiling thinly. 'I'm not deaf.'

'The microphone is very sensitive,' the surveillance man told
them. 'It'll pick up a whisper. But it's only any good for about a
quarter of a mile, any further than that and you'll break
contact.'

They both nodded.

'Miller, you keep in touch with us using this,' Gibson said,
handing him a compact Motorola two-way. 'As soon as Terri
makes contact with the killer on the phone, as soon as he's given
the location of the rendezvous, you let us know.'

Miller nodded.

'What sort of distance are we talking about with the two-
way?' he asked.

'Three or four miles,' said the surveillance man.

'Reece will be in the car with us in case you have any
problems,' Gibson said, indicating the other policeman who

258

turned red once more.

He looked at his watch.

9.06 p.m.

'Terri, it's my guess that he'll bounce you all round London to make sure you're not being tailed,' said the DI. 'From one location to the next. Just make sure you tell Miller everything the killer tells you.'

'I'm not stupid,' she said quietly.

'No, and neither is the bastard who's after you,' snapped the policeman. 'Miller, if by some chance you do lose her then let us know straightaway. There'll be cars standing by.'

Miller pulled the hip flask from his pocket and took a hefty swig.

'Before you ask, Stuart,' he said. 'I *do* need it.'

'I was going to ask if there was any to spare,' said the policeman wearily.

Miller grinned and handed him the flask, watching as he drank from it, wiping his mouth with the back of his hand. He handed it back. Miller, for his own part, pulled the .38 from his belt and checked that it was fully loaded.

'Remember,' Gibson said, 'it's only to be used if you've got no possible alternative.'

'It's not you who's going to be going up against him, Stuart,' Miller reminded his former colleague.

A heavy silence descended, broken by the DI.

'It's time we took our positions. You leave when you're ready. Just make sure you're at those phones at Hammersmith by ten.'

'I will,' Terri assured him. 'Maybe I should have my camera crew with me,' she added, her attempt at humour failing to lighten even her own spirits.

Gibson and Reece left them alone in the room.

'Maybe it ought to be me who has the gun?' Terri said.

'Why? You'll probably try to interview him, not shoot him,' Miller said sarcastically.

Terri exhaled deeply and wandered across to the window, looking out into the darkness.

'He's imitated the killing methods of eight other murderers,' she said. 'I wonder who he's thinking of copying next?'

'Whichever killer specialized in TV reporters, I should think.'

Terri laughed humourlessly.

'Perhaps I should get you to look at one of *my* photos,' she suggested, a trace of sarcasm in her voice. 'You can tell me whether or not he's going to kill me.'

Miller didn't answer.

Terri continued gazing out into the night.

Gibson slid into the passenger seat of the Astra and glanced across at Chandler who was puffing on a Rothmans.

'Don't lose him,' the DI said.

'Why, in case the killer gets the girl or you lose your job?' the DS answered, smiling crookedly.

'If I go down, Chandler,' Gibson hissed, 'I'll make bloody sure I take you with me.'

The DS took one last drag on his cigarette then ground it out in the ashtray. A plume of smoke rose mournfully to join the cloud which already filled the car.

In the back seat Reece was fiddling with the two-way, checking frequencies.

'We're ready,' he said. 'It's up to Miller and the girl now.'

In the hotel room Miller and Terri checked their watches. She fastened her jacket, ensuring that Miller could still hear her. He told her that he could hear her heart beating through the earpiece.

Miller watched her leave, waited five minutes then took the lift down to the ground floor, walked out and slid behind the wheel of his own car.

'Moving,' he said into the two-way, and swung the Granada out into traffic.

It was 9.37.

Fifty-six

The man glanced at her as he passed, slowing his pace slightly, but he continued walking, on towards the ticket machines.

Terri swallowed hard and looked first at her watch then at the row of phones before her. Two or three were broken, the shattered receiver of the one closest to her dangling by the cord. Litter was piled in the bottom of some booths, and a beer can, blown by the wind, rolled gently back and forth, the metallic rattle echoing around the virtually deserted entrance to the station.

The tiles on the floor were coated with filth. The place smelt like a urinal.

Terri shuffled her feet and waited, glancing at the pieces of paper which were stuck inside the black-painted canopies that covered each phone. Numbers to ring. Names. As if each booth were some kind of miniature bill board for people to advertise in.

Phone this number for a sensual massage, said one.

Fresh young model, another proclaimed.

She glanced at each one.

Black Dominatrix wants willing slaves, screamed a third, written in yellow ink.

There was a familiar rumble as, below her, a train pulled in.

Terri glanced at her watch again.

Almost ten o'clock.

Would he ring on time?

Which phone would ring?

She pulled up the collar of her jacket and waited.

261

Miller took another swig from his hip flask and pressed the earpiece more firmly into his ear. All he could hear was the low thudding of Terri's heart.

She had spoken briefly as she'd climbed out of her car, but that had been more than ten minutes ago. He hadn't heard a word since, only the rumbling and rustling as she moved, fastening and unfastening her jacket. He looked at the dashboard clock.

9.58.

The two-way beside him crackled loudly and Miller snatched it up.

'Any contact yet?'

He recognized the voice as Gibson's.

'Nothing,' he told the DI.

There was a long silence and Miller looked at the two-way, wondering if the policeman was going to speak again. Above him, traffic rumbled noisily over the flyover and he cursed as a plane went over, adding its own deafening sound to that of the cars and other vehicles which swept past him.

He heard something in the earpiece.

Terri's voice. Distant and crackling as if someone were screwing up a paper bag beside her.

'. . . which one he'll use.'

Miller tapped the earpiece, muttering angrily to himself when he found that some of her words were slipping away.

'. . . almost ten. I hope you can hear me, Frank . . . calling soon . . . this place . . . deserted.'

'Jesus Christ,' Miller hissed, snatching up the two-way. 'Gibson, come in. The bloody signal from the microphone is breaking up.'

'Can you still hear her?' the DI wanted to know.

'At the moment yes, just about.' He looked at the dashboard clock once more.

9.59.

Terri's voice came in again, hissing in his ear along with a rasp of static which made him wince, but at least it was clearer this time.

'I wish he'd hurry up and ring, I'm freezing,' she said.

Miller took another swig from his hip flask.

'Almost time,' Terri said again.

There was another crackle of static. Miller banged the wheel in fury.

Her voice sounded thin, broken up by the static.

10.00.

'Come on, come on,' he hissed, as the sound crackled even more loudly in his ear.

Silence.

He snatched up the two-way.

'Gibson, I've lost the signal,' he barked. 'I can't hear her.'

Fifty-seven

Miller was half-way out of the car when he heard Terri's voice again.

'Thank God,' he whispered, then into the two-way, 'She's transmitting again.'

He clambered back into his car and started the engine, listening to the instructions which were coming through the earpiece.

'He wants me to go to a place called Gateway Towers,' said Terri. 'It's in Shoreditch. It's a block of flats, it's been empty for about six months. I hope you're hearing me, Frank.'

'Loud and clear,' said Miller, guiding his car out into traffic.

'Have you got the destination yet?' Gibson asked.

Miller didn't answer.

'Can you hear me?' the DI repeated. 'Have you lost the signal again?'

Still Miller remained silent, more intent on trying to pick out Terri's car in the mêlée of traffic ahead of him. The tail-lights of other vehicles looked like so much neon in the darkness and he blinked hard to clear the hazy film which seemed to have settled over his left eye. The haziness cleared and he drove on.

'Miller.' Gibson's voice was more urgent now. 'Can you hear me?'

Finally he picked up the two-way.

'I hear you.'

'What the hell are you playing at? Couldn't you hear me?' Gibson rasped. 'Did she give you the location? Where is he going to meet her?'

Miller hesitated a second longer.

'The Band Stand in Kensington Gardens,' he said quickly, then switched off the radio.

In the pursuing Astra Gibson shook the two-way violently.

'Miller,' he shouted.

'He's turned it off,' said Reece.

Gibson gritted his teeth angrily.

'Why, for Christ's sake?' he snarled, then he reached across Chandler and grabbed the radio in the car. 'All units to Kensington Gardens, the Band Stand.'

'But we promised them no interference,' said Reece.

'This isn't a game any more,' snapped Gibson angrily. 'And I also want all units to be on the look-out for a dark brown Mini Clubman, registration number OVV 368P, and a silver-grey Ford Granada, registration number SHK 665Y. They're to be stopped on sight.' Gibson sat back in the passenger seat, his face set in an expression of determination. 'Now we'll see,' he muttered.

Miller tossed the two-way onto the back seat and drove on. As he did so, he pulled the .38 from his pocket and once more checked that all the chambers were full.

He drove on.

Bob Johnson had sat looking at the phone for what seemed like an eternity, a slight smile on his face, but now he got to his feet, pulled on his jacket and headed for the door. He guessed that the journey would take him about thirty minutes.

John Ryker had slammed the receiver down, almost snapping the object in half. He ran a scarred hand through his hair and paced back and forth agitatedly, the anger seething within him.

It was time to settle things once and for all.

He headed towards the door, picking up his car keys on the way.

The time had come.

Fifty-eight

The concrete and glass edifice of Gateway Towers thrust upwards into the night sky like an accusatory finger.

It was a derelict. A monument to high speed building and quick profits. The manufactured leviathan rose from the street below as if pushed from the bowels of the earth by some primeval force.

The deserted building stood in total darkness.

Terri brought the Mini to a halt and climbed out, fumbling on the back seat for the torch which she had remembered to bring. It was large and felt more like a truncheon, and the weight reassured her as she approached the main doors of the high-rise. The glass in the doors and windows as high as the fifth floor had been broken. Some of it lay on the pavement outside but most was inside the building. Covered by a layer of dust in which Terri fancifully thought she could have carved rather than written her name.

She pushed the front doors which swung back to admit her, swallowing her up. The blackness closed around her and with it came the stench of neglect and decay. Of urine and excrement. Of stale vomit. For if no council residents were allowed to live in the tower then it had become something of a sanctuary for the down-and-outs who lived in the area. It was their empty bottles and cans that littered the entrance.

Terri moved further into the hall, her footsteps muffled by the thick carpet of dust. It clung to her like filthy snow and she put a hand over her face in an effort to prevent the swirling dust from penetrating her nostrils too badly.

Spray-can Picassos had been busy on the vast canvas offered

by the block's walls. Drawings seemed to vie with one another in offensiveness. Graffiti, some scrawled on with charcoal, some painted on, offered various observations on life in the gutter:

MAGGIE IS A FUCKING BITCH
THE QUEEN IS DEAD

Terri moved towards the lift, the doors of which gaped open like a yawning mouth. She recoiled quickly as she saw a pile of excrement in one corner of the disused car.

To her right was a flight of stairs and it was these she began to climb, the torch beam cutting through the darkness, particles of dust twisting and swirling in the light. Here she moved more slowly, aware of how loud the sound of her high heels sounded in the oppressive silence. She took the stairs slowly, eyes focused ahead, ears alert for any sound of movement.

'I hope you can hear me, Frank,' she whispered. 'And I hope you're close. I'm almost at the landing to the first floor. No sign of anyone yet.'

She reached the landing and peered down the corridor which led to the now empty flats. All the doors were securely locked, and after trying the first five or six Terri decided to go up another floor. She turned a corner and found that the stairs were on her left this time. She shone the torch over them, advancing slowly.

Something moved above her.

On the floor above she heard movement and, for long seconds, froze.

'I think he's here,' she said softly, aware of her blood rushing in her ears, her heart pounding against her ribs. 'I'm going up to the next floor.'

As she began ascending, Terri thought how ridiculous the situation was. She was alone in the derelict building except for a man who had murdered nine people and now, instead of turning and running for her life, she was climbing higher to meet him. The logical move would have been to get out, but instead she continued to climb.

'I really hope you're close, Frank,' she whispered once more.

She reached the second landing.

'I'm on the second floor now,' she said. 'Ahead of me, two of the doors are open. I'm going on.'

Miller checked his speedometer and noticed that the needle was nudging forty-five, but he didn't slow up. He had heard every word uttered by Terri since she'd entered the derelict tower. He was less than five minutes drive from it now. He dared not slow up.

He didn't even notice the police car pull out behind him.

The driver of the pursuing vehicle peered through the darkness at the car, a frown creasing his forehead.

'Silver-grey Ford Granada,' he said to his colleague. 'What was that number we were told to watch for?'

His companion repeated the registration number.

'Christ, you'd better call in. I think we've found him.'

The two cars sped on.

'What the hell does he think he's playing at?' snarled Gibson to himself. 'Why did he tell us *this* location?'

He gripped the car radio tightly then flicked the transmitter switch.

'Are you sure it's the same car?' he asked the policeman.

The uniformed man repeated the registration number.

'What's he doing in Shoreditch?' Gibson said angrily. Then into the radio: 'Look, you keep on his tail, don't lose him. There'll be more men there in a few minutes but you're not to apprehend the driver of that car. Is that understood?'

Gibson banged the dashboard angrily.

'I should have known,' he said quietly. 'Come on, Chandler, turn this car around and let's go, otherwise we're going to end up with two more bodies on our hands tonight.'

'Two?' said Reece, looking puzzled.

Gibson didn't answer. He allowed his own hand to move to the bulge inside his coat where the 9mm Browning Automatic nestled in its shoulder holster. He looked at his watch. It was 10.47.

Already he had the unshakeable feeling that they were too late.

Fifty-nine

The first of the doors opened easily, swinging back on hinges that hadn't tasted oil for many months. The high pitched squeal made Terri wince and she looked around anxiously, the torch beam cutting swathes through the impenetrable blackness.

She paused in the corridor for a moment then looked inside the room. Apart from a couple of empty cardboard boxes, it was empty. In fact, the building reminded her of a gigantic, futuristic crypt. Silent and forbidding, a home for shadows.

And perhaps something more tangible.

Ahead of her the second door opened a fraction and Terri froze, aiming the torch at the movement, trying to pick out shapes in the cold white light.

From beneath her she heard footsteps.

And now ahead of her she saw signs that the dust which coated the floor had been disturbed.

Someone had walked this corridor before her. And recently too.

She advanced cautiously towards the open door, feeling a chill breeze nipping at her face while below her silence descended again.

Terri reached the open door and pushed it, directing the torch inside.

A dark shape moved in one corner of the room and Terri barely stifled a gasp.

The cat hissed at her and dropped the mouse it had been holding in its jaws. With one leap it bounded up on to the window-sill, eyes glowing yellow in the light of the torch.

Terri let out a relieved breath and turned away from the door.

At the end of the corridor two firedoors led to another flight of steps which she knew would take her up to the third floor. She paused a moment, noticing that the dust was not disturbed ahead of her. In fact, she was so taken with this latest discovery, all other thoughts seemed to leave her mind. She directed the torch at the floor.

Behind her, another of the doors opened slowly.

Miller took the steps two at a time, stumbling twice in the enveloping blackness, cursing as he fell on the stone steps, but he picked himself up and ran on, the .38 now gripped in his fist as he hurtled towards the next flight. Towards Terri.

Terri moved ahead slowly, torch aimed ahead of her, unaware of the dark shape which was moving into the corridor behind her, moving away from the room as if detaching itself from the blackness. She heard no footsteps because the dust disguised them.

She heard only silence and the thudding of her own heart.

Until finally, she heard the voice.

'Terri.'

She spun round, torch dropping from her terrified fingers, shattering on the ground, but in that split second before the light went out she had seen the face of the man who now barred her way.

The face of the man whom she had expected to find in this place tonight.

Bob Johnson was smiling.

Sixty

In the darkness of the corridor, Johnson was almost invisible. The only light came from the open door of the room, illuminating his features as he moved towards her.

Terri took a step backwards.

'I've been waiting,' he told her.

She continued to back away, glancing past Johnson towards the head of the stairs beyond.

She heard the sound of footsteps.

Growing louder.

Johnson heard them too and his face twisted in anger.

'What's going on?' he rasped.

Terri said nothing but merely continued her retreat, moving slowly through the dust which stuck to her shoes and swirled around her feet like noxious fog.

Johnson's hands tightened into fists and he glared at Terri, the knot of muscles at the side of his jaw throbbing madly.

'We were meant to be alone here,' he hissed.

The sound of footsteps was growing in volume.

From below, the beam of a torch bounced across the wall in an erratic pattern as Miller drew nearer.

He reached the landing, gun in one hand, torch in the other.

'You fucking bitch,' snarled Johnson, looking first at Terri then at the advancing Miller. 'You set me up.'

'Kill him, Frank,' Terri screamed, throwing herself to the ground.

Johnson let out a roar of rage and lunged towards Terri, but Miller steadied himself and fired.

The shot sounded thunderous in the confines of the corridor, the noise reverberating around the deserted building as if it had been some kind of echo chamber. The muzzle-flash flared brilliant white, blinding Miller momentarily, but he squeezed the trigger once more, the .38 bucking wildly in his hand as it spat out its lethal load.

The second shot caught Johnson in the chest, to the right of his sternum.

The bullet shattered two ribs as it powered into him, tearing its way through a lung before exploding from his back, punching an exit hole the size of a fist. Blood and gobbets of lung tissue sprayed from the wound as Johnson went down, his life fluid spilling in a widening pool in the thick dust.

Terri screamed and rolled away from him as he shot out a hand in an attempt to grab her leg, forcing himself up onto his knees as Miller took aim a third time.

He hesitated, terrified of hitting Terri in the darkness but her screams of fear seemed to spur him on and he fired again.

His next shot hit Johnson squarely in the back, pulverizing a kidney and ripping away a sizeable piece of flesh. Blood spurted from the wound, and as he opened his mouth to shout his pain, Johnson tasted blood in his mouth. Seconds later it spilled over his lips. He fell forward, face down, his hands twitching spasmodically.

Miller lowered the revolver slowly and shone the torch over the prone body, allowing the beam to rest on the bloodied face. His eyes were open but already beginning to glaze over, particles of dust settling on the whites. A trickle of blood was running from his left nostril, like a crimson ribbon.

Miller edged his way around the body, extending a hand to help Terri to her feet. She grabbed him, almost knocking the gun from his grasp, and Miller heard her sobs as she clung to him. Without taking his eyes from Johnson's body, he supported her past the bullet-torn carcass towards the stairs. Looking back as he reached them, staring for long seconds at the body. Then, together, he and Terri began to descend.

Her sobs slowly subsided and she paused to wipe her face, wiping both tears and dirt away.

'Are you all right?' Miller asked, his hand aching from the

vicious recoil of the .38.

She nodded.

Outside they heard the sound of a police siren.

'How the hell did they find us?' Miller mused aloud, slipping the gun back into his pocket. He put his arm around Terri's shoulder and they walked the remaining few steps to the first floor landing.

Beneath them they heard the first of the policemen come crashing into the building.

Behind them, they were oblivious to the fact that Bob Johnson, his clothes soaked in blood, now stood watching.

For unbearable seconds he stood there, supported by the balustrade, his breath coming in wheezing gasps where the bullet had torn open his lung. But then he gritted his teeth, his eyes narrowing in rage, and with a roar of rage he launched himself at the couple.

It was as if Johnson had been fired from a catapult. He flew through the air, momentarily defying gravity, his blood-spattered body seemingly suspended on invisible wires until he crashed into them. Knocking them both to the ground.

The impact stunned Miller and he felt a jarring pain in his skull as his head was slammed against the concrete steps. Blood burst from the cut which opened on his forehead, and as he rolled over, reaching for the .38, he felt strong hands being fastened around his throat.

Despite his wounds, Johnson seemed to possess almost superhuman strength, and he dug his thumbs into Miller's throat, simultaneously banging the effects man's head against the concrete. Miller blinked hard as white light flashed before his eyes. He struggled to reach the gun and succeeded in pulling it free of his pocket but Johnson released his grip long enough to grab Miller's arm, shaking it until the revolver flew from his grasp and went skittering away down the stairs.

Terri, herself dazed from the attack, struggled after it, looking back to see that Miller was weakening rapidly.

She heard the police pounding up the stairs but her only concern was finding the gun.

In the gloom she fumbled about, her hand finally closing

around the pistol. Terri scurried back up the stairs, using both thumbs to pull back the hammer on the weapon, drawing closer to the insane tableau before her.

Johnson raised Miller's head a few inches from the ground then slammed it down with a force that threatened to split his skull. Blood was now spreading from beneath Miller's head and he felt sick, waves of unconsciousness now flooding over him. It felt as if someone was pumping his head full of air. He tried to breathe but the thick dust filled his nostrils and all the time those huge hands gripped his throat and squeezed.

Miller found himself looking up into the maniacal face of Johnson. It was a face that belonged to a madman. His features were twisted, spattered with blood, but, as Miller fought back as best he could, those features began to dissolve before him. He was blacking out.

He saw, through a red haze, Terri standing behind Johnson, the gun lowered, pointing at his head.

Then he was sure that it was all over. He felt his bowels loosen. Felt his senses slipping away from him.

Terri pressed the barrel of the revolver against the back of Johnson's head and fired.

The explosion was deafening.

From such close range the result was devastating.

The top of Johnson's head seemed to explode like a volcano, the portions of his skull propelled by the bullet rising into the air along with an eruption of blood and sticky brain matter. His mouth fell open and locked in that position, his eyes still open as if registering surprise that half of his head had been blown away. Fragments of bone and thick slicks of blood spattered the wall, mingling with the flux of brain to form a monstrous collage.

Beneath him, Miller was aware of the crimson mess showering his face, but it seemed not to bother him. He was too close to unconsciousness for that.

All he knew was that the vice-like grip on his throat suddenly eased as Johnson pitched forward, crashing to the ground on his face, revealing the hole in the back of his head. Miller could have fitted both fists inside it.

Terri dropped the pistol and lurched against the balustrade, peering down into the blackness to see two uniformed policemen charging towards her. They were speaking but she didn't hear the words.

Neither did Miller, he rolled onto his side, away from the corpse of Johnson. When he tried to swallow Miller felt agonizing pain in his throat and he massaged his Adam's apple with one bloodied hand. He smelt the stench of blood, of excrement. Dust filled his mouth and nostrils as he rolled onto his stomach but he was past caring.

He blacked out.

Sixty-one

'What motive did Johnson have for committing the murders?' said Miller, tentatively touching his bandaged scalp.

'How much did *you* know about him, Terri,' Gibson wanted to know.

She could only shrug.

The policeman exhaled deeply and rubbed his eyes. He glanced up at the wall clock.

It was almost 1.15 a.m.

'Maybe this isn't the time to start sifting through this mess,' he said, softly.

'The killer's dead, Stuart,' said Miller. 'Isn't that all that matters at the moment?'

'I'd like you both to come in tomorrow and make full statements,' Gibson said. 'How are you feeling, Frank?'

Miller touched his head again.

'I'm all right,' he said. 'Nothing a drink won't cure.'

He and Terri got up from the table where they'd been sitting and made for the door.

'You look like *you* could do with some sleep too,' Miller observed, looking at his former colleague.

Gibson shrugged and got to his feet, opening the door for them. He watched them walk down the corridor towards the lift then he turned back into the room and looked at Chandler. The DS was shuffling uncomfortably in his seat, unable to maintain eye-to-eye contact with his superior.

'It looks as if you'll have to wait a lot longer for my job now, doesn't it?' Gibson rasped. 'This case is wrapped up. All the angles and the motive might still be out of our reach at the moment, but like Miller said, we've got our killer. Bad luck, Chandler.' The DI smiled and pushed the door open, motioning his colleague to leave. 'Now get out, before I kick you out.'

The DS got to his feet and hurried from the room.

Gibson crossed to the table and sat down once again, looking at the photos of Johnson, and of his victims.

So, it was over at last.

He almost smiled. Apart from the paperwork.

Miller swayed uncertainly as he stood beside his car, a sudden stab of pain from his injured skull causing him to suck in a sharp breath.

'Maybe I'd better drive,' said Terri, walking round to the driver's side of the Granada. She slid behind the wheel and unlocked the door, letting Miller inside. He allowed his head to loll backwards. She studied his profile for a second, noticing how drained of colour he looked. 'The doctor did say that you weren't to be left alone for the next twenty-four hours. Have you got a spare room?'

Miller smiled but didn't look at her.

'Thanks for the offer,' he said. Then, looking at her, 'There's something else I ought to thank you for too.'

Terri looked vague.

'You saved my life,' he told her. 'Johnson would have killed me too if you hadn't found that gun.'

She didn't answer but merely started the engine and swung the car out of its parking space. Despite the late hour, the streets were still relatively busy and Miller guessed that the trip home would take about thirty minutes.

'What will you do now?' he asked as she drove. 'About work? I mean, with Johnson gone . . .' The sentence trailed off.

'They'll be looking for someone to take his place,' Terri said.

'What about you?'

She shook her head.

'I don't think I'd want the job. I think I'll take a couple of months off, try to forget about it all. I know that won't be easy.' She almost smiled. 'Maybe I'll sell my story to the newspapers and retire on what they pay me.'

277

Miller didn't answer.

Terri looked across at him and noticed that his eyes were closed.

'Frank,' she called softly, reaching across to touch his hand.

Miller didn't wake up until they were five minutes from his home.

He stretched, his bones cracking loudly, then apologized for dozing off. It must have been the bang on the head, he reasoned. At least the nagging pain which had been gnawing at his skull seemed to have eased somewhat. Terri parked the car in the road and the two of them walked to the front door of the house. Miller found his keys and unlocked the door, slapping on the light as he entered the hall.

'Jesus Christ,' he gasped, staring at what confronted him.

Terri could not find the breath to scream, her eyes bulged madly in their sockets, riveted to the vision which greeted her.

Suspended in the middle of the hall, hanging from a thick rope which had been secured to the banister ballustrade, was the body of a woman.

She had been expertly and painstakingly flayed so that not one inch of skin remained to cover the network of muscles and bones beneath.

It took Miller just a second to realize that the bloodied figure was the one which had been stolen from his house two days earlier.

It was as Miller moved towards the model that John Rÿker stepped into view.

He was carrying a large double-edged knife which glinted menacingly in the light.

Ryker smiled crookedly.

'Welcome home.'

Sixty-two

'Shut the door, Terri,' Miller said quietly, his eyes never leaving Ryker.

'Do as he says, Terri,' Ryker echoed, chuckling. He eyed the TV reporter approvingly. 'I've seen you before haven't I? On TV? Very nice.' Then he turned his attention back to Miller. 'I told you the other day that we had business to attend to but you wouldn't listen, would you?'

'It was you who wrecked my house?' said Miller but it sounded more like a statement than a question.

'Let's cut the bullshit, Miller, I want my money now,' Ryker snapped.

'And I told you before I haven't got it.'

The older man stepped forward, bringing the knife up.

Terri stepped closer to Miller.

'What money is he talking about?' she wanted to know.

'Money for services rendered,' Ryker said to her, without taking his eyes off Miller. 'Money for helping to make him one of the best effects men in the business, money for supplying him with props.' He chuckled and reached for the leg of the model. 'Money for risking my fucking neck.' Ryker pressed the knife into the thigh of the dangling model, cutting deeply from femur to kneecap. He prised the latex open as if he were a surgeon, then, using the razor-sharp point, he carved a large portion of the rubber skin away, revealing what lay beneath.

'Money for robbing graves,' Ryker snarled and tore open the model's leg.

Hidden beneath the latex but now visible was real human flesh.

279

It was pale and shrivelled but well preserved. It gave off little or no smell.

As Ryker spoke he carved away more of the prosthetic flesh.

Miller could only watch as more of the real body beneath was exposed.

'"I need a heart, Ryker,"' the older man mimicked, sardonically. '"Get me one, I'll pay you well. I need a baby, Ryker. Get me one. Get me a body, Ryker. Get me an arm, Ryker".'

He tore off a large piece of the latex, exposing the lower abdomen of the dangling corpse. The flesh was mottled blue and green in places and now both Miller and Terri detected a powerful smell of decay which had previously been masked by the fake flesh.

Ryker slashed wildly at the corpse, hacking off one of the fingers.

Terri moved to one side, edging slowly away from the door, her eyes never leaving Ryker as he hacked and slashed at the body.

'Get my money, Miller,' he snarled. 'Or I'll carve you up like this bloody dummy.' He looked at Terri. 'You *and* your girlfriend.'

Miller took advantage of the brief respite, and as Ryker turned to look at Terri he stepped forward, shoving the corpse as hard as he could.

The grisly object swung forward and slammed into Ryker who was knocked flying by the impact.

The knife fell from his hand and skidded across the floor.

He leapt for it, his hand reaching for the deadly blade, but Miller too reacted quickly and brought the heel of his shoe crashing down on the older man's outstretched fingers.

There was a loud crack as two of the digits were shattered and Ryker yelped in pain, rolling away, trying to get to his feet.

The body, propelled by Miller's push, continued to swing back and forth like a monstrous pendulum.

Miller ran at the older man, hitting him with his shoulder, the impact sending him hard into the wall.

Ryker grunted, winded by the collision, but he steadied himself against the nearby table, his hand closing around the tall glass vase which occupied its centre. Hefting the ornament before him like a club, he advanced, holding one side, wincing every time he sucked in a breath.

Still the corpse swung to and fro, each fresh movement bringing with it the stench of decay. The sightless eyes gazed at the tableau below indifferently.

'I'll kill you,' hissed Ryker and ran at Miller, bringing the vase down with bone-crushing force.

Miller moved, but not quickly enough.

The heavy piece of crystal struck his shoulder and he sucked in a painful breath as he felt his collar-bone snap. A white-hot pain enveloped his upper body and his left arm suddenly went numb. Every time he flexed his fingers it felt as if someone were sticking red hot needles into his flesh, but he rolled back, that injured arm reaching for the fallen knife.

Terri could only look on helplessly as Ryker hurled the vase down at Miller.

Miller instinctively raised his arm to shield his face and felt another horrendous impact on his forearm this time. The vase shattered, showering him with crystal splinters, some of which cut his face.

Ryker was upon him immediately, driving a powerful kick into his groin.

Miller doubled up, but as he did so his hand closed over the shaft of the knife and he sprang forward, driving the blade deep into Ryker's thigh.

The body-snatcher shrieked and clutched at the weapon, trying to tug it free, feeling it rasp against bone as he did.

From the amount of blood which erupted from the wound Miller was sure that he'd severed his attacker's femoral artery. A great red fountain burst from the torn leg, spattering Miller and the wall behind him. He drew his hands across his eyes to clear his view, seeing Terri approaching the stricken Ryker from behind clutching part of the broken vase.

She struck hard, driving the jagged edges into his face, watching as he fell backwards, still trying to wrench the knife from his thigh.

Terri stood watching as Miller rolled on top of Ryker,

reaching for the knife, using all his strength to rip it out. It came
slowly, tearing muscle and sinew as it did so. But finally the
glistening blade was free and Miller raised it above Ryker whose
face was now a bloody ruin, pieces of glass still embedded in it.
One lethal shard had gouged away part of his upper eyelid, and
every time he blinked a sticky flux of vitreous fluid and crimson
would spurt out.

Miller found his own vision was clouding. He was hesitating.

'Do it,' screamed Terri. 'Kill him.'

Miller grabbed Ryker by the chin, and with one powerful
thrust buried the knife in his heart.

'Kill him,' Terri shrieked again, almost knocked flying by the
body which still swung its steady path back and forth.

She stood mesmerized by the bloody spectacle before her
transfixed as Miller put all his weight behind the blade, pushing
it deeper into his opponent's body, ignoring the gouts of blood
which splashed him as the heart pumped madly, expelling its
thick contents with the force of a high-pressure hose.

He felt Ryker's body jerking beneath him as he stabbed again.

And again.

Miller rolled onto the floor beside the punctured body, his
breath coming in great racking gasps, his nostrils filled with the
overpowering coppery stench of blood and the more pungent
odour of excrement. His shoulder was throbbing mightily and
he winced as he prodded the broken bone.

Terri remained motionless, her gaze fixed on the body of
Ryker, her eyes flicking backwards and forwards, taking in
every detail.

'Terri, call the police,' Miller said, trying to raise himself up
on one elbow.

She didn't answer.

Miller wondered if she might have gone into shock, but when
he looked at her he felt a cold chill run along his spine. He felt as
if someone had pumped ice into his veins.

Terri Warner was smiling.

She was kneeling beside the body of Ryker, a broad grin on
her face and Miller noticed with disgust that she had dipped one
index finger into the dead man's chest wound. She withdrew the

282

dripping digit, ignoring the blood which ran up and stained her blouse.

She licked the crimson fluid with a slow movement of her tongue.

Miller felt sick.

Not only because of the pain he was feeling and the sight he had just witnessed but because, in that second, the realization struck him.

'Terri,' he whispered softly, struggling up onto his knees.

She merely looked at him, that insidious grin plastered across her features, her lips stained with blood. But it was her eyes which he found most disconcerting.

The unblinking stare which seemed to bore into him.

'You killed him,' she chuckled. 'It's easy isn't it?' She laughed and Miller felt the hairs at the back of his neck rise.

'You murdered the others,' he said. 'You killed those eight people.'

'Nine,' she corrected him. 'I killed that policeman in my flat too. He'd found the tapes.'

'I don't understand,' Miller said, transfixed by that blazing gaze.

'The messages on the answering machine,' she told him. 'I recorded them myself. That's why the police could never trace them. I put them in the machine myself. I recorded them all at the TV studios, Johnson let me have free run in there. He thought a lot of me.' She chuckled again.

'But how did you know that Johnson would be at the flats tonight?'

'Because *I* called him. *I* told him to be there. I knew he'd do it for me.'

'Oh Jesus,' Miller gasped softly. 'But why the killings?'

'You could never understand, Frank. No one can ever understand the fascination of death. I've had it ever since I was a child. In the beginning I was frightened of it but then I came to understand it. To love it. Its power. Its inevitability. Taking someone's life is probably the greatest power that anyone has. The ability to kill. The others had it too. Haigh, Manuel, Sutcliffe, Nilsen. All of them. I wanted to feel that power too, I wanted to feel what they had felt when *they* killed.' She paused to look at Ryker's body. 'Haven't you ever wanted to kill someone? To see them die? To watch them die? No other reason, just to watch. That power is inside everyone. There's a piece of every person that's capable of killing, but they hide it, they push it away, hide it in the backs of their minds and pretend it doesn't exist. But it's there and it never goes away. That desire to kill someone, sometimes a person you know, is in every human being. How many times have you rowed with someone and felt like killing them? How many people hate their relatives enough to kill them? How many would murder their neighbours if they had the chance? When you find out that someone has been talking behind your back, don't you feel like doing something to them? Like I said, the power is in us all. It's just that most people deny that it's there because they're ashamed to admit it's there.'

Miller listened dumbly, his eyes never leaving Terri as she faced him across the body of Ryker. The corpse was the only thing between them.

And the knife was still embedded in its chest.

Waiting to be picked up.

'I can't call the police, Frank,' she told him. 'Not yet.'

'You're going to kill me?' he asked.

She smiled.

'When you stabbed Ryker, didn't you feel that sense of power? You *took* his life. It makes you like God, Frank, able to decide who will live and who will die.' Her expression suddenly hardened, and in that split second Miller saw her hand dart forward towards the knife.

He lashed out, his punch catching her full in the face, the impact knocking her onto her back. Blood ran from her broken nose and she moaned feebly as Miller crawled towards her, looking down at her face.

She smiled crookedly as she looked up at him and, with a roar of rage, Miller drove another blow into her bloodied visage, this time cracking her jaw.

The impact knocked her unconscious.

Miller sat back on his haunches, his breath coming in gasps.

His injured shoulder was still throbbing but he seemed oblivious to the pain. His attention was focused on Terri.

Above him, the swinging body had finally come to a halt. It twisted and turned silently on the rope.

Sixty-three

When the police arrived Miller was sitting in his lounge drinking.

He heard the banging at the front door but finished what was left in his glass before getting slowly to his feet.

On his way across the hall he stepped over the body of Ryker. The corpse was already stiff with rigor mortis, the spilled blood now congealed into a sticky crimson porridge.

Miller touched his injured shoulder and winced painfully, pausing a second before he opened the door.

The leading policeman blenched as he saw Ryker's body lying in its puddle of congealing gore, but his superior pushed past him followed by a couple of ambulancemen. As Miller made his way back to the sitting room he saw the uniformed men lifting the corpse onto a stretcher.

Miller offered the policeman a drink but he declined. Miller looked at the man appraisingly. He looked as tired as Miller felt and had to keep rubbing his eyes periodically.

'Were you alone in the house when the attack happened?' the policeman asked.

Miller nodded and re-filled his own glass.

'Did you know the man?'

'We'd met a couple of times,' Miller said wearily. 'We worked together once.' He downed a sizeable mouthful of whisky, feeling the amber fluid burn its way to his stomach.

The questions continued and Miller answered each one dutifully, watching in amusement as the officer in charge wrote down his answers almost verbatim.

'You say the attack took place about 1.30,' said the

policeman, looking at his watch. 'That's almost four hours ago. Why didn't you contact us sooner?'

Miller shrugged.

'I must have blacked out,' he said, rubbing his shoulder.

The policeman chewed the end of his pen for a moment then flipped his notebook shut.

'There's an ambulance waiting outside to take you to hospital. That shoulder needs seeing to.'

Miller smiled thinly and finished his drink.

'I might need to ask you some more questions,' the policeman said.

'No sweat. Ride in the ambulance with me,' Miller said, wandering into the hall. 'Just give me a minute, will you?'

'I'll wait for you outside,' the officer said and walked out.

Miller waited until he was out of the house then turned and headed down the short corridor towards his workroom. The key was in the door so he turned it and walked in, shutting it behind him.

The flayed woman was back in her place, fresh latex now covering the parts which Ryker had exposed.

The severed head in the tray on top of the filing cabinet stared blankly at him.

The burn victim looked on impassively.

The work had not taken as long as he'd expected and he looked on with pride.

Seated in the far corner of the room, her body completely encased in latex, was Terri Warner.

Miller had carried her to the workroom and then, quickly but expertly, he had stripped her and covered every square inch of her flesh with his own prosthetic creation. The face he had distorted to mask her real features. She now sported an assortment of boils and sores, all moulded from the liquid rubber with matchless skill.

He had blocked her nostrils and mouth with cotton wool while he worked, finally covering her face with a mask of rubber.

She had already suffocated before he got that far.

The knock on the door startled him and he stepped away,

287

allowing the newcomer to enter.

The policeman looked into the room, scanning each one of the grisly creations.

'One of the men outside said you were in films,' the officer said. 'Special effects isn't it?'

Miller nodded, watching as the policeman looked at the creations with something akin to admiration.

'How the hell do you make them look so real?' the man wanted to know.

Miller looked across at the body of Terri Warner and smiled.

'Trade secret,' he said quietly.

'He that is without sin among you, let him first cast a stone . . .'

Luke 8:7

'We all need scapegoats, someone else to blame for what we're really feeling. Anything, as long as we don't have to face the truth.'

Anon.